CW01510458

NIGHT TERROR

A NOVEL

Jeff Gunhus

This book is a work of fiction. Names, characters, businesses, organizations, places, events, and incidents either are a product of the author's imagination or are used fictitiously. Any resemblance to actual persons, living or dead, events or locales is entirely coincidental.

Copyright 2014 by Jeff Gunhus.

All rights reserved. Published in the United States by Seven Guns Press. No part of this book may be used or reproduced in any manner whatsoever without written permission except in the case of brief quotations embodied in critical articles and reviews.

Printed in the United States of America

Cover design by Eric Gunhus
Edited by Mandy Schoen

Library of Congress Cataloging-in-Publication Data
Gunhus, Jeff
Night Terror / Jeff Gunhus
ISBN-13: 978-0-9899461-4-8
ISBN-10: 0989946142

ALSO BY JEFF GUNHUS

ADULT FICTION

Night Chill
Night Terror
Killer Within

MG/YA FICTION

Jack Templar Monster Hunter
Jack Templar and the Monster Hunter Academy
Jack Templar and the Lord of the Vampires
Jack Templar and the Lord of the Werewolves

NON-FICTION

Reaching Your Reluctant Reader
Wake Up Call
No Parachute Required
Choose The Right Career
The Little Book Of Secrets

Praise for *NIGHT CHILL*

"...unforgettable, exceptional debut. A primitive ritual and an ancient secret threaten a family's safety in this heart-pounding tale of horrific madness, Guaranteed to trigger night sweats along with a childlike, irrational fear of the creaky attic, Jeff Gunhus's *Night Chill* will not disappoint horror fans."

  - Foreword Clarion Reviews - 5 STARS

"Gunhus delivers a taut supernatural thriller...the powerful Nate Huckley terrifies, and the assorted cast of human antagonists add to the white-knuckle tension. All the chops of an action-packed horror tale."

  - Kirkus Reviews

"I see a lot of book synopses that claim works by lesser known authors are King-like or that their writing style is similar to Koontz. I always take these with a grain of salt. But in this case, it is very true."

  - A Goddess Of Literature

"Night Chill seems to have it all for the horror fan/supernatural lover. It's got a beautifully laid out mystery that spans centuries and involves something terrifying for any parent out there...I highly recommend Night Chill and it's one book that shouldn't be passed up."

  - The Mind of Tatlock

"What an amazingly, heart pounding, non-stop, emotional, creepy THRILL RIDE! I can't remember the last time a book pulled me in a wouldn't let me go, but this one did from start to finish."
   - *Monique J King*

"A long time reader of Dean Koontz, I would dare say Night Chill was up there with some of the best from Mr. Koontz. Plenty of twists and turns that kept me just wanting to keep reading."
   -Aussie Kindle Fanatic

"A delicious compilation of 2 parts Dean Koontz, 1 part Stephen King and a pinch of Robin Cook."
   - *Sarah Lowery*

"This book kept me on the edge of my seat from the very beginning to the very end. The story goes in a whole different direction then I expected it to."
   - *Rosemary Fink*

"Really an absorbing read on a long winter's weekend. I couldn't ask for more from a book of this genre. Thanks to the author for writing it."
   - *P. McGimsie*

"Captivating from start to finish and hardly time to catch your breath. The horror builds until the very end and the climax leaves you worn out from the journey."
   -Clifton R Byrd

For Nicole

Who knew I had books like this in me

And married me anyway

The battleline between good and evil runs through the heart of every man.

-Aleksandr Solzhenitsyn

The belief in a supernatural source of evil is not necessary; men alone are quite capable of every wickedness.

-Joseph Conrad

Fear is pain arising from the anticipation of evil.

-Aristotle

SCIENTISTS INVESTIGATE MASSIVE SINKHOLE IN WESTERN MARYLAND

PRESCOTT CITY, MARYLAND (ASSOCIATED PRESS)

Residents of Prescott City, Maryland were awoken Tuesday morning by an earthquake, the effect of a massive sinkhole in a nearby abandoned mining operation. The cave-in produced tremors measuring 3.9 on the Richter scale and were recorded as far away as Baltimore and Washington DC.

"The mine had been abandoned for nearly eighty years. During that time there was no monitoring, so this cave-in was likely a long time in coming," said Dr. Brooks Hardy, a geologist at the University of Maryland. "Area residents can expect small aftershocks over the next several weeks as the lower strata settle into a new equilibrium," warned Dr. Brooks.

The Midland Sheriff's office has declared the site off-limits, issuing a warning that trespassers will be prosecuted.

EX-NAVY SEAL INVOLVED IN SHOOTING RAMPAGE REMAINS AT LARGE
MIDLAND, MARYLAND (REUTERS)

Joseph R. Lonetree remains at large after a brazen escape from county jail in Midland, Maryland in which he subdued two deputies and took local businessman Jack Tremont hostage. Tremont had been in custody at the time on an unrelated charge of which he was ultimately acquitted. On October 5th, Lonetree was apprehended by authorities after he used an arsenal of semi-automatic weapons to open fire on law enforcement officials stationed at Midland General Hospital. Using explosives hidden on his person, he escaped jail on October 6th, taking Tremont hostage. Tremont subsequently escaped unharmed.

The unexplained disappearance of Sheriff Ross Janney and Deputy Nick Sorenson on the day of Lonetree's escape has led authorities to speculate that the two may have become the ex-Navy SEAL's latest victims. Other missing persons that have previously been discussed as suspected victims in Lonetree's alleged killing spree are Prescott City residents Max Dahl, James "Jim" Butcher, Scott Moran, and his daughter Cathy Moran. Chief Sullivan declined comment when asked whether he was willing to officially list Lonetree as the suspect in all six disappearances.

Chief Sullivan instead issued the following public warning: "Any information regarding the whereabouts of Joseph Lonetree should be immediately reported to local police. He is considered armed and extremely dangerous and should not be approached under any circumstances. Law enforcement continues to work diligently to find this murderer and bring him to justice. It's only a matter of time."

EDITORIAL: TEN-YEAR ANNIVERSARY OF CAVE-IN SHOULD REMEMBER THE FALLEN

PRESCOTT CITY, MARYLAND

Marking the anniversary of the massive limestone cave collapse that literally shook our small town ten years ago, environmentalists and big business are about to square off in court over ownership of the site.

While many Prescott City citizens have united behind the idea of turning the area into an ecological park, Smithco International, the Canadian mining conglomerate that owns the site, has resisted pressure to sell the land. "Advances in extraction techniques can transform a played-out mine into a valuable asset in a single day. We have no interest in selling at this time."

However, while they play Monopoly, many of us in Prescott City find the anniversary a painful reminder of the disappearances which occurred simultaneously with the cave-in.

Midland Sheriff Ross Janney, Sheriff's Deputy Nick Sorenson, Max Dahl, James "Jim" Butcher, Scott Moran, and his daughter Cathy Moran all went missing during this time and their bodies were never recovered. While many believe they were underground at the time of the cave-ins, others continue to suspect foul play.

Suspicion at the time was placed on ex-Navy SEAL Joseph Lonetree who, despite a nationwide manhunt, was never found. While Lonetree remains on the FBI's Most Wanted list, it's little consolation to the families of Prescott City who lost so much.

Yes, the mile of rusting chain-link fence still surrounding the cave-in site is an eyesore. But the way the anniversary seems to have forgotten our dead is a sore on our conscience of which we should be ashamed.

Editorial Staff – Prescott Gazette

Chapter 1

Charlie Winters didn't scream. Not because the pain had stopped, because it hadn't. Every nerve in his body was still on fire, bursting with electric signals to his brain that the bag of meat, sinew, and bone that was supposed to protect it was being systematically destroyed. Pound by pound, his flesh was eaten. Ounce by ounce, his blood was guzzled down.

No, his screams stopped only because his vocal cords were raw and bloody and had ceased to function. None of the dozen or so attackers had bothered to silence him when they started the feast, and Charlie had screamed and screamed until he could do so no more.

Even with his throat filled with blood, he still tried to cry out, expelling a spray of red mist. The men feasting near his head enjoyed this and breathed in the vapors of his bloody exhalation. One of the men's thick fingers dug into Charlie's left eye socket and scooped out his eyeball, giving a quick yank to pop it loose from the strand of nerves attached to it. Charlie felt another man put his lips around the empty socket and suck hard at the juices inside his head. Nails clawed at and then ripped off the small pad of meat on his cheek, a delicacy on ten-year-old boys as much as it was on suckling pigs.

Charlie closed his eyes and begged for death.

An hour earlier he had been a regular boy, just like anyone else.

But then again, he knew that wasn't really true. He'd never been like anyone else. And now it had finally cost him.

Chapter 2

The woman didn't look evil, but there was no better word to describe her. Charlie Winters would wonder later how he could have missed sensing her earlier than he did. It was equivalent to normal people walking halfway through a field only to look down and find themselves thigh-deep in a pile of rotting animal carcasses, the stench hitting them like a wave. After retching their stomach contents, they would question both their senses and their sanity. How could they have missed such a smell? How could they have not felt their feet sinking into the liquefied soft tissue?

Charlie's senses were better than a normal person's. Way better.

It had started when he was only a baby, a fact he knew because he still remembered every second of this life since the moment of his birth. It was a long time before he understood that such a memory was not a normal thing. Other people, normal humans, could not remember the first feeding at their mother's breast. The hot pain of circumcision. The first glimpse of sunlight as they left the hospital. So many firsts, memories as clear to Charlie as what he'd had for breakfast that day.

Inside those memories, the echoes and shadows of his other unusual senses lingered. The ability to sense emotion. To pick up on intention. Sometimes these abilities strengthened what he observed in the physical world. His grandparents' cooing excitement over him matched an internal warmth that felt the same as sunshine. His father's thoughtful stares mirrored Charlie's sense that his dad would do anything to protect him, to provide for him. Even if there was an undercurrent of trepidation that vibrated like a single out-of-tune string on a guitar, the other intentions drowned it out and gave Charlie a sense of comfort. This was very different from his mother, whose kind smiles and soft features once masked a nearly constant desire to kill him.

Her thoughts had alternated between putting a pillow over his head and dropping him down the basement stairs. In darker moments, when his father was gone overnight for a business trip, she would consider carving up her child with a knife. Even going as far as pulling a cleaver from the block and slowly running her sweaty palm down the length of the blade. She never did this in front of him, but that was part of his gift. He could see through her eyes. Feel her emotions. Know her dark intentions. And understand that the threat of violence was very, very real.

But as much as she fantasized about it, his mother didn't kill him. In fact, she never so much as laid a finger on him in anger. Slowly, over time, the dark thoughts faded, and the light inside his mother came to match her soft eyes and the beautiful mouth that sang to him and called him sunshine. A normal person might never have been able to forget the darkness and might never have trusted the woman who once considered taking a ball-peen hammer to his forehead, but he wasn't normal people. He was special. And it was that specialness that showed him the truth in her absolute love for him once the veils of shadows had fallen away from her like someone passing through heavy curtains.

Much later, Charlie read about a condition called post-partum depression and understood where the dark had come from. It hadn't been his fault. Or hers. It was the depression that spawned the evil thoughts. And he liked to think it was her love for him that pushed them back enough to keep him safe.

Even after she recovered, he could sense when she felt pangs of guilt about those days. They were like electric bolts jolting through her. When those moments happened, and they could happen at any time, he would come up and hug her, kiss her on the cheek and tell her how much he loved her. At first, she cried harder when he did it, and he sensed her guilt grow even stronger. Later, she puzzled over how he timed the affection to her thoughts. Over time, the puzzling turned to suspicion, even fear that somehow he knew. After that, like with all of his special gifts, he learned it was best to hide.

But he hadn't hidden his powers well enough.

If he had, then the woman who called herself Mama D would never have come looking for him.

5

Charlie only lived two blocks away from school and, after a long discussion, his parents had decided he was allowed to walk home by himself. Solon looked like a hundred other small towns scattered across Iowa: mostly one-story homes clustered around a main street consisting of a gas station, a couple of family diners, and a bar or two. Joensy's, home of Iowa's Largest Tenderloin, had moved out a year earlier to a strip mall in nearby Coralville, leaving an empty shell in the center of town. The one traffic light blinked yellow since there wasn't enough traffic to really bother slowing anyone down. But on that Tuesday, right after school, Charlie wished the light had turned red for him and stopped him from crossing the street to where the woman waited.

She was dressed like anyone else in town. Blue jeans. Black sweater covered up by a heavy winter jacket. Knit cap and cheap Wal-Mart gloves. She wore sunglasses, so Charlie couldn't see her eyes. Maybe if he had he would have noticed her staring at him as he walked toward her.

He didn't recognize her, but that wasn't too unusual. Solon felt like the boondocks, but it was close to Iowa City and other towns, so seeing someone new didn't really raise any eyebrows. Still, he was curious, so he reached out with his mind to take stock of her intentions.

Nothing.

It felt like a wall was erected around her.

He pushed a little harder against her mind, but it held firm. This unnerved him because it was the first time it had ever happened to him.

As he walked past her, she reached out, glove removed, and grabbed his wrist. Her skin was hot. Feverish.

She pulled him to her and lifted her sunglasses, giving Charlie a good look at her. He guessed she was younger than his parents, probably in her twenties. She had an exotic-looking face with high cheekbones and wide, thick red lips. Her skin was pulled tight against her facial bones, and he got the sense that her skin was somehow *thinner* than it was supposed to be. But it was her eyes that caught his attention. Just like the skin was somehow thinner, the woman's eyes were somehow *deeper* than eyes ought to be. Dark blue with dilated pupils that seemed to see right into him. He couldn't decide if she was the most beautiful woman he'd ever seen—or the most terrifying.

He pulled back on his wrist—but she held on tight.

It's not nice to go pokin' into other people's heads, Charlie-boy.

He froze. Of course he'd heard people's thoughts before, but not like this. He wasn't eavesdropping. She was talking directly to him. He pushed as hard as he could against her mind and felt a second of satisfaction when he saw her smile disappear, replaced by a look of concentration.

Ohh…you're a strong one, my lil' Pesh. You'll do jus' fine. I'm Mama D. We gonna be friends.

Charlie knew better. He knew in his bones that this woman was danger. The kind with a capital D. But a second later he found that he wanted nothing more in the world than to please her. He couldn't help himself. She purred at him like a cat as she whispered words of encouragement. No, he didn't *hear* the words, he *felt* them. Smooth and soft and supple. Pouring over him and through him in a way that made him want to do whatever

7

she told him. She let go of his wrist and walked down the sidewalk, her brow furrowed in concentration.

C'mon, Pesh. Mama D's gonna take good care of you.

Deep inside, a voice screamed at him to run. To find an adult to hide behind until this woman, this monster, went away. But the voice was nothing more than a fire alarm in the middle of an inferno.

A van turned the corner farther up the street and rumbled toward them. It rolled to a stop and the side door slid open to reveal a man, the same one who would hours later pluck Charlie's eye from its socket and munch on it like an olive.

He didn't grab him. He just moved aside to make room as Charlie climbed into the van all by himself and took a seat in the worn leather chair. Mama D got into the front passenger seat as the man in the back slid the door shut.

The man in the driver's seat handed Mama D a sword, which she stroked affectionately. She turned in her chair and looked at Charlie with disapproval. "Seat belt, Pesh. I don't want you gettin' hurt if we're in an accident."

The driver, a man named Jimmy who Charlie suddenly knew liked pecan pie and pornography with large black girls, waited until he had buckled his seat belt before easing down on the gas pedal and pulling the van back onto the road. And then, impossibly, Charlie's eyes grew heavy, so heavy, until he couldn't keep them open no matter how hard he tried.

I'm so tired, he said with his mind to Mama D.

I know, Pesh. We all are, Mama D's voice purred back. *You need your rest. Sleeeep now. Don't you worry 'bout nothin'. I'll wake you up when we get there. I can promise you that. You do believe my promises, don't you, Pesh?*

Charlie nodded. He did believe her. Absolutely. And with that thought, a wave of weariness washed over him, causing him to sink deeper into his seat and lean his head against the window. He stopped fighting it and simply gave in to the tiredness that had seeped into his body.

As the van hit Highway 1 leaving Solon, speeding up until the barren, harvested fields rushed by in a blur of dead color, Charlie Winters fell into a black, dreamless sleep. It was eight hours before he woke up in a different state, lying prostrate on the trash-covered concrete floor of an abandoned warehouse, screaming as his flesh was torn from his bones and devoured in front of him.

Chapter 3

Darin Johnson feasted, ripping skin and flesh with his teeth next to the others. Mama D had taken the choicest cut as was her right, but she'd been generous and had left a lot of the kid's power in his blood and meat. The little guy didn't have much on his bones, but his specialness made it one of the finest meals they'd had in a long time. Maybe all the way back to the Watkins girl in the early '80s. Now *that* had been a special meal.

Still, Mama D had been right when she'd promised them a treat. Finding power in a boy was unusual and, after eating only females for the last few decades, the novelty heightened Darin's senses. Still, he couldn't help but think, *what if this power had been born into a girl?*

As good as the meal was, they all knew the power would have been exponentially greater if little Charlie Winters had been born Charlene instead. Darin's mouth salivated at the thought.

Still, the meal was undeniably incredible. He gorged himself on the boy, working carefully around the brain and heart so that the kid stayed alive until the very end. Once he died, the power would wink out and the kid would just become meat and blood. None of them would touch the body once that happened. They weren't cannibals, for God's sake.

Darin tilted his head back to lower a long piece of intestine down his throat. Just as he did, he caught the flash of the van's headlights off the polished edge of a tomahawk. A second later, the blade sank into the skull of the man next to him, cleaving it in half. The men around Darin reacted quickly, launching themselves at the attacker with bloodstained teeth and clawed hands. But the tomahawk swung brutally between them, slicing through one man's throat, sinking into another's eye socket.

Then a second shadow attacked. Not with a tomahawk, but with two machetes, one in each hand, flashing through the air, landing precision blows. One through a man's forehead. The other to a man's chest, ripping through his heart.

While the others fought back, Darin turned and ran. He tripped on a body and fell hard. He scrambled to get up but slipped on the blood-covered floor. Then strong hands grabbed him and pulled him to his feet. He struggled but the hands moved quickly and a second later he was in a painful headlock. The world spun as his captor turned. He saw all the others laid out on the floor,

11

their bodies ripped apart.

Standing in the middle of them was a large man with long, black hair tied into a ponytail. His square face turned toward him and Darin saw pure hate in the man's eyes. With that one look, Darin knew with certainty that the others had been lucky to die so quickly. There was a promise in the man's eyes. And that promise was that very soon, Darin Johnson would wish he had been killed along with the others.

Chapter 4

Joseph Lonetree surveyed the carnage. He wiped clean the edge of his tomahawk and caught his reflection on the blade. Using his shirt sleeve, he wiped away the blood splattered across his face and neck. The distorted image on the steel still showed his square jaw and deep eyes that gave him a haunted look in the harsh light. As an ex-SEAL, he was an expert in dozens of weapons, some of them the most sophisticated weapons ever created by the military-industrial complex of these United States of America. But over the past few years, the tomahawk had become his weapon of choice. What had started as a call-back to his Sioux heritage had turned into a genuine appreciation for the weapon's effectiveness. Besides, it felt appropriate to use an ancient weapon when hunting an ancient adversary.

He looked up at Nick Sorenson holding the prisoner. Sorenson was the fellow SEAL who'd followed him down the supernatural rabbit hole over a decade earlier with the business in Prescott City. Sorenson was five years younger than him, sharp, and wired tight. He carried himself in a way that men knew not to mess with him, and women knew he wasn't going to be around for long. As a result, he rarely got into fights and even more rarely went home alone at the end of the night. After Maryland, he'd stuck with Lonetree without discussion. There was work to do, and they intended to finish what they started. Neither of them had guessed then that ten years later they would still be hunting.

Sorenson stuffed a gag in their prisoner's mouth and shoved him to the ground. He gave a quick nod to Lonetree that he was five-by-five, wiped his machetes on one of the men at his feet, then slid the weapons back into the sheaths he wore on his belt. He and Lonetree began to turn over each body to inspect the faces. But Lonetree had already taken stock and knew the bad news. There were only men among the dead. She wasn't here. Mama D had gotten away again.

"I'll check their van," Sorenson said.

While Sorenson jogged over to the men's van, Lonetree knelt beside the victim's half-eaten carcass. The soft tissues were gone, all organs except the heart and brain ripped from his body. Even so, as Lonetree looked him over, a single blood-filled eye rolled in the skull until it settled on Lonetree.

*Please…kill…me…*said a voice in his head.

Lonetree's stomach turned. He'd seen a lot in his life, more than most could have imagined, but this was almost more than he could handle. Somehow, impossibly, the boy was alive.

Please...it hurrrttss...

The voice sobbed. It was in his head but it was just like he would expect the kid's actual voice to sound if his throat hadn't been ripped out. High-pitched. Full of fear and pain. For the love of God, it was just a little boy.

P...p...pl...please...

In a sudden connection with the boy, Lonetree understood how this had happened. He understood because the boy understood and he was in Lonetree's mind, telling him. Begging him.

Whatever Mama D had done to the boy had changed him. Unless his heart or brain were destroyed, he would go on living. Go on suffering.

Ple...pl—

Lonetree sank the tomahawk into the boy's skull. The lone eyeball froze in place, then drifted to one side and stared past Lonetree.

Sorenson called out from the van. "She's not here."

Lonetree yanked the tomahawk out and gently ran his finger over the boy's face, closing his eye.

"But you're going to want to see this," Sorenson said. He walked up to Lonetree and handed him a road atlas, the old-school version popular before GPS. It was for the entire United States. Lonetree didn't see the significance until he noticed what page it was opened to.

Maryland.

And circled with a black felt pen was a large section of Western Maryland. Within the circle was the small town of Prescott City. Scribbled next to it was a date. Three days away.

15

Lonetree handed Sorenson the atlas and turned to where their prisoner sat cuffed on the floor. He twirled his tomahawk in his hand as he walked up to the man and pulled out his gag.

"What's your name?" Lonetree asked.

"Darin. Darin Johnson," the man said, eyeing the tomahawk.

"Darin, you're going to tell us why Prescott City is circled on this map," Lonetree said.

Darin grinned, a sudden confidence appearing on his face. It was clear he felt he had a bargaining chip in this game. "If I tell you, what will you—,"

The man screamed as Lonetree swung the tomahawk down and sliced off the front half of the man's right foot.

"Goddamn," Darin screamed. "What're you doing? Let's talk."

"We are talking," Lonetree said.

He swung the tomahawk and severed three fingers from Darin's right hand.

Darin sobbed and screamed all at once. Lonetree felt a flicker of sympathy for the man, but it only took a quick glance over at the boy's body to get rid of that.

"I don't think you want me to have to ask again," Lonetree said.

"Y…you can…go…to hell," Darin managed through his pathetic mewling.

"Yeah, I'm probably going to hell, but something tells me you're going to get there first." Lonetree leaned down by the man's head, the edge of the tomahawk blade a hair's width away from Darin's eye. "Now listen good," Lonetree whispered. "It's up to you how fast this goes.

Should we start again? Why is Prescott City circled on this map?"

An hour and many creative ways to induce pain later, Lonetree felt he had everything he could get from Darin Johnson and allowed Sorenson to decapitate the asshole and send him on his way to his date with the devil.

Darin hadn't given them a complete picture, but Lonetree didn't think the man knew enough to give that to him anyway. What little Darin did know, he'd told them. And what he'd told them wasn't good news.

Right afterward, Lonetree and Sorenson left the warehouse, climbed into their gear-filled Suburban, and immediately began driving east.

Back to Maryland.

And back to the Tremont family.

Chapter 5

Jack dreaded what he was about to do. He steered the Lincoln Navigator through the stone pillars of the Prescott City Cemetery, his mind still searching for some excuse to get out of the meeting ahead of him.

His emotions must have been transparent because Lauren reached out from the passenger seat next to him and grasped his hand. He gave it a quick squeeze, comforted as always by her presence.

The noise in the media about the ten-year anniversary of the madness they had endured together had reopened old wounds. While the experience had tested them, it had ultimately reforged their bond, no small miracle given what had happened to their family. The pressures and stress of what they had endured weren't exactly material they could hash out in counseling. But the years of marriage therapy in California before their move to Western Maryland, before the murderous Nate Huckley had intruded into their lives, had given them a good blueprint to follow as they sorted through it all.

In long, late-night conversations, they'd forced the demons out into the light of day. Her feelings of guilt for accusing Jack of abducting Sarah, his feelings of betrayal when he had needed her trust the most, their shared sense of disbelief over what had happened down in the caves.

This last was particularly hard for them to overcome since Lauren had never been down to the caves. She'd never seen anything of the powers they'd been up against. Based on the evidence she'd seen with her own eyes, their little girl had been abducted by an insane cult of real people, no supernatural explanations necessary. Hearing Jack describe what he'd seen in the cave, what he'd seen Sarah do, was hard for her scientific mind to accept. She claimed that she believed Jack, but he wondered whether she really did or if she just chocked the whole story up to some kind of psychological coping mechanism.

Of course, their greatest concern had been Sarah. While she'd recovered fully from the shotgun wound from Dr. Mansfield, it was her emotional recovery that most worried her parents. But she proved to be the most resilient of all of them, helped by her mind that had mercifully blocked any memory of the cave or much before it. And, given the mysterious events surrounding her abduction and rescue, there'd been no shortage of people asking her questions. Law enforcement, Child Protective Services, and her parents all wanted to know what she remembered. But they all received the same answer. Nothing.

Even now, ten years later, Sarah's last memory was seeing her rubber ball bouncing down the hallway at Midland Memorial Hospital while she waited for her mom. The next thing she knew, she assured everyone who asked her the same question over and over, was waking up in the hospital as a patient.

Late at night, when the screams of men being ripped apart filled his head and every dark shadow in the house seemed to hide the grotesque, malformed body of the shaman from the caves, Jack envied his daughter. And thanked God she had been given this one mercy.

He almost wished Lauren would forget. She often spoke of her endless worry that her little girl's memories would come back in flood later on and what that would do to her. The same doctor's mind that had earned Lauren's PhD from Johns Hopkins set her sights on understanding the science behind what was happening in Sarah's brain. She had immersed herself in all available literature on repressed memories and sought out audiences with the top experts in neuroscience and psychology. While her credentials alone were a strong calling card, the half-truth she told about her story was enough to open any door. Her daughter had been abducted, shot in the chest with a shotgun, and barely rescued by her father moments before her abductors were buried alive under thousands of tons of rock in the Prescott City sinkhole. The geological wonder had made national news, and that helped bring instant recognition and sympathy to her situation. The only problem she told Jack about was the lack of good answers she'd received.

Jack had watched as Lauren's drive to understand their daughter's condition teetered on the edge of mania. Used to the hard science of her own discipline, she grew increasingly frustrated with a scholarly field based on theories and, in her mind at least, pure conjecture. After hundreds, possibly thousands of hours of research, Lauren's conclusions were the same ones Jack had reached over a single evening's Internet search.

No one knew why repressed memories occurred in some people and not others. Sometimes the memories returned. Sometimes they didn't. Sometimes they only partially came back. Sometimes there was a trigger. Sometimes there wasn't. Basically, the common line in all the research was the simple fact that the brain was a more complicated and powerful machine than science could yet comprehend.

Jack had been thankful when Lauren called off her search and simply accepted Sarah's lack of memory for the gift that it was. They had no control over whether her memory might return. All they could do was understand that it might happen at some point in the future and, if and when it did, be there to support her.

Jack made a right turn toward the back of the cemetery. They worked their way through the curving path, past the nubs of stone worn down by wind and weather from Prescott City's earliest days, toward the shiny, modern granite slabs marking her more recently departed souls.

He glanced in the rearview mirror at Sarah in the backseat. She was staring right back at him in the mirror, her bright blue eyes piercing him with an intensity she'd picked up since that night in the cave. As soon as they made eye contact, her eyes softened, and she gave him a smile. The gesture was so pure and full of love that it caught him off guard, and his eyes welled with tears. He grabbed his sunglasses and slid them on, embarrassed by his fragility. When he looked back in the mirror, Sarah was staring out of the window at the passing rows of headstones, her light blond hair glowing in the morning sunlight.

She wasn't a little girl anymore. Only sixteen years old and beautiful enough that she drew looks from grown men wherever she went, leaving her dad to scowl at them for noticing her. At least there hadn't been any boyfriends yet. Jack wasn't sure how he was going to handle that when it came.

"I wish Becky was here," she murmured.

Lauren looked back at her. "I know, sweetie. I do too. You can call her after school, okay?"

Sarah was silent for a few beats before answering. "Why does she need to go to boring school anyway?"

"She's almost done. If she gets into Georgetown, she'll be closer," Lauren replied.

Jack grinned. What had started as a mispronunciation of *boarding school* when she was younger had become Sarah's term for her sister's school outside Baltimore. That had been another challenge for the Tremonts. After Sarah's rescue, Becky had trouble settling back into a routine. Night after night she woke up to nightmares about Sarah's abduction. About Nate Huckley at the rest stop when he had shown up in the middle of the thunderstorm. About the night Jack had almost taken a baseball bat to Buddy, the family dog.

Jack and Lauren had talked about moving to give them all a fresh start, but Sarah overheard their conversation one night and broke down into inconsolable tears. She begged and pleaded for them not to make her move, her voice taking on an edge of panic that neither of them had ever heard from her before. Jack held her while her whole body shook as if she were chilled to the bone. Without thinking it through, he'd promised his little girl that they wouldn't move. As he made the promise, he saw Becky staring at him, tears welling in her eyes.

The idea for a solution came from Becky herself. She had gone to stay near Baltimore with one of Lauren's friends, Sushma Bhasin, during the crisis of Sarah's abduction. In the process, she had become fast friends with Sushma's daughter, Nouri, who attended McDonough, the prestigious boarding school, and who had convinced Becky it was the absolute coolest place to go in the universe.

Becky had been eight when she first asked to go. Lauren was the hardest sell, but it made sense. Both of their girls had been through a lot, but there was no denying that Sarah, repressed memories or not, had borne the worst of it. When they gave Becky the news that they would let her go to boarding school if that's what she wanted, she'd screamed with excitement and thanked them. Jack felt a pang of guilt over her feeling so afraid at her home that she wanted to leave that badly. But later, he overhead Becky on the phone with Nouri in a hushed conversation about boys and the nearby beaches. He wasn't sure whether to feel relieved or more concerned.

It was hard to believe that ten years had passed, and she was now graduating in the spring.

"I see them," Sarah said, her voice rising.

As they came around the bend, Jack saw them too. A woman in a black dress and two teenage girls, all with long brown hair, holding hands. Kristi Dahl and her daughters, Julie and Jesse.

He swallowed hard and prepared himself to play his role in this ongoing charade where he honored Max

Dahl as a loving husband, father, and friend. Jack had decided ten years ago that the truth would only hurt those Max left behind, so he'd kept the secret of the man's true nature to himself.

Still, as he looked at the sad faces awaiting them, he couldn't help wonder how they would react if they knew the truth about Max. The man didn't deserve to be mourned, but his family didn't deserve to be subjected to the truth. As Jack looked for a parking space, he resolved once again to pretend to honor Max the friend and do his damn best to forget Max the sadistic child killer.

Chapter 6

Jack parked the car near the Dahls. The family got out and exchanged hugs. Kristi's eyes were red from a night's worth of crying. Maybe a decade's worth as far as Jack knew. Jesse was sullen as she accepted Jack and Lauren's condolences, but her eyes sparked when she saw Sarah. They had been good friends before the horrific events, but since that time they had become inseparable. Julie held her mother's hand, and the group walked the small distance to Max Dahl's grave.

As they approached, Kristi began to sob. Jack felt bad for the loss of Max the husband and Max the father. On many days, he even missed Max for the friend he had become to Jack after their move from California. What he didn't miss was Max the cult-member who had stood by while Huckley and the others plotted to abduct and sacrifice Sarah in their ritual with the Source.

Jack closed his eyes, hoping it appeared he was holding back his emotions. In fact, he was. But instead of sadness and grief, he held back disgust and anger.

A mental image of Max disintegrating in front of his eyes flashed before him. Teeth tumbling from rotten gums. Skin thinning until blood simply oozed out from his pores. Eyes filling with blood and bursting like old, bruised grapes. It was justice served, but it gave Jack no feeling of satisfaction. Max had ultimately sacrificed himself for his daughter, gifting her the stolen life force from hundreds of sacrificed children to repair her diseased heart. It was another month before the doctors admitted she was miraculously cured, but Max died knowing he'd saved her. Jack was glad he'd found the humanity to make the gesture, but wished he'd died not knowing. After what he had done, he didn't deserve to be his little girl's hero. He deserved the hell he most certainly found himself in.

"He knew the first time he met you at Piper's that you were going to be a great friend," Kristi said, wrapping her arm in his. "He just knew things about people, you know?"

"He was a great guy," Jack said, hoping the tremor in his voice would be mistaken for sadness. "He loved you and the girls more than anything." *At least that part was true.*

Kristi broke down and cried at the comment. Lauren wrapped an arm over her shoulder until she collected herself. "I'm sorry," she finally managed. "I told myself I wouldn't do that. Not in front of the girls."

"It's okay," Jesse said. "We all miss him."

This set Kristi off on a harder cry. She wrapped her arms around her girls, pulling them into a tight hug. The Tremonts stood quietly by, Lauren wiping tears off her cheek. When Kristi pulled back, she had herself in control.

"Thank you both so much for being here. It helps Jesse. It helps…" Kristi broke into tears again. "I'm sorry. I'm sorry…"

"There's nothing to be sorry for. You cry as much as you want," Lauren said, dabbing at her own eyes with a tissue.

"Having it all over the papers and the news has made it hard," Kristi said. "I can't believe it's been ten years."

"Ten years of perfect health for Jesse," Lauren replied. "Focus on that."

"You're right, not even a cold," Kristi said, sniffling. She stood up a little straighter and blew her nose into a tissue. "It's a true miracle. It's like God took Max but gave me Jesse back."

Jack felt a knot form in his stomach. There was no God involved in the transaction—that much he knew for sure. Kristi and Lauren continued to speak to one another, but the conversation was lost to Jack. The words faded, like a TV playing in the background, as his eyes wandered over the gravestones.

While they were memorializing Max's death, it was also a day marking how close they had come to losing Sarah too. The brush with death still gave Jack chills at night, but the terror had passed. He and Lauren were closer than they had ever been in their marriage. They looked at the anniversary as a turning point, a time to leave the nightmare of Huckley and Janney and all the other murderers behind them. Even his guilt over Melissa Gonzales, the little girl he'd struck and killed with his car in California, had been laid to rest with the girl's ghostly visitation to forgive him. It was time to move on, once and for all.

But then he saw a lone figure standing on the far edge of the cemetery. Even with a long black jacket and a hood pulled over his head, Jack immediately knew who it was. The man raised a hand in salutation and then took a step sideways so that he was hidden behind a tree. Jack's sense that the worst was behind him and his family shattered into a million pieces.

Lonetree was back, and that could only mean one thing.

The worst was still to come.

Chapter 7

"Jack? Would that be okay?"

Jack's attention snapped back from the edge of the cemetery to Lauren and Kristi. By the looks on their faces, it wasn't the first time they'd asked him the question. Lauren appeared concerned, even following the direction he'd been staring to see what had disturbed him. Only he knew there was nothing there for her to see. Not anymore.

"I'm sorry, I was just thinking…you know…about Max," he said.

Lauren slid her hand into his in what would appear to Kristi as a comforting gesture. But Lauren knew the real story about Max's involvement, so her eyes seemed to ask the real questions on her mind. *Is everything okay? Is there any danger? Is Sarah safe?* Jack knew she would see right through him and know that the answers to those questions were not the ones she wanted.

"Lauren offered to take the kids to school and drive me home," Kristi said. "Would that be alright?"

"She shouldn't drive like this. Not today," Lauren said, her voice reluctant now but resigned to the commitment she'd already made.

"Yeah, of course. I'll take your car and we'll make the switch later," Jack said, trying not to sound too eager. "Unless you need it right away."

"No, we can just figure it out later." Kristi pulled Lauren into another hug. "Thank you both again. I didn't think today was going to be this hard."

Jack fidgeted next to them, his mind filled with clichés of comforting things to say. A platitude about time healing wounds almost worked its way out, but instead he chose to keep his mouth shut and let the silence fill the space.

Kristi gave him a quick hug and a thank you and then reached out for Jesse's hand to walk toward the Navigator. Sarah took her friend's other hand and Jack and Lauren followed behind.

"Everything okay?" Lauren asked as Jack handed her the keys.

Jack leaned in and gave her a kiss on the cheek. He lingered there and whispered in her ear, "Lonetree's here." Lauren's body went stiff. "Try not to worry. I'm going to see what—"

"What if someone sees you with him?"

"No one's going to see us," Jack assured her. "Except for all these dead people." Lauren shuddered and pulled back. They had experience with dead people behaving badly. "Sorry, bad joke. But you know how paranoid he is. He wouldn't do anything to put us at risk."

"But—"

"He saved our lives, Lauren. All of our lives. If he's here, it means either he's in trouble or we are."

Lauren nodded. "Okay. Keep your phone on. Call me when you're done talking to him."

"You got it, boss."

Lauren scanned the cemetery but shook her head. Even Jack now saw nothing but tombstones and leaf-strewn landscaping. With a piercing look at him, she climbed into the SUV and started the winding trail back to the main road. As he watched them leave, Jack found himself hoping his unspoken platitude was right. Maybe for the people in the car, time would heal their wounds. He could only hope there was some truth in the idea.

He turned back in the direction he'd seen Lonetree. He was surprised to see the big man step out from behind a marble mausoleum half the distance from where Jack had first seen him. Lonetree had covered almost seventy yards without Jack noticing. The SEAL sniper hadn't lost his touch.

Jack scanned the tree line as he walked toward Lonetree, wondering whether Nick Sorenson was watching over them in case the police or FBI had somehow gotten the drop on him. If they had, Jack pitied the poor officers who tried to bring him in. Jack had bonded with Lonetree during their fight against Sarah's abductors in the way he imagined soldiers bonded together after facing certain death together. Still, even with that bond, he felt a healthy amount of fear for Lonetree's terrible capacity for violence. Like a wild animal, he was unpredictable. That trait made Jack keep up his guard and made him happy to be an ally and not an adversary. He fully intended to keep it that way.

Lonetree met him halfway. While the Native American had features that seemed chiseled from stone, Jack was relieved to see a smile on the man's face. It looked more like a grimace, but Jack had spent enough time with Lonetree to know it was about as happy a look as he could manage. For the first time since seeing him, Jack relaxed a little. Perhaps this was just a checking-in visit after all.

"Last time we talked you were going to retire down in Mexico," Jack said, holding out his hand.

Lonetree shook it, pulling Jack into a chest bump that nearly knocked him over. "I should have done it. Sipping margaritas with the señoritas would have been a hell of a lot more fun than what I've been doing."

"You know they're still after you, right?" Jack said, feeling a little ridiculous mentioning the obvious. "With all these ten-year anniversary stories, you've been in the paper quite a bit. Kind of risky coming back here."

"I needed to see you," Lonetree said.

An ice ball formed in Jack's stomach and churned. "You could have just called."

"Are you kidding? Don't you read the news? The NSA listens to everything. If I called you, they'd have that recording over to whatever limp biscuit at the FBI's in charge of my case within an hour. Not that they'd believe what I have to tell you anyway."

The ice ball went from a slow churn to a full, raging spin cycle in his gut. "What's going on?"

Lonetree locked eyes with him. "You know what I've been doing since the cave, right?"

Jack nodded. "There are more people out there like Huckley and his group."

"Not as many as there were ten years ago." Lonetree smirked. "Sorenson and I caught up with a lot of them. Didn't go well for the bad guys."

"But that's not why you're here," Jack said, feeling impatient.

Lonetree nodded. "There's this group. The worst out there." He paused and looked away. "They're coming here. They're coming for Sarah."

Jack's head spun and his stomach turned over on itself. Bile rose in the back of his throat, and it was everything he could do to keep from throwing up his breakfast. Lonetree reached out a hand to steady him, and he grabbed onto it. He sucked in a few deep breaths, forcing his brain to process the information and accept the new reality.

"Lauren and Sarah," he said, looking in the direction where the Navigator had driven off.

"Don't worry," Lonetree said. "I wouldn't have let them leave if I thought they were in immediate danger."

Jack took a deep breath, fighting down the panic that rose in his chest. Even though every instinct told him to sprint back to the car and chase after Lauren, he knew he couldn't do that. He had to think this through. He had to come up with a solution. And to do that, he needed more information.

He steadied himself and stood upright. He looked Lonetree in the eye.

"Tell me," Jack said. "Tell me everything."

Chapter 8

Lonetree liked that Jack found his resolve in a matter of seconds after hearing the bad news. It didn't surprise him so much as reaffirm his faith in the man. He'd learned not to underestimate Jack Tremont, especially when the welfare of his family was involved. Still, he knew this would be a hard blow, especially given that so much time had passed. While Lonetree had been living with this grim truth since days after the escape from the cave, Jack had been wrapped in a thick cocoon of blissful ignorance. A cocoon Lonetree had been only too happy to let be as long as he could.

Since the death of his brother, Lonetree's existence had come to mirror his name. Well, at least the lone part. A tree would imply that he was able to form roots, take hold somewhere and thrive in one spot. But that wasn't him at all. No, anything more than a few days in one place caused him to get antsy. Being a fugitive from the law was a lifestyle that suited him. Don't make friends. Don't stand out. Don't sleep in the same place more than one night.

The fact that he was doing exactly what God had put him on Earth to do made the lifestyle even easier to bear. There wasn't any hardship or indignity he couldn't endure in order to do what he loved.

Hunting bad guys.

Especially these guys. Child-killers. Devourers of souls and flesh.

Al-Qaeda and the Taliban he'd fought during his tours in Iraq and Afghanistan had been villains, worthy of the particular kind of justice he dished out as a SEAL. But these guys were more than villains. They were evil. Pure and simple.

There was no dose of humanity lurking behind the façade. A Taliban fighter might have been forced into duty to protect his family. A terrorist could have been a doting father and husband who had his worldview tangled into something sick and twisted by a drone accidentally killing half his village. But if that father was trying to kill US soldiers, Lonetree had no scruples about putting a .50 caliber bullet through his brain. Still, Lonetree could differentiate between an enemy and evil. No matter how hard the United States military sold it, they were not always the same thing.

This time, they were.

As he stood in front of Jack, he struggled over where to start his story. He wanted to explain everything, but they didn't have time for that. Yet he knew from Jack's expression that he wasn't going to let Lonetree get away with simplifying it too much.

"Let's go for a drive," Lonetree said. "This might take a while, and I don't like to stand outside for long. Uncle Sam has too many things taking pictures up there."

"I see your paranoia is alive and well," Jack said as they walked back to Kristi Dahl's car.

"When some random guy shoots up a place and no one dies, local police are called in. Same scenario but it's a SEAL sniper with a decade of combat under his belt…well, let's just say other resources are utilized in that search."

Jack glanced to the sky as he opened the driver's door. "Is it safe for you to be here?"

"No," Lonetree admitted. "But it's not my safety I'm worried about. We don't have a lot of time. You drive, and I'll give you the down and dirty version of what's going on."

Jack nodded and climbed into the car as Lonetree got into the passenger seat. Firing up the engine, Jack hesitated before putting it into gear. "Does Sorenson need a ride?"

Lonetree's eyebrows rose in surprise, but he smiled. "No, he has our vehicle on the other side of the cemetery." *Good, Jack,* Lonetree thought. *I hope you've been keeping sharp because after you hear what I'm about to tell you, you'll realize you're going to need every advantage we can get to keep you and your family alive.*

Jack shifted the car into gear. "Well, stop being such a pussy and tell me what's going on."

Lonetree laughed, a deep, rolling sound, more of a grunt than anything else. "I've missed you, Jack. It's good to be back. I'll tell you, but you're not going to like it."

Lonetree began his story. By the time they reached the main road, Lonetree knew he'd been right. His friend didn't like what he had to say. Not one bit of it.

Chapter 9

Sarah didn't like being in the car with Mrs. Dahl. Her sadness was like a hole in the passenger seat that pulled the oxygen from the air until it was hard to breathe. Between Mrs. Dahl, the trip to the cemetery, and all the publicity in the news recently about the ten-year anniversary, Sarah felt like she would suffocate under the pressure.

She pushed the button to slide down her window but her mom had it locked. She called them safety locks, but Sarah knew they were really called child safety locks. And that was how her mom still thought of her. As the baby of the family. A designation that didn't come without its perks. Between recovering from her gunshot wound and with Becky away at boring school, Sarah had wrapped her parents around her little finger right after her abduction. Late night TV? Sure. Ice cream every night? No problem. Need to miss a day of school because you're tired? Of course, sweetie.

She had to admit, the first couple of months had been pretty sweet. But that was before reality set in. Once it was clear that she would make a full recovery, then the rules started to come back. Not all at once, but one at a time Mom and Dad redrew lines in the sand. She complained, of course. Tried for some sympathy. She had been six when it first happened, after all. But, truth be told, she didn't really mind the rules. It made her feel normal again. Like things could go back to the way they were before Nate Huckley had lured her into his hospital room and taken her to the caves and to the Source.

After lying to so many adults, she had almost convinced herself that she had no memory of what happened in the cave. Almost. In reality, she remembered every moment she spent underground. She remembered the men grabbing at her arms and legs. How they hungered for her death. The pain of the shotgun blast.

But most of all, she remembered the moment of connection with the shaman when he drew power from her to break free of his stone prison. In those few seconds she saw into his black heart and teetered on the edge of his bottomless well of hate and anger. It was only the power of the women around her, the skeletons in the cages, which had prevented him from destroying her. And now the shaman was dead and she lived. But the memory of that connection was hard to bear, coming back to her sometimes in her nightmares. Sometimes in the light of day as a cold shiver passing through her body. A whisper in the back of her mind. A soft sound calling her name. Beckoning her to come to the earth. To lie in a grave, close her eyes, and sleep.

Saaaarrraahhhh.

Saaaarrraahhhh.

Part of her wished she could confide in her parents, but she knew keeping the truth from them was the right thing to do. She sensed the relief they felt from believing she had no memory of that terrible night. It was a kindness she enjoyed giving them. She hoped that she would never have to tell them the truth.

Some days were harder than others to carry the burden. She'd learned to cope and block most of it out, but sometimes the dreams felt too real. Sometimes the voices in her head didn't stop when she opened her eyes, even when she turned on all the lights in her room and sat on her bed, hugging her knees to her chest and humming songs to drown the visitors out. Some of the voices were insistent though. Like the one from the night before. A young boy, nine or ten, who wouldn't let go no matter what she did. He wanted to tell her how he'd died, but she didn't allow it. She didn't want to hear about that. The only thing that got through loud and clear was him telling her to be strong and to see things through to the end. She assured him she would, not having the slightest idea what he was talking about.

Sarah found herself wishing that voice was with her now. Anything to distract her from the feeling she had from being in the car with Mrs. Dahl. The hole inside her friend's mom felt too much like what she'd experienced in the cave. It was cold and helpless. Nothing but empty despair. And the thought that the hole would swallow her and devour everything she was and everything she would ever be made her tremble in her seat. It was so bad that for a second she considered telling her mom everything right there on the spot.

But by the time her mom pulled the car in front of the school, the feeling passed. She was just desperate to escape the car and get some fresh air. She opened the door while the car was still rolling.

"Sarah, what do you think you're doing?" her mom snapped.

Sarah climbed out of the car, pulling her book-heavy backpack behind her.

"Sorry, Mom. Don't want to be late." She spoke quickly so her mom wouldn't notice the raw emotion in her voice. She shouted a quick, "Love ya!" as she shut the door and walked away from the car, praying that she wouldn't hear her mom's voice calling her back. No voice came, but her mom gave her a short honk of the car's horn as a goodbye. Sarah plastered a fake smile on her face and spun around to give her mom a quick wave.

Instead she was looking right at Mrs. Dahl in the passenger seat. Only now she wasn't Mrs. Dahl at all. She was a bloody corpse propped up against the window, her head smashed in on the right side so that blood and bits of brain were splattered all over the inside of the car.

But even with the horrendous injury, Mrs. Dahl was still alive. She lifted her head off the window and turned to Sarah, her shattered jaw hanging low and loose.

With her left hand, Mrs. Dahl reached up and pulled down on her chin, prying open her own mouth. The broken jaw came unhinged and, with a violent twist, she tore it from her face.

There was something inside the mouth. A black ball that swirled and moved like liquid metal. Suddenly, it gushed from her mouth like vomit, a torrent that filled the car, leaking out around the windows and doorframe. Sarah knew it was the despair coming to get her. It was the darkness that had been looking for her since the cave.

She held her backpack in front of her like a shield and dropped to the ground, screaming at the top of her lungs, ready for the blackness to slam into her, to consume her, to destroy her. She screamed and screamed, and waited to die.

Chapter 10

"But I still don't get how that's possible," Jack said, making the turn to the freeway onramp. "So, let me get this straight. You accept an ancient shaman from Central America locked in a limestone cave in Maryland, transmuting his blood into a life force that gives those who drink it heightened powers and immortality, but you don't get this?" Lonetree asked.

Jack shook his head. It was all crazy, every bit of it. But somehow his brain had coped with the insanity by categorizing it as an aberration. A one off. Or at least something so rare and impossible that there could never be another of its kind for centuries. Like a thousand-year flood. Or an extinction-level rock slamming into the Earth from the cold reaches of space.

But here he was, just a few years out from his last experience with the impossible and it was already knocking on his door again. Only that wasn't right. It wasn't impossible. The Source had been real enough. The weeks of trying to rationalize what he'd seen in the cave had yielded nothing for his efforts. No matter how hard he tried, he couldn't explain away what he'd experienced. Once the impossible became possible, the solid lines he once saw between truth and fiction had dissipated like smoke rings blown into the wind. He realized he was resisting Lonetree's story not because he didn't think it was possible, but because every fiber of his being was begging that it wasn't true.

"I saw it with my own eyes, Jack," Lonetree said. "Trust me, I wish I hadn't."

"Do they have a shaman like Huckley and Mansfield did?" Jack asked.

Lonetree leaned back in his seat. It was the first question Jack had asked since they left the cemetery that seemed to accept the premise. This was happening. This was real. "There is a center to it all. A woman. Goes by the name Mama D."

"What does the D stand for?"

"Don't know. Who gives a shit?" Lonetree growled. "All I know is she makes Huckley look like a kitten. You want to slow down a little? Getting pulled over by the local yokels wouldn't be so good for me right now."

Jack looked down at the speedometer and saw that he was edging up past ninety miles per hour. He eased back on the accelerator. They weren't really going anywhere, just driving to avoid being seen, but the tension was obviously getting to him.

"Worse than Huckley? How is that possible?"

"We tracked her down using my brother's research in his notebooks. He didn't really know anything about her, all he had was a theory that the Source wasn't the only manifestation of this evil. He had pages of information tracking abductions in the Southwest. Some on the West Coast. He thought he saw patterns there. Something that pointed at another cell of these creatures."

"But aren't there hundreds of thousands of kids who go missing every year? How could you find a pattern with so many?"

"Over eight hundred thousand kids under eighteen go missing each year. Out of all the missing kids, ninety-seven percent of them are recovered."

"That still leaves over twenty-four thousand kids. There's so many."

"That ninety-seven percent is a pretty good number. It's up from sixty-two percent in the early nineties when the National Center for Missing and Exploited Children started doing its work. Before that, local law enforcement had sole jurisdiction in abduction cases. The states didn't even talk to each other back then."

Jack nodded as he took the off-ramp, ready to circle back on the freeway toward town. "That's why Huckley and his crew hunted in Pennsylvania and West Virginia. By spreading out their kills, they avoided bringing attention to themselves."

"Fortunately, that's harder now that law enforcement is a little more savvy. Sorenson has a buddy in the Bureau, so we were able to get the data points for the last ten years. Each year, they've identified around a hundred and fifty deaths with abducted kids."

"What about the rest of the ones not recovered?"

Lonetree shrugged. "Disappeared. Some probably dead. Some sold into the sex trade. Others, just sixteen-year-olds getting the hell away from their parents."

Jack remembered a story Lonetree had told him in the caves about his alcoholic father. He wondered if he had been one of the sixteen-year-olds who disappeared from home without a trace. "But the abducted kids who were murdered. There was a pattern there?"

"There were a couple of false starts. Me and Sorenson tracked down some run-of-the-mill kiddie killers first."

"What did you do with them?" Jack asked, immediately wishing he hadn't.

Lonetree looked at him with an arched eyebrow. "Do you really want to know?"

"No, not really," Jack said.

"Let's just say we took care of the trash when we found it," Lonetree said. "But finally we picked up the trail of this other group."

"How?"

"It's kind of hard to explain," Lonetree said, sounding a little uncomfortable. "I get feelings sometimes. Kind of like intuition. Nothing like it must be for Sarah, but along those same lines."

Jack flinched at his casual grouping of Sarah with himself. "She's not like that. Not since the cave. All that's stopped." Lonetree sat studying Jack for an uncomfortable length of time. "I'm serious. She doesn't even remember the cave at all. And there haven't been any *incidents* since then."

Lonetree just kept staring him down. Jack wilted under the scrutiny.

"You don't believe me?" Jack asked.

"No, I can tell that you believe that's the truth," Lonetree said. "I just wonder why she's lying to you."

The car tires thumped along the rumble strip on the side of the freeway as Jack veered off course. He turned the wheel and straightened them out.

"She's not lying to us. Why would you say that?"

Lonetree held up his hands. "Hey, maybe I'm wrong." His tone clearly indicated he didn't think he was.

"She wouldn't lie to us. Not about that," Jack snapped. Lonetree sat in silence, watching him. Finally, exasperated, Jack said, "Why don't you finish your story?"

"Like I was saying, we picked up this group's trail and hunted them for months. It was only a week ago that we caught up to one of them. A low-level guy, Eddie Greer. Funny, you'd think a guy who'd been around over two hundred years would have more of a backbone, but Eddie gave us everything we wanted without needing much persuasion. I guess immortality can make you fear death even more."

"Did he tell you they were after Sarah?"

Lonetree shook his head. "No, but he told us about Mama D. How she was always on the look-out for kids with special gifts. Psychic powers and such." Lonetree paused to see if he would get a reaction from Jack. When nothing came, he continued. "He told us she'd found a new kid. A really special one. But he didn't have the details yet. It wasn't how things worked with Mama D. We decided to use him to get to the rest of the group, but it didn't work out. We screwed it up, got there too late and the kid died. Mama D got away."

Jack heard the bitterness in Lonetree's voice. He knew better than to ask for more details. "I'm sorry," Jack said.

"Yeah, me too," Lonetree murmured. "We caught one of the bastards alive. After a little persuasion, he told us what he knew."

Jack suppressed a shiver, imagining what kind of tactics a persuasive Lonetree would likely use. "And he told you they were coming for Sarah?"

Lonetree shook his head. "We found a road atlas. And on the map, someone had circled Prescott City. When we asked our friend about it, he just knew that they were supposed to be in that town on that date. Not a day before so they wouldn't raise any suspicion. Mama D would contact them then with instructions."

"And what were they planning on doing once they got here?"

"Mama D told them she was on the trail to finding a special treat for them. That she didn't have it yet, but she would by that date and she would bring it to them."

"That's it?" Jack asked.

Lonetree looked confused. "What do you mean, that's it?"

"You said they're coming for Sarah. You don't know that."

"Jack..."

"Maybe they're coming to the sinkhole. Maybe the Source is still a presence there or something. I don't know."

"You're reaching," Lonetree said.

"I'm reaching? You came here saying they're after Sarah. There's no proof. This whole thing could just be a coincidence."

"A coincidence? Let me lay it out for you a little better. Mama D seeks out kids with psychic abilities. Somehow she feeds off that power and in the process transmutes their blood just like the shaman did. Then her followers devour the flesh while the kid's alive. And whatever Mama D does to them keeps them alive while their body is consumed."

Jack stared at Lonetree, horrified. "As terrible as that is, Sarah doesn't have any powers. I told you that."

Lonetree looked at him, his exasperation softening into sympathy. "But you're wrong about that. And I think you know you are."

Jack swallowed hard but he held on to the mantra that had given him so much comfort over the past ten years. He repeated it in his head.

She doesn't remember anything.
She's normal again.
She doesn't remember anything.
She's normal again.

Jack met Lonetree's stare. "That's all behind us. She's just a normal girl," he said, hating how weak his voice sounded.

Lonetree shook his head. "No, Jack," he said. "Your little girl is anything but normal. And the sooner you accept that, the sooner we can start figuring out how we're going to protect her."

Chapter 11

"Sarah, stop. Sarah, it's okay."

The soundtrack of her screams scratched to a stop. She looked up and saw Jesse crouched beside her, concern on her face. This wasn't the first time Jesse had seen her disappear into herself, cowering on the ground like a dog about to be beaten.

"Was it out loud?" Sarah whispered.

"Was what out loud?"

"My...my screaming?"

Jesse shook her head. "I heard you whimper a little, that's it. Was it a bad one?"

Sarah took a long, shuddering breath and risked looking up at where her mom's car had been. It was already gone down the street. Her mom hadn't seen her collapse to the ground like an idiot. That was good. If she had, she would have taken her in for tests and more conversations with psychologists who thought they were so much smarter than she was with their trick questions and petty manipulations. She had Jesse to confide in and that was enough.

"Yeah, it was pretty gross," Sarah said.

Jesse scrunched up her face. "Do I want to hear about it?"

Sarah shook her head, trying to pass it off like it was no big deal. No, she didn't think Jesse wanted to hear about what she had just seen happen to her mom. She usually told Jesse everything, but this was one vision Sarah decided to keep to herself. It was already a tough day for her best friend; adding a vision of her dead mother didn't seem very fair.

As she braced herself to get up, a pit formed in her stomach as she realized what she'd done. She motioned for Jesse to come closer to her.

"I peed myself," she whispered, her face flush with embarrassment.

But Jesse had been on this road with her before. There wasn't even a second's flash of judgment or pity in her friend's eyes. Sarah might as well have told her that she needed a Kleenex to blow her nose. Jesse was just simply there for her, no matter what. It was why Sarah loved her so much.

"How much?" Jesse asked.

"A lot."

"It's OK, right? No biggie. I have gym clothes in my bag. You walk with your backpack in front of you and I walk behind you. Straight to the bathroom."

Sarah nodded, stood up, and brushed off her

knees.

"Looks like you bitches are gonna be late to class. And here I thought you were both so Goddamn perfect," said a deep-throated voice behind them.

Sarah groaned. Mitzy Berlin. She was a girl as far as the anatomy between her legs was concerned, but she was all guy otherwise. Broad, linebacker shoulders, a heavy, squared chin, a wide, flaring nose. Her thin hair hung straight in long greasy strands concealing most of her zit-covered face. Her voice sounded fake, incongruously masculine and old for her sixteen years, but it was the voice that God in His good judgment had given her. She used it to great effect to boss and bully the kids at Prescott High School. Of course, she didn't stop at using her voice. While shredding a little kid's self-esteem was always a rocking good time, nothing really took the place of a solid beat-down.

"Saw your names in the paper," Mitzy sneered. "Think you're famous now or something?"

Sarah knew all about Mitzy Berlin, more than she ought to have known, and she knew she wanted no part in her game. Especially as Sarah stood hiding the patch of urine spreading in her crotch. She gave a quick look around and found out what she was sure Mitzy already knew. There were no teachers or adults anywhere nearby.

Sarah grabbed Jesse's jacket and pulled her along, doing her best to not make eye contact with the girl.

But Mitzy grabbed Jesse's jacket as they tried to slide by and yanked her backward. "Don't ignore me," Mitzy said. "That's just rude."

"Hi, Mitzy," Jesse said, trying to kill with kindness as she always did.

"Hi Mitzy," Mitzy mimicked. "Why are you so happy? Your dad's *dead.*"

"Stop it, Mitzy," Sarah said.

"Everyone in town is talking about it again with the anniversary and all. They're saying he was part of some cult or something. Liked little girls." Mitzy brushed back Jesse's hair from her face with a pretended intimacy. "I bet he liked you plenty, didn't he?"

Sarah watched as her friend's happy demeanor slowly crumbled. Her eyes filled with tears and her lower lip trembled.

"Leave her alone," Sarah said, stepping between Jesse and Mitzy.

"You're not much different. What did they do to you when they took you? Did they touch your private parts? Is that why you two are always together? So you can lesbo out and touch each other like those men did? Like your daddy did?"

"I'm warning you," Sarah said through clenched teeth. "Leave us alone or you'll regret it."

"Oh my God," Mitzy said, stepping back. She broke out into an enormous smile usually reserved for people who won the lottery. "Did you pee your pants or something?" She looked a little closer and pretended to sniff the air. "You did. You pissed all over yourself!"

Sarah felt her face grow hot. "Shut up."

"Don't tell me to shut up, you little slut. I'll smack you in the face."

Sarah clenched her hands into fists. She heard a distant rumbling, like the sound of an avalanche rolling toward her, chewing up trees and rocks on its way downhill. Impossible to stop. "You better leave us alone."

"Maybe that's what those men did. Is that what

happened? Did they piss all over you and you liked it? Is that what happened? That's why you peed on yourself, isn't it? Cuz you like it so much, you little lesbo."

The rumble in Sarah's head grew louder. Something told her she still had time to run away from the sound and escape. But looking at Mitzy's acne-pocked face and her sneering mouth, she didn't want to escape. No, she wanted to teach Mitzy a lesson.

C hapter 12

"Y ou're not going to tell anyone about this," Sarah said, her voice unnaturally calm. It was enough to unnerve Mitzy, who took a hesitant step back. "Oh yeah? Why's that?"

"Because if you tell anyone, I'll tell everyone about Roscoe."

Mitzy looked horrified. "What did you say, you little shit?"

"I'll tell them all about your mom's boyfriend. The one who used to sneak into your room when you were a little kid. I'll tell them about all the things he did to you. The nasty, terrible things."

"You don't—"

"Even worse, I'll tell them about the time your mom walked into the room. You remember that, right?

She saw him. And what did she do?"

"H…h…how do…"

Jesse pulled at Sarah's arm. She was bawling. "That's enough. Stop."

But Sarah didn't want to stop. She wanted to hurt Mitzy the same way Mitzy had hurt so many other kids. The rumble was all around her now, filling her head. She wanted to keep going. "Your mom saw everything, Mitzy. You know she did. And now I know it."

"No…"

"She looked right at you, remember? Saw the tears streaming down your face while her boyfriend grunted on top of you. And what did she do?"

Mitzy stepped backward. All the toughness sapped from her, she looked small and pale. "No, please don't."

The sound in Sarah's head was a roar now, the sound of rushing water mixed with a thousand maniacs laughing. "She closed the door. What mother does that, Mitzy? What kind of mother sees her daughter getting screwed by her boyfriend and just walks away? I'll tell you. A mother that doesn't love her daughter. A mother that hates her—"

"Arrrhghg!" Mitzy screamed, a guttural sound of pure rage. She ran at Sarah, her face twisted into a grotesque mask. She looked like an animal, snarling with bared teeth. Her hands out like claws.

Jesse stepped in her way. Mitzy smashed a hand into Jesse's face, skin from her cheek and forehead piling up under her fingernails. Jesse fell to the ground, crying out as she held the bloody scrapes.

Mitzy charged past her. She didn't care about Jesse Dahl. It was Sarah she wanted. And she wasn't just going to give her a few scrapes. She was going to put her in the

56

hospital. Hurt her so bad that she wouldn't ever even think about telling the world her secret. Maybe even kill her if that's what it took.

Sarah knew these thoughts as clearly as if they were her own. And they scared her.

The sound in her head became a panicked scream. Like a steam whistle exploding next to her eardrum, but on the inside of her head. She knew she was in real danger from Mitzy, but the pain in her head dropped her to her knees. The world strobed in flashes of bright light. It took all of her power just to put her hands in front of her face. She had to block the punches and kicks coming her way.

But nothing came.

She waited, her hands still in front of her face, eyes squeezed shut, trying to push the noise in her head away so she could at least function to protect herself. It worked. The sound ebbed away, growing softer with each heartbeat. When she opened her eyes, she couldn't believe what she saw.

Mitzy Berlin was sprawled on the ground in front of her. Eyes wide open. Panting for air. Spasms wracking her body. Blood gushing from her nose and ears.

Sarah stared dumbly, not understanding. Then Jesse had her by the arm. Her voice sounded distant. Like it was underwater.

"Stop it. You're killing her. Stop doing it."

Sarah slowly turned to Jesse. There was blood on her face from Mitzy's nails, but the cuts were almost healed. As Sarah watched, the skin on each wound closed in on itself and smoothed over. Gone. Sarah never got tired of seeing that happen.

"Sarah! Stop it. Let her go!"

In a daze, Sarah realized her friend thought she

was responsible for hurting Mitzy. The girl's body jerked on the ground like it had electricity passing through it. Spittle turned to foam at the corners of her mouth.

You're going to kill her if you don't stop.

The voice came from inside her, the same place where she heard other people's thoughts. But something told her this wasn't anyone nearby. It was a boy's voice, young and high-pitched. But there was something different about it that she couldn't quite figure out.

Is that what you want? the boy said, unnervingly matter-of-fact. *Do you want to kill her?*

It's not me, Sarah told the voice. *I'm not doing it.*

"Sarah, I'm begging you. Stop!" Jesse screamed.

She's almost gone…last chance. Once a killer, always a killer. Then you'll be Huckley. Then you'll become the Source.

Sarah flinched away from the words like she'd just been burned with a flame. She stumbled backward and grabbed her stomach. On her knees, she vomited on the school's front lawn, heaving and heaving until she thought her ribs would snap apart.

Chapter 13

An ambulance was called and Mitzy was loaded onto a stretcher and taken to Midland General Hospital. Officially, the word from the teachers was that Mitzy Berlin, poor girl, had suffered an epileptic episode and would be right as rain after a few days' rest.

But the whispers in the hallways of any institution are where the real truth is told and schools are no exception. In hushed conversations, students and faculty alike wondered what role Sarah Tremont and Jesse Dahl had really played in Mitzy Berlin's sudden medical issue.

No one had seen it happen, which meant everyone could imagine their own version of events. Little pieces of gossip fueled the flames. Ned Burnett had seen Sarah bawling her eyes out as the ambulance drove away, saying *I'm sorry, I'm sorry* over and over again. Tina Walsh saw Jesse in the girls' bathroom scrubbing blood off her face, but didn't see any cuts or scrapes. *So whose blood was it?*

Even Mrs. Sibolski who taught tenth-grade English had her tidbit of information that made its way into the rumor mill. And this one was really weird. When the school principal had called Mitzy's mom at work to tell her what had happened, she was told that Mrs. Berlin herself had suffered a seizure at work and had been taken away by ambulance. *Over ten miles apart and they had seizures at exactly the same time. What are the chances, you know?* said Mrs. Sibolski to anyone who would listen.

There were no conclusions to be reached. Only rumors to spread and theories to share. No one thought of asking Sarah and Jesse directly. Even before this, the girls had been given a wide berth by both students and teachers. Because on a primal level, right on the edge of consciousness, there was an unspoken truth that everyone understood and respected.

Sarah Tremont was not normal. Not normal at all.

Chapter 14

Lauren looked out her window and saw the ambulance arrive at the emergency room entrance below. A lot could be decoded about the severity of the injury on board by the behavior of the driver and paramedics. In this case, the ambulance rolled to a slow stop and the driver waited a few seconds before opening his door. Even then, he waited a few more seconds before jumping out, stretching his arms, and then walking to the back of the vehicle. The back doors opened and the gurney slid out as the paramedics extended the legs to the ground.

The lack of urgency could either bode well for the patient, or indicate the fight was already over and this was a DOA, dead on arrival. But even from the third floor, Lauren could see that the young girl on the stretcher was awake and moving her hands as she answered the paramedics' questions.

As a mother, Lauren was relieved that the girl didn't seem to be in pain or distress. Probably a simple broken bone or an allergic reaction cured with a simple dose of epinephrine. That meant there was likely not going to be a call from the ER for her help. It was part of her arrangement with the hospital in exchange for the space and independence they provided her. She was left alone to do her research but would consult as needed on cases that either surpassed the ER docs' abilities or took them outside of their comfort zones.

The truth was that she looked forward to those calls and it was really the only reason she had kept her lab in the hospital to begin with. Back when her medical career had taken her down the research path with the Centers for Disease Control, she'd missed the interaction with patients. While the deaths were heartbreaking, the times when she felt a part of saving someone's life and restoring what could have been a fractured family gave her a gratification that couldn't be found in the CDC's electron microscopes.

But intellectually she knew that while medicine on the retail level might make her feel better about herself, there was work to be done that could save thousands of lives. Maybe millions. She was just happy the new hospital administrator, Dr. Elaine Hofstra, who had taken over for the deceased Dr. Mansfield, had agreed to let her set up her lab here. A sizeable donation made by the Jack and Lauren Tremont Foundation to the hospital had certainly helped grease the wheels a bit. The prospect of that much money and access to one of the preeminent medical minds in the country had been too good to pass up, especially given all the unpleasantness that had plagued the hospital when she first took over. Missing bodies. An attempted murder in the hospital. Even a shoot-out in the parking lot, for Chrissakes.

Still, when the delivery trucks began to arrive with hundreds of thousands of dollars' worth of specialized lab equipment, Dr. Hofstra had raised an eyebrow. When the security company arrived to place high-tech locks on the lab, she finally voiced her concerns about the kind of research Lauren intended to conduct.

Lauren heard the woman out, even admired her for her diligence, and then pointed to the terms of their agreement that Lauren was to have absolutely no oversight by the hospital board or administration. She didn't have to threaten withdrawal of the foundation funds; it was implied. They settled on a periodic third-party review of Lauren's storage and safety procedures by the CDC. Dr. Hofstra was content with the compromise and Lauren knew the right people at the CDC to give her a clean bill of health based on her word. Everyone was happy.

She only wished the research itself had been going better.

The lab wasn't large, maybe thirty by forty feet. The perimeter was lined with countertop where every instrument from a full lab could be found. Beakers, intricate forests of test tubes, centrifuges, microscopes, all the good stuff. On one wall was a large wire mesh cage divided into one-foot by one-foot boxes with solid metal walls between them. This cage was ten boxes wide and four high. Over half of the boxes crawled with large hairless rats. Bred for research, the hairless rats looked like tiny alien creatures with folds of excess skin, beady black eyes, and twitching noses. On the bench across from the cage were seven plastic boxes, each containing a dead rat carcass. Next to each of them was a vial of blood labeled with a reference number.

Lauren raised a recorder to her lips as she crossed the room to the dead rats. "Trials 333 through 339 have failed. 100% mortality rate within thirty-six hours of injection. Test animals exhibited immediate and prolonged post-injection agitation." *Maybe the agitation was from the scalpel you took to their skin,* she thought to herself. She pulled on plastic gloves and picked up the rat in the box labeled 333, turning it over in her hands. There was a long incision along the rat's spine. "Three three three. Dorsal incision exhibits no regenerative growth." She picked up the next one to the same result. "Three three four. Dorsal incision exhibits no regenerative growth." A few minutes later she'd reached the last one and recited the same words seven times.

"Perfect," she said to herself. "Putting Neosporin on the cuts would have healed them more than this."

She prepared the dissection trays for each rat. It would take time but she had to be thorough. It was not only in her nature, but it was good science. And since she was breaking about a hundred rules laid out by the CDC and the American Medical Association, she felt like she should at least do the science right.

She had considered hiring a few technicians to help with her workload, but she would have to lie to them about the research they were doing. Even then, if the proverbial shit ever hit the fan, whoever was associated with her little enterprise would likely never work in a lab again. She knew the risks and was prepared to take them, but it wasn't fair to subject others to the same risks without their knowledge. Jack, of course, knew what she was doing. He'd argued that she ought to take her research to the CDC, but she'd won him over in the end. She knew exactly what would happen if she brought this to the CDC. She knew the protocols in place, and the results would be unacceptable. There would be a time to bring them in, but not yet. Not while she was still trying to figure out what was going on and whether it really might be the panacea she hoped.

She sliced open the first rat and poked through the liquefied remains of its internal organs. Just like the three hundred and thirty-two rats before it, this one yielded no real insights into why the most recent serum had failed. There was no differentiation between this and all the other subjects in the way the serum had attacked the soft tissues and yet left the brain untouched. Her previous work on hemorrhagic fevers had given her expertise to draw upon regarding rapidly deteriorating flesh, but this was unlike anything she had seen before.

No matter how she manipulated the serum, she couldn't keep it from attacking the body it was supposed to protect. She'd employed all the tricks from her days of working on vaccines. Recombining RNA receptacles. Hardening protein strands. Even Trojan-horsing the compound inside an existing vaccine. But always to the same result. A painful death for her ugly, little rats.

She leaned back in her chair and rubbed her tired eyes. There had to be a way, she just needed to keep at it. She tried to think of how she was going to replenish her supply of raw material for use in her serums. She was down to her last couple of cubic centimeters and that would be used up making the next batch. It was a tricky situation and underscored just how illegal her lab truly was.

But it was for the greater good. If she was successful, she would change the world. Millions would be cured of disease who might otherwise die. Perhaps tens of millions.

It was worth the risks. Just as she did every couple of years, she just had to manufacture a reason to get a few more vials of Jesse Dahl's blood.

Chapter 15

Jack sped up the stairs to Prescott High School's front entrance. When he'd gotten the phone call from the school nurse, his heart ended up in his throat as he waited for the woman to explain the reason for the phone call. Lonetree had assured him the danger from Mama D was still a day or two away but Jack's first thought was that the ex-Navy SEAL had miscalculated. That the school was calling to report Sarah missing. That the whole thing was starting over again.

But the nurse didn't say those things. Only that Sarah wasn't feeling well. Sick to her stomach was all. She mentioned something about Sarah witnessing another student's epileptic seizure and that it had disturbed her. If Jack hadn't been so relieved that Sarah was safe, he might have asked a few more questions about why the school hadn't seen fit to call him or Lauren if their daughter was shaken up by something she had seen. The nurse seemed happy to skip right by the issue, probably having reached the same conclusion.

Jack had dropped Lonetree off at a gas station in town. They'd exchanged phone numbers and Jack promised to call after getting Sarah. As he drove away, he saw a black SUV swing into the gas station and roll to a stop to let Lonetree climb in. Jack realized Nick Sorenson must have been following them the entire time and he hadn't even noticed.

Jack made his way through hallways lined with dented lockers and terrible artwork from Prescott City's aspiring junior artists. The scent of Pine-Sol hung in the air. It occurred to Jack that every school had the same smell, but that it didn't do much to impart a clean feeling. The smell seemed to suggest there was something grimy and dirty being masked over, like the way a diseased person's room was scrubbed with disinfectant after they died. He shook himself from the morbid thoughts and quickened his pace, eager to get Sarah and get out of there.

His phone rang right before he opened the door to the nurse's office. Through the window he saw Sarah sitting on a low sofa in a small waiting room. Her color may have been a little off, but other than that she looked fine. He held up his iPhone and saw that it was Lauren requesting that they Facetime. He groaned. For him, Facetime was the most awkward thing in the world. He felt a little guilty for not liking the technology. Easy-to-use video calls had been promised by sci-fi movies since the 1950s. It had taken well over half a century for it to finally show up and now that it had, he found he preferred a regular old phone call. He felt foolish holding his phone up in front on him, basically taking an extended selfie. It had been great to use with Becky at boarding school, but he found day-to-day use annoying.

He stopped outside the closed door, tapped the screen to accept the call, and waited while the video connection was made. After a couple seconds of delay, he saw Lauren in a lab coat, hair pulled back, her lab behind her. Whatever device she was using to make the call was on some kind of tripod on the counter. She leaned in too close to the camera, making her face look enormous.

"I just got your message. Damn ringer was off," Lauren said. "Are you there yet?"

Jack was glad he had the audio going through the Bluetooth on his ear. He was sure the teenagers at Prescott City High used stronger words than *damn*, but it still felt like strong language on school property. "Yeah, I'm right outside the nurse's office. I can see her through the window. She's fine. See?" He toggled the camera so it showed Lauren a live feed of Sarah. She looked up and waved. Jack couldn't help but think Lonetree was crazy. There was no way his little girl with the long blond hair and gentle blue eyes had lied to him about her special powers being gone. The more he thought about it, the more ridiculous it sounded. Jack reversed the camera again. "See, all good."

She leaned back in a rolling desk chair, looking relieved.

"Thank God. Your message about L—"

"About leaving early this weekend?" Jack interrupted. He took seriously Lonetree's warning that there were significant resources being used to hunt down the ex-Navy SEAL. In light of all the NSA stories on the front pages of the newspapers, it didn't seem too much of a stretch to imagine their phone calls might be recorded and stored in some server farm somewhere. "Why don't we talk about that when you get home? Can you knock off early?"

She looked concerned but seemed to pick up his hint not to talk about Lonetree on an unsecure line. The world tilted at an angle as she picked up the phone and carried it across the lab to a shiny stainless-steel machine.

"Okay, I just need to set up this next batch," she said, putting the phone on the counter as she opened the machine to reveal an array of test tubes. Jack recognized the machine as a high-tech sterilization unit with scalding heat, infrared, and every other bug-killing treatment science could devise. He thought of it as the world's most expensive dishwasher. Sarah began plucking test tubes out of the device. "If I hurry I can leave in fifteen minutes. Where do you want to meet?"

"Can you skip a batch?" Jack asked. "I think we should meet up as soon as possible." He looked back through the window and saw Sarah watching him closely. He felt a little guilty for making her wait. He turned around and faced the hallway so Sarah couldn't read his lips. "I think Sarah needs our help," he whispered.

"I'll hurry," Lauren said. "I'll just take…just…"

Lauren knocked a test tube off the counter, reaching for it as it fell to the floor. There was the sound of glass breaking, and then Lauren's scream filled his earpiece. It took him a second to realize he was hearing the sound in stereo, half through his Bluetooth and another almost identical scream, with his other ear. Coming from inside the nurse's office behind him.

Jack spun around to see Sarah holding her left forearm, screaming out in pain.

He ran into the room and kneeled next to her just as the school nurse, an older lady with a bad dye job that gave her raven-black hair, came out from the back room. She gave him a scathing look, as if he had been the one to hurt his daughter.

"What happened?" the nurse said, inspecting Sarah's forearm.

Sarah kept screaming, staring at her forearm like it was a foreign thing.

"Nothing, I—I was outside the room. Talking on the phone." He reached out for Sarah but she jerked away from him.

"Don't touch it," she screamed.

"Calm down, honey," the nurse said. "Let me see. Did you get stung by something?"

Sarah took a shuddering breath and pulled her hand from her forearm. Jack expected to see a mark of some kind, but there was nothing there. Sarah fell silent as the nurse inspected it. She looked up at Sarah, confused.

"Honey, I don't see—"

"*Fuck! Shit! Goddammit.*"

The small, tinny voice came from the Bluetooth earbud that had popped out of Jack's ear when he ran into the room.

The school nurse eyed him disapprovingly and Jack shrugged.

"My wife," he said, as if that explained everything. One eye on Sarah, he popped the earbud back into place and looked back at the phone. It took him a few seconds to get the orientation but he figured out that the phone was on the floor and he was staring up at the ceiling. To

71

one side was a white cabinet door. His stomach sank as he saw it was smeared with blood.

"Lauren!" Jack called out.

"I'm okay," she shouted back. "Just cut myself a little. Getting a Band-Aid."

Jack relaxed a little. He reached out to Sarah and she held out her arm for him.

"I'm okay, Daddy," she said quietly. Almost embarrassed. "Can we go home? I don't feel well."

"Of course," Jack said. He looked to the nurse. "Do I need to sign her out or anything?"

The nurse shook her head. "I'll take care of it." She gave Sarah a little pat on the head. "Feel better, okay? Ice cream and TV should help."

Sarah gave her a weak smile for the effort, but Jack could see she wasn't herself. He thanked the nurse and they walked out into the hallway together.

"I'm back. Is Sarah all right?" Lauren said in his ear.

Jack raised the phone again and saw the screen was black with the message: *Weak signal. Image should return in a moment.* He could hear Lauren but couldn't see her. "Yeah, I think so. What happened to you? I saw the blood on the wall."

"I was hurrying too fast. Dropped a test tube and tried to catch it instead of just letting it fall. Glass went into my arm."

"Jesus, good thing it was sterilized."

"I'd throw a tech out on their backside if they made that mistake. So stupid."

"But you're okay?"

"I'm going to need to go down to the ER to get some stitches."

The iPhone indicated the video was reconnecting. He watched it, eager to see her face and gauge for himself if she was underplaying how bad it was. The image came back and he saw her face. He could tell she was in pain, but it wasn't terrible.

"Let me see it," Jack said.

"I'm fine."

"Hey, you're the Facetimer here. Let's use the technology."

She hesitated and then the image slowly spun away from her until it was pointed at a blood-soaked bandage.

Wrapped around her left forearm.

Exactly where Sarah had felt her pain.

He stopped walking and stared at his little girl, walking in front of him. She stopped, turned, and stared right at him. He couldn't explain how, but he could just *feel* that she was aware he had just connected the dots.

Sarah had felt her mother's pain. Over twenty miles away, and still she had felt it.

"Jack? Are you there? Can you still hear me?"

Jack ignored the voice in his ear. He just stared at Sarah. And she stared back. The pretense was gone. They both knew and there was no point in hiding it.

She walked back to him and took his hand in hers. "I'm sorry, Daddy."

Tears sprang to his eyes. He reached out and scooped her up in a hug. She was just his little girl. No matter what powers were inside of her. No matter what she was capable of, she was just his little girl.

"You have nothing to be sorry about," Jack whispered.

She leaned to his ear to whisper something back.

A thousand times in her life, she had leaned in and whispered, *I love you, Daddy*, into his ear. God, he wished that was what she said.

But she didn't.

Sarah leaned in so close that he felt her breath against his skin, and whispered, "Daddy, who's Mama D and why does she want to hurt me?"

Chapter 16

Mama D stepped from the house into the swelter of the Texas heat. She looked out over the rough desert landscape covered with low brush and hardy cactus. It appeared flat for as far as the eye could see, but she knew that was an illusion. When you got down into the thick of it there were any number of washes and gullies scraped out by ages of weather. Natural funnels and conduits for the rare occasions when the West Texas sky ripped open and drenched the desert with a year's worth of rain in a matter of minutes.

Mama D enjoyed seeing Mother Nature assert herself like that. She enjoyed it when black, roiling thunderclouds appeared on the horizon and slid over the landscape with a sense of terrifying purpose. The temperature dipped and the wind stirred. Animals found shelter because the primordial brain still understood what man in his sophistication seemed to have forgotten. Nature was something to be feared, its fury uncontrollable.

Though she didn't truck much with the psycho-babble bullshit slung around in twenty-first century America, Mama D had pondered her fascination with storms and come up with her own theory. She associated herself with their power. Their anger. Their resolve to sow destruction.

Mama D pulled the piece of paper from her pocket and reread the names scrawled there. Over a dozen men killed at the Charlie Winters feeding. That Indian Lonetree again. He had gotten close to her this time. Too damn close. After the new feeding was over, she was going to solve that problem. Have him hunted down and brought to her alive so she could remind all of her followers the most important truth they would ever know. Just like the storms, Mama D was a Goddamn force of nature.

This was true back before she became Mama D.

This was true even before the Pastor, although he certainly had a part in making her who she was today.

Before she was Mama D, her parents brought her before God as Annabel Elizabeth Deschautes. On that auspicious day, they handed her to a sinner with a pastor's collar to half-drown her in a baptismal fount in front of a hundred witnesses. As soon as his rough-calloused hands touched her bare skin, she saw every evil, vile thing the pastor had ever done. The cat he'd beaten to death with a baseball bat when he was seven, pretending it was his kid brother instead. The shove at the top of the stairs that sent that same brother tumbling down, snapping his spine

76

and putting him in a wheelchair as a drooling vegetable. The same brother who the pastor rolled out in revival tents across the South to cry tears over and use to get money to pour out of his congregants' pockets and into his own. Then there were the kids. Dozens of them. His hands all over their privates, fiddling, poking, jerking. Mostly boys, but a few girls just to prove to himself he wasn't a pervert or anything. Because that would be a truly irredeemable sin.

All of this rushed into Annabel Elizabeth Deschautes as the man raised her up in front of the congregation, his hand secretly rubbing between her legs under the baptismal gown, the diseased prick getting off on doing it in front of everyone without them knowing. Although she could not yet speak, she knew with absolute clarity that her destiny was to grow up strong and then come back and kill the son-of-a-bitch for all that he had done and for all that he would do.

The year was 1921 and she was six months old.

A decade later, she used an old cavalry sword from the pastor's own house and a pair of pliers to pay him back. She sliced him open with the blade, beginning a lifetime infatuation with using a sword on her victims. But she didn't cut him deep. She had no intention of moving too fast. She cut him just enough to give her a good edge to work with. It was hard work, but she peeled the man's skin from his body over a two-day period, then watched as insects and rodents feasted on his raw, bloody flesh. As she did all this, she basked in the comfort that comes from a promise well-kept.

To make the event really special, she brought the brother along to watch. Annabelle reached into his mind and found most of him still in there, an intact soul trapped in a destroyed body. He thanked her over and over, then, with a shit-eating grin on his face, watched the writhing, pulp of tissue that was his brother roll around on the ground, trying to get away. But when the man died, she felt both cheated and ashamed. Two days of unimaginable pain didn't seem like enough penance. She pledged to get better and make sure the next one lasted a more appropriate length of time.

When she reached back into the brother's mind to apologize for ending the fun too soon, she noticed something she hadn't before. Inside him, buried under the gauzy layers of brain damage, was a spark similar to the fire that burned inside of her. The gift. The power that made her able to read minds, influence behaviors and, if she was angry enough, to actually cause things to move with her mind.

She poked at it, called to it, and the spark responded. It shone bright, flickering as if from the exertion of making itself seen. Annabel had an image of a shipwrecked passenger on a sinking lifeboat waving frantically at a ship passing nearby on the open ocean. Slowly, she realized the image didn't come from her mind. It came from the spark.

And she knew what it wanted.

She felt a twinge of regret when she slit the brother's throat, but she got over it the second she put her lips to the cut and the hot rush of blood poured into her mouth. She had no idea where the impulse came from, only that something took hold of her and nearly forced her to do it. When she felt the spark enter her through the blood, she understood. The power wanted to live. The spark worked its way toward the fire inside her chest and disappeared into it to become an indistinguishable part of the whole. She breathed in deeply and sensed her increased power. The thought that came to her next was the same thought that led even the strongest of men into the hands of the devil named addiction.

If one felt this good, more would feel even better.

More and more and more. Men, women, sinners, saints, anyone who had even the slightest spark turned her head and drove her to distraction until she could consume what made them special and add them to her own fire. A few years of this and the blaze inside of her was an inferno, burning out of control, bordering on chaos.

Then a man came and everything changed. He came to add her fire to his own, only to find himself locked onto something much more powerful than himself, the dog who finally caught the car and wasn't sure what to do with it. She tried to kill him, to turn the hunter into the hunted and take his fire for herself, but he was stronger than anything she had faced before and the attempt nearly killed her instead. As did the second time she tried to kill him. And the third.

She found his power almost irresistible. She was a jonesing drug addict in front of a pile of pills that promised a greater high than anything else on the market. But after the fourth attempt to overwhelm him nearly destroyed them both, they settled into an uneasy truce. The man had information she needed. And, in the end, she served a purpose for him too.

He taught her how to bring her cravings under control, how to tamp down the urges when they were too dangerous, how to slake the blood thirst. He explained what he knew about the shadow world in which they both lived.

She learned that many were born with the gift, but that fear and shame caused them to push it down until it withered inside of them. That's why, he explained, hunting children made the most sense. Their fire was stronger and there was less chance of violence they, as the hunter, couldn't control.

The group he worked with hunted as a pack, serving a master that could amplify the spark and give them a gift of immortality. She scoffed when he claimed to be over two hundred years old. Laughed until he allowed her the barest glimpse into his mind, filled with images of nineteenth century America. She took the opportunity to try another attempt to explode open his mind and swallow his fire in one ravenous gulp, but he shut the door quickly, shaking his head at her in mock disappointment. She shrugged but didn't apologize. She knew he'd expected no less from her.

They hunted together, the man enjoying the flair she exhibited by her use of a sword. They focused on children with the gift unless they came across the rare adult with enough spark to make the risk worthwhile. He always let her have the spoils of the hunt, watching her carefully when she fed, an odd expression on his face. So used to reading minds, she was out of practice reading body language and facial expressions. But after a week of this, she finally realized what the look was. Curiosity mixed with resentment. The man couldn't feed. When he'd come for her, he wasn't trying to steal her fire, he was trying to capture her to bring her to someone who could. The master they served didn't just amplify the spark; it was the only way the man could drink the fire. He was no more than a slave.

NIGHT TERROR

One night, in the middle of a Louisiana bayou, after feeding on twin sisters under the full moon, encircled by oak and bitterroot covered with nests of Spanish moss, Annabel followed two urges. She turned to the man and slid her dress off her shoulders and dropped it to the ground. Annabel knew she was beautiful. Only seventeen, her body was that of a woman's, not a girl's. The effect of the moonlight on her smooth, perfect body, full breasts heaving with anticipation, would have reduced most men to idiots. But the man didn't move from his spot. It wasn't until she produced her sword that he walked toward her. As he approached, she dragged the blade across the top of her breast, producing a flow of blood that looked purple in the strange light of the moon.

The man lost his control and lurched forward, licking the blood from her skin, placing his mouth over the incision, pulling at it with all the intensity of a starving infant. Annabel felt the blood drawn out of her, feeling the pull through her vascular system until there was a tugging sensation on her heart. She was a little shocked at the intensity, but found she could will her body to slow what the man could take. And she knew blood was just the carrier for what he really wanted. Carefully, she allowed a small part of the fire she took from the twins to go with the blood. She was reminded of a saying: the Lord giveth and the Lord taketh away. She thought the more accurate saying to be, the Lord giveth because the Lord had already taketh away. As she held him suckling at her breast, she knew she was the Lord in this saying.

When he was done feeding, they fell to the ground and Annabel followed through with her second impulse. With the man half-mad with the rush of the new spark, it was easy to get from him what she wanted. The sex was rough and feral, animals locked together, scraping and grinding toward climax.

When they were done, they laid together, staring at the stars and the endless possibilities they represented. She imagined the years ahead of her with the man, hunting, developing their abilities, exploring their bodies together. For the first time since she was pulled screaming from her mother's uterus, she didn't feel utterly alone. She took his hand and offered to let him stay, to allow him to serve her the way he served his master he called the Source.

The way he smiled at the suggestion unnerved her. It wasn't amusement, but pity that she saw in his eyes. The way one looks at children when they speak of things they could not possibly understand. She knew in an instant that the gift she gave the man paled to what the Source provided.

A wave of excitement passed through her that something so miraculous existed, followed immediately by the nauseating understanding that the man would not stay with her. A rage filled her as she realized she was being denied. He reached out to kiss her lips and she slapped him hard across the face. He rocked back but didn't retaliate. He simply pulled on his clothes and stood. Finally, he said to her, "Stay safe, Mama D. Keep what I gave you safe. There might be a time when I need it back."

Then he left, never to be seen again. He left nothing behind. No phone number. No forwarding address. No clothes. No single item that might fit into his parting words.

Nate Huckley left nothing behind except her new name and the baby growing inside her.

Mama D turned back toward the house, a noise shocking her out of her reverie. She realized that her hands were protectively covering her abdomen and she dropped them to her sides. After eight decades, she hated that she still held on with any fondness to the memory of that night.

She opened the door and walked back inside through the entryway, past the kitchen, down the hallway until she came to a heavy steel door with a bar across it, like something in a medieval castle. Inside, something was destroying the room. Wood cracked and popped. Glass broke. The door shuddered as things were hurled against it.

"Shhh, Pesh," Mama D called out, picking up one of her favorite swords leaning against the wall. "Settle. It's all right. Settle now. Mama's here."

The noise stopped, replaced by a scraping sound right on the other side of the door. After a few moments, that was replaced by a high-pitched whine, similar to a dog begging to go outside.

"There," said Mama D. "That's a good boy. Now step back from the door so Mama can come in."

Another shuffle.

Mama D slid the bar away from the door and twisted the heavy black key in the lock. She pushed the door open into a dark room, the sword at her side.

"I'm here, Pesh," Mama D said. "Everything's okay. You gotta trust me on that. You do trust your mama, don't you?"

Mama D stepped inside the room, her eyes adjusting to the light.

"C'mon baby. Time for us to go. There's someone in Maryland I want you to meet. You're gonna love her. I

83

promise."

A grunting noise came from the back of the darkened room.

"She's good people. I hear she knew your daddy." She walked to a chest of drawers and pulled out a pair of boxer shorts. "C'mon, let's get dressed and go see her, all right?" Nothing moved. "It's a long way away. You get to go bye-bye in the car."

Still nothing. Mama D sighed. She put the sword's edge to her wrist. "Okay, but you're being a very naughty boy today. Mama doesn't like that one bit, you hear me?"

A large shadow ran toward her, the size of a small man, knocking things out of the way, reaching her just as the blood dripped from her wrist. Mama D looked up at the ceiling as the shadow latched onto her and sucked at the gash, a pang of guilt passing through her because she didn't want to look at the creature drinking her blood. She hated that she couldn't stand to look at her own child.

"Shhh…it's all right. Everything's gonna be all right soon," she whispered more to herself than to Pesh. "We got a special prize waitin' for us in Maryland. And, if your daddy was right, it's gonna change everything."

Chapter 17

"Careful," Lonetree growled, grabbing the door handle as the Ford Expedition bumped down a dirt road. "You're not driving an armored Humvee."

Sorenson grinned and twisted the wheel to dodge a large rock in their path. "You know, my grandma complains about my driving too. You sound just like her."

"Very funny."

"No, I'm serious," Sorenson said. "I don't know why I didn't see it before. Every day, you're starting to act more and more like her."

"I can still kick your ass."

"You're kinda looking like her too. I noticed your man-boobs are hanging a little. Just like Grandma's."

"Your grandma has man-boobs?" Lonetree said.

"That's just wrong."

Sorenson let out a huge laugh. The path got tough for a bit so he concentrated on his driving, bouncing them around brutally. The forest around them showed the signs of an early winter. Lonetree remembered the same area on fire with color the year before, but now it seemed dead and lifeless. The leaves that still clung earnestly to their branches were brown and wilted. They matched his mood.

After navigating around rocks and fallen trees, the road opened back up and Sorenson relaxed a bit. "Do you think Tremont will stick it out and fight?"

Lonetree shook his head. "No, I don't think he will. Would you?"

Sorenson mulled it over. "If I only knew what he knows right now, then probably not."

"You think I should have told him everything," Lonetree said. It was a statement, not a question.

"You must have your reasons," Sorenson replied. "I'd be dead a dozen times over if I made a habit of second-guessing you. It just seems…I don't know…"

"C'mon, Nick. You can't tell me you're going to start pulling punches now. Just say what you're thinking."

"It just seems wrong not to tell him," Sorenson said. "He's going to find out eventually."

"Maybe…maybe not," Lonetree said. "Besides, I could be wrong." Sorenson eyed him skeptically, taking his eyes off the road for a beat too long and hitting a rut at the wrong angle, bottoming out the undercarriage. "Jesus, want me to drive?"

"That's okay, Grandma, I want to get there sometime today."

Lonetree looked out at the trees streaking by his window. "Grandma my ass," he muttered under his breath, knowing Sorenson would enjoy thinking the good-natured ribbing was getting under his skin.

The back and forth with Sorenson was appreciated and sorely needed. For the last ten years, moments of fun and levity had been few and far between. He wondered if he would have been able to survive the journey without Sorenson around to keep him sane. The younger man had followed him unquestioningly, even leaving the SEALs against Lonetree's wishes when Lonetree had come home looking for his brother's killers. It was his most valued relationship. Given the dark business they conducted now, it was fitting that their bond had come from an equally dark, troubled place.

Lonetree first met Sorenson as a young demolitions expert tasked to his SEAL team. Contrary to SEAL standard operating procedures, Lonetree had been allowed to go into the fight as a one-man operation, hunting high-value targets for long periods of time. It's not that he couldn't function as part of a team. In fact, when the mission called for it, he excelled at it, often functioning in a leadership capacity. It's just that he'd been most effective on his own, slithering through the networks of caves in Tora Bora, Afghanistan looking for Al-Qaeda, or searching for members of Abu Sayyaf deep in the Indonesian jungles. And then there were the rumors about him. They were always the same, and always came with an equal mix of fear and wonder.

It was said that Lonetree knew things. He sensed a sniper attack seconds before it happened. He knew an IED placement even when it was buried perfectly and there was no way he could have seen it. He could track anyone through any terrain, even in a full rainstorm, even after dogs lost a trail.

The truth was most of his instinct came simply from good soldiering, not some kind of Indian magic like people whispered about. He admitted there were moments of what he called inspired instinct, moments when he did feel things that he couldn't logically explain away. But he didn't think much of it. Such moments of instinct weren't uncommon among soldiers. Hell, even civilians could relate to spinning around after feeling someone watching them, only to find that someone was off in the distance. It was an experience nearly every human had and yet science had no explanation for it.

So, he rationalized that his feelings were no more than what every person felt from time to time. Only maybe he was a little more tuned in because, as one of the perks of constantly worrying a bad guy is about to put a bullet in your ear, all of his senses were hyped up every waking moment.

But he never tried to dispel the rumors either. It helped that men assigned to his team felt a little extra confidence. Comments like, *A little Indian juju never hurts* weren't uncommon. Lonetree held a special position in a world of tough men who weren't easily impressed and he used it to his advantage. He also liked that people gave him a wide berth when he walked through a room and that his commanding officer seemed relieved when he requested to go on missions alone. A therapist would likely argue his desire not to rely on others came from being raised by a single alcoholic father in the middle of the poverty of the reservation. Lonetree didn't look that deeply into it. He just liked to work by himself. Get in, kill the bad guys, get the hell out.

That all changed when he met Nick Sorenson. More like when Nick Sorenson sought him out and lodged himself as a permanent pain in Lonetree's ass.

Chapter 18

There had been other young SEALs who had tried to get close to Lonetree. Stories of warriors like the strange Native American were exactly the kind of stories soldiers loved to tell so they spread far beyond his unit. Lonetree knew that the stories had become so fantastical and exaggerated that he might as well have been an honest-to-God superhero for all the powers ascribed to him. Every few months, one of the young pups sought him out and tried to befriend him.

The day Sorenson was assigned to Lonetree's operational unit, the younger man sat down at the table where Lonetree was characteristically eating alone, introduced himself, and stated, "I think the stories about you are a bunch of horseshit. All the magic mumbo jumbo anyway. I think you're just a better soldier than the rest of these assholes and I want to learn everything you know."

Lonetree hadn't looked up from his plate. Didn't even acknowledge the man's presence. Seconds stretched into minutes. A few minutes became ten. Then Lonetree was done with his food and, still without even looking at Sorenson, got up, tossed his plate in the bin, and left the mess hall. It didn't take a sixth sense to know he was being followed. The kid was right behind him, a few yards back, not trying for any kind of discretion. And that's where Sorenson stayed for the next nine days, usually no more than a few yards away. While the unit was still on call, they were on a two-week rest rotation and it was pretty quiet, enabling his newly acquired shadow to keep up with him pretty easily. If Lonetree was in the weight room, Sorenson was doing the same exercise a few benches down. If Lonetree was doing a ten-mile run, Sorenson was twenty yards behind him. If Lonetree was on the range, Sorenson showed up there too.

After being initially annoyed by the whole thing, Lonetree decided to have a little fun with the kid. He pushed his runs harder than he normally would, noticing Sorenson fell back to fifty yards or so, but still kept up. He stayed up two nights in a row, practicing disassembling his weapon over and over again while he let his mind wander. He suppressed a grin when Sorenson nodded off while reassembling his own weapon at his bunk, dropping pieces to the floor. The kid scrambled after them, cursing up a blue streak.

Next, Lonetree switched from the hot mess hall food to the Meals-Ready-to-Eat, MREs, they ate on missions, barely tolerable dehydrated food and flavored protein paste. The food was designed to keep you alive, but there was nothing positive to be said about the taste. True to form, Sorenson copied him and, with a sour face, pulled the tinfoil covers off his MREs while he sat in the middle of the mess hall surrounded by men eating barbequed ribs, chicken, mashed potatoes, and bread lathered up with butter. Uncle Sam might miss the boat on a lot of things, but he's figured out that a well-fed soldier is a happy soldier. Not so much for Sorenson, who scraped at his MRE with a plastic spoon while his buddies made fun of him at every meal.

All of that had been fun, but it got real in a hurry when their team was called up for an operation. Ten minutes after the call came in, five of them, including Lonetree and Sorenson, were on a helo in full tactical screaming toward a high mountain village where some high-value terrorist target had been IDed in a Taliban stronghold. Lonetree glanced at Sorenson as they all performed their gear check. Part of Lonetree regretted the sleep deprivation game he'd been playing with the kid, but he was a SEAL. A couple nights' missed sleep shouldn't make a difference. He hoped.

They landed five clicks from their target and made the hike in short order. It was the middle of night with no moon, making their state-of-the-art night-vision goggles an enormous advantage. The US military likes to say it owns the night. If that was true, then the SEALs were the monsters that hunted in that night.

The village was actually no more than a compound of five squat, mud huts nestled into the base of a hillside. Lonetree separated his team into three. A sniper who took a high position for recon and force protection. A two-man team that would sneak around to the far side of the target in case someone decided to make a run for it. He and Sorenson on point to kick in a door or two and look for the bad guy.

As they split up, Lonetree whispered to Sorenson, "You okay?"

"Five-by-five," Sorenson said, no sign of stress in his voice. "Let's get this guy."

Lonetree liked what he heard. The kid was cool under pressure. Focused but not tight. So far, anyway. They had barely entered the kitchen and they were about to jump right into the frying pan.

He crouched to the ground, giving the rest of the team a chance to get into position. Something was bothering him though. He was getting one of his feelings. He adjusted his night-vision goggles to infrared and scanned the mud huts. Nothing. Still, he felt the presence of danger. And fear. *No shit,* he thought to himself. *You're doing an extraction in the middle of a Taliban-controlled area in the Afghan mountains.* Still, there was something wrong.

Lonetree gave Sorenson a hand signal and they moved forward in a two-by-two covering approach. The night-vision goggles cast everything in an unearthly green hue, but it made the moonless night feel like daytime. He switched his goggles to thermal and immediately saw that only one of the five huts was heated. Bingo.

He and Sorenson took a position by the door. He paused as the rest of the team made their calls in his ear that they were in position. *Bravo, go. Charlie, go.* Lonetree nodded and Sorenson kicked in the door. Lonetree tossed two flash-bang grenades into the hut and Sorenson and he both covered their eyes so the bright flash wouldn't blind them. They waited a beat and then entered the hut one at a time with guns raised.

JEFF GUNHUS

Chapter 19

The hut was a charnel house.

Naked bodies hung on meat hooks spaced every few feet on the walls. All men. The spikes pierced through each shoulder so no vital organs were injured. The bodies were mutilated in grotesque ways. Ragged amputations. Deep lacerations crawling with maggots. Noses, ears, and lips cut or seared off with flames. Genitalia mangled beyond recognition.

In the smoke from the concussive grenade, it was hard to see at first with a fireplace on the far wall the only light in the hut. But within seconds the most horrific part of the discovery showed itself. They were alive. All of them. Some screaming. Some crying. Others just lolling their heads side-to-side, drool hanging from their chins. But all somehow still alive.

Lonetree caught movement to his right and spun, ready to fire. It was a single man, wizened hair bunched into thick mats. A long beard hung to his chest, divided in two down the middle and braided like he was some kind of crazed pirate from a carnival ride back home. His eyes shone with a maniac's certainty, bright and on fire, like they held a truth that had to be shared. He stood with his hands up, just next to his ears, a sneering grin pasted to his face.

Sorenson called out *clear* behind him. The rest of the hut was empty.

"Speak English?" Lonetree asked.

The man nodded once.

"Why are these men here? Why are they being tortured?"

The man laughed, a deep grunting noise filled with phlegm. "Tortured? No, they are released." The man's English was heavily accented but better than Lonetree expected.

"Released from what?" Sorenson asked.

The man smiled and looked lovingly at the men skewered to the walls. Almost as if he were jealous of them. "From lies. Everything to them is revealed and small bits are passed on to me. Truth hides inside pain. But you know this…Joseph Lonetree."

Lonetree froze. He saw Sorenson whip his head in his direction.

"How do you know my name?" Lonetree demanded.

"How does the wind know the name of the trees?" the man said.

Lonetree felt like he'd been punched in the stomach. That saying was his father's. He'd heard it a thousand times growing up. This son-of-a-bitch was in his head. The man grinned wider, enjoying Lonetree's reaction. Lonetree pulled his knife from his side. "Time for some truth," Lonetree said.

But before he could step toward the man, a heavy weight settled on his wrist. Then his entire forearm. An intense pressure that squeezed and kneaded his muscle until it pressed on his bone. The sensation spread to his elbow, then up his arm to his shoulder. Lonetree grunted from the pain and staggered backward. It felt like a python had wrapped itself around his arm, but there was nothing there. The man's grin had turned into a sneer, his face twisting in concentration. Lonetree's knife hand slowly turned toward him. Lonetree fought it, straining with everything he had.

"Stop!" Sorenson shouted.

The man didn't even glance at him. He barked in perfect English, "Orders are to bring me in alive. You always follow orders. Don't you, Sorenson?"

The pressure had reached Lonetree's throat so he barely got out the next words. "T…take…him…"

Sorenson instantly fired. The back of the man's head disappeared in a red mist. The force of the large-caliber bullet at short range lifted the man off the floor and threw him backward against the wall next to the fireplace.

"Yeah, but I take my orders from him, asshole," Sorenson said.

Lonetree's earpiece came alive.

Shot fired. Shot fired.

Alpha. What's your status?

Lonetree cleared his throat. "Target down. Hut secure. Stand-by."

He looked over at Sorenson. The kid might have been holding it together almost better than he was.

"So this is the kind of shit you get into, huh?" Sorenson asked.

"Sometimes," Lonetree said.

Sorenson nodded toward the walls. "Look at that."

Lonetree stepped to the nearest men hanging from the walls. He went to the one who was least mutilated and poked him with his gun. Nothing. He reached up and felt for a pulse. The next one he checked was the same. Dead. All of them. Somehow they had been connected to the man Sorenson had shot. "Probably a mercy. Let's get the hell out of here."

"Don't have to ask me twice," Sorenson said.

"Coming out," Lonetree radioed to the rest of his team.

Roger that.

Sorenson held up a log from the fire and gave Lonetree a questioning look. They both knew that operationally, setting a massive bonfire was the wrong thing to do. Lonetree looked around the room at the desecrated bodies.

"They probably all come from families," Sorenson said. "Do we want wives to find this? Kids? It's one thing to lose someone. It's another to know *this* was done to them. "

Lonetree nodded. He crossed over to the fireplace and grabbed his own burning piece of wood. Together, they set everything flammable they could find on fire. Soon, the inside of the hut was a raging inferno. They ran out of the hut to keep from sucking down too much smoke, and straight into incoming gunfire. There were tracer rounds so Lonetree knew exactly how close to death he came with the first salvo. He dove for cover as bullets pinged off the hut behind him and seared past his head. A burst of fire exploded from Sorenson's M16 as he took his own cover behind a boulder. There was a second's pause in the incoming fire, then a single shot with the distinctive crack of an M24 rifle. A man's cry filled the air, followed by a heavy *thud*. The SEAL sniper had done his job. Lonetree took advantage of the break and ran for one of the other mud huts. Sorenson laid down covering fire then followed right behind Lonetree in a classic two-man advance.

Then all hell broke loose. A rocket-propelled grenade flew right at them, streaking by and exploding a mud hut behind them. As if a signal, the hillside to their right lit up with over a dozen muzzle flashes. This was more than a guard spotting their approach and sounding the alarm. It was a Goddamn ambush.

"Heavy fire. Heavy fire," Lonetree called into his throat mic. "Rally point 3-1-2. Move. Move."

Lonetree laid down a withering line of fire as Sorenson retreated, then turned and did the same for him. He thought he heard gunfire north of their position and figured the other half of his team was fighting their way out too. As he ran, he caught a bullet in his right leg. The impact spun him around and dropped him to the ground. His head smashed against a rock hard enough to make the world disappear for a second. But the white-hot pain in his leg brought him right back to consciousness.

How does the wind know the name of the trees?

It wasn't the cleric's voice. It was his father's. As clear as if he were crouched down next to him, whispering in his ear. Lonetree turned to look for his dad, but saw

Sorenson instead.

"C'mon, gotta go!" Sorenson yelled.

Lonetree accepted Sorenson's help and pulled himself to his feet. The bullet in his leg hurt like a son-of-a-bitch, but he was a SEAL and SEALs don't feel pain like other people. At least that's what his instructors at Coronado at BUD/S school had convinced him to believe.

The other members of his team appeared from behind them, bringing the full power of their weapons to bear on the Taliban fighters. Lonetree dropped to a knee and did his part, lighting up the hillside with his M16. The fight was over in under thirty seconds. There was no celebration, no high-fives. Once the immediate threat was neutralized, the SEALs gathered their injured commander and made their way efficiently to the LZ for their helo ride home.

No one asked what happened in the mud hut. No one questioned why Lonetree and Sorenson had killed the target. Or why they had seen fit to set the mud hut on fire. The after-action report the team later filed was totally mundane, a work of art in bureaucratic smoke screening. Lonetree got patched up, lucky that the bullet only passed through the meat of his leg. And life went back to what it had been before the mission.

The only difference was that when Sorenson stepped out of his tent in the morning, Lonetree was there, leaning on a crutch, waiting for him. They didn't discuss it, set terms, or enter any agreement. But with one look, there was an understanding between them. Lonetree would teach. Sorenson's job was to learn. It worked for as long as it worked, and then it would be over.

As they walked together to the mess hall for some hot chow, Lonetree revealing that the MREs had just been a way to mess with Sorenson, neither of them could have realized the dark places their relationship would take them.

The SUV smashed into a rock and nearly cracked Lonetree's head against the passenger seat window, bringing him out of the past. Yes, he valued Sorenson more than anything. He just wished the bastard would learn how to drive.

Chapter 20

"Terrain's getting bad," Sorenson said, slowing the SUV down to a crawl. "I think we're on foot for the last bit."

"Thank God," Lonetree said. "I'm driving back."

Sorenson parked the vehicle, took out the keys, and stuffed them in his pocket. "If you can get the keys, old man."

"It'd take me all of thirty seconds."

"I dunno. You've taught me all your tricks."

"That's what you think," Lonetree said with a smirk. He opened his door and climbed out. They were close to the spot. He could feel it.

Sorenson followed him as he picked a path through the trees. After about ten minutes, it opened up and they stopped to survey the small valley.

"What do you hope to find here?" Sorenson asked.

"Nothing," Lonetree replied, eyeing the crumbled ruins of the barn where Huckley and his group had used an elevator to access an old mining shaft. At the end of that shaft had been the cave where unspeakable horrors had taken place over centuries, culminating in the night when Sarah Tremont had enabled the shaman-creature to escape. Jack had been the last to see it, battling the monster all the way to the top of the shaft before it was smashed back down to the bottom of the cave by the elevator machinery and covered with millions of tons of rock.

"I hope we don't find anything at all," Lonetree finished.

Chapter 21

Lauren sat quietly in one of the triage stations with the curtain pulled as Nurse Haddie stitched up her forearm. She didn't want to make a big deal about the injury, especially with Dr. Hofstra on the prowl looking for reasons to get involved with her business. While the initial donation to the hospital had greased the wheels for Lauren's lab, her complete independence and total secrecy irked Hofstra to no end. Lauren was sure that she would use the injury for some play for more oversight. Nurse Haddie had been watching Sarah when she was abducted so she was always eager to do Lauren a favor.

"This is pretty nasty. Are you sure you don't want another doc looking at this?" Nurse Haddie asked.

"No," Lauren replied. "I poked around in it when I was upstairs. There's nothing much to worry about in there."

Nurse Haddie shook her head, obviously thinking of Lauren digging through her own deep laceration to inspect it for ligament damage. "Girl, you crazy," Nurse Haddie mumbled, pulling her suture tight.

Lauren looked over the stitches and nodded her approval. "You do good work."

Nurse Haddie beamed. Lauren didn't give out many compliments. "And how're your girls doing? I haven't seen them in forever."

She was right. Neither of the girls wanted anything to do with Midland General after what they'd experienced here. "They're doing good. Becky's almost done at McDonough now."

"I heard. I don't think I could do that. Couldn't bear to send my baby away." Nurse Haddie made the comment conversationally as she went about finishing the stitches. After a few beats, Lauren noticed the woman stiffen as if she realized that the words probably had come out a little judgmental. "I didn't mean it like that. I just—"

"It's fine, Haddie," Lauren said. "Really. It's been one of the hardest things to get used to. Honestly, I hate it. But she just couldn't get back into the swing of things up here after the…you know…and Sarah didn't want to move…so…"

Nurse Haddie put her hand on Lauren's. Lauren almost flinched and was glad she caught herself before she did. Nurse Haddie smiled. "It's okay, Dr. Tremont. You're doing the best you can for your girls. Everyone knows that." She leaned in conspiratorially. "All the nurses like you, you know. The other docs are pretty much ass-wipes, but you're okay."

Lauren burst out laughing. "Just okay?"

"Well, you're still a doc," Nurse Haddie said. "So, okay's about as good as it's gonna get."

"Then I'll take it," Lauren said. This time she put her hand in the nurse's. "Thank you. And thank you for keeping this little injury under wraps."

"No problem. Hofstra has a total hard-on for you. I don't know why you don't—"

The thin curtain whipped back, opening the triage bay to the rest of the ER and revealing a red-faced Dr. Hofstra. "Why doesn't she what?"

Nurse Haddie cut the last bit of excess suture and stood up. "All done here, Dr. Tremont. I have rounds to get to."

She tried to leave, but Dr. Hofstra held out an arm to block her. "Please see me in my office after your shift, Nurse Haddie."

Nurse Haddie nodded then pushed past her.

"Leave her alone, Elaine," Lauren said once Nurse Haddie gone. "She didn't do anything."

"That doesn't matter," Dr. Hofstra snipped in a way that made it clear it mattered quite a bit to her. "I came for your expertise. It's the girl they brought in earlier. Mitzy Berlin."

"I know the name. She goes to school with Sarah."

Dr. Hofstra sniffed the air. "She came in earlier today, suspected epileptic seizure. The problem is that the mother was taken to St. John's earlier today. There's a problem with their CAT scan so they just transported her here. Same symptoms as the daughter."

"A seizure?" Lauren asked. "Something environmental? Some kind of contaminant they were both subjected to?"

"Or pathogen," Dr. Hofstra said. "The mother has what look like burns on both her arms. Her coworkers didn't notice them when she came to work and no one saw how she got them."

"Could have been chemical. Hair salons have colorants that could cause burns in concentrated form."

"Maybe. I just need to know what kind of precautions I need to take here."

Lauren thought about Jack and Sarah waiting to meet her. Jack had sounded concerned on the phone. With Lonetree back in town, concerned wasn't good. Still, she didn't like the sound of two unexplained seizures from the same family. "I'll take a quick look before I leave."

Dr. Hofstra pursed her lips and frowned at Lauren's stitched-up arm. "Did that happen in your lab?"

Lauren stood. "Yes, but everything is fine. It was a test tube that had just been disinfected."

"I'd like to sit down and discuss safety protocols. I think it's time we—"

Lauren nodded as she edged away from her. "Absolutely, let's set up a meeting." She left the triage area, calling out over her shoulder, "We'll have to set it up later. I'm going to check on those patients."

She didn't have to see Dr. Hofstra's face to imagine the sour expression. If she thought Dr. Hofstra was purely concerned for the well-being of her staff and thought her lab was some kind of threat to them, she'd be more sympathetic to her. In reality, she was clearly anxious to find out what Lauren was up to and have the hospital somehow participate in the project.

Not for the first time, Lauren considered whether she ought to go through the regulatory red tape to create a lab outside of the hospital. But for the supplies she needed and the access to CDC resources required for her work, an independent lab would be exposed to a lot more scrutiny than she wanted. As hard-nosed as Hofstra was, she wasn't beyond looking the other way if she thought there was some benefit for her in the end. Even so, Lauren doubted the straight-laced Dr. Hofstra would be pleased at all to find out what Lauren had cooking in her lab. If it was up to her, she never would.

Besides, seeing interesting cases on occasion was something she wasn't ready to give up. It grounded her and reminded her that medicine was not about lab experiments, but about real people who needed help. She checked her watch and picked up her pace, striding through the hallway to Debbie Berlin's room. She hoped it was a routine case so that she could get on the road, but she had a nagging feeling that she wasn't going to be that lucky.

Chapter 22

Debbie and Mitzy Berlin were in separate rooms on the second floor. Lauren donned a mask before entering Debbie's room, her first nod to the possibility that some unknown pathogen could be at work. In her previous life, the one before she and Jack both decided to put their family and their marriage before their careers, Lauren had traveled the world in her work with the CDC, chasing down the silent killers like Ebola, hanta, swine flu, and avian influenza She'd walked into mud huts filled with patients bursting with hemorrhagic fevers and seen rivers filled with the bloated bodies of the dead. Given those experiences, she wasn't too worried about looking in on a suburban Maryland mom.

Debbie was propped up in the bed, looking upset at the world. She was still dressed in street clothes, too-tight jeans and a sequined shirt that showed more cleavage than Lauren cared to see. A sprawling tattoo of roses and barbed wire drew her eyes to her right breast so that she felt embarrassed for gawking. Debbie's hair was an impossible burnt orange color with blond highlights, possibly the worst coloring job Lauren had ever seen.

Her chart said she was thirty-one, but it had been a hard three decades. Bags hung beneath eyes marked with crow's-feet, noticeable even through the heavy layer of makeup covering her face. She was hooked up to a blood-pressure cuff on her arm and a heartbeat monitor was snapped onto her finger. White bandages covered her arms. As soon as she saw Lauren, she swung her legs over the edge of the bed and looked at her impatiently.

"I wanna get outta here," Debbie said. "You can't keep me here. I know my rights."

"We'll get you out of here as soon as we can, Mrs. Berlin."

"That's Miss."

"Excuse me?"

"Ms. Berlin. Been four years and my boyfriend can't seem to find his way to a jewelry store." The joke came out flat. Lauren wondered how many times she'd used that line.

"I'm sorry, Ms. Berlin. We're just trying to understand the cause of your seizure so that we can—"

"Seizure?" Debbie barked. "Who said anything about a seizure? I just fainted is all. Look hon, I had a few drinks last night. Probably a few too many if you want to know the truth. I cut hair so I'm standin' on my feet all day. I just didn't drink enough water is all."

Lauren looked at the records in her hands. "The paramedics said your coworkers described a full epileptic seizure. Full-body. Eyes rolled back. Foaming at the mouth."

"Foaming at the mouth. Un-fucking believable. Who said that? Darla? That twat. She has it out for me."

"And these burns on your arms," she said, motioning to the bandages. She nodded toward them, seeking permission to look at the wounds. Debbie rolled her eyes but nodded. Lauren carefully unwound the gauze. The skin from Debbie's wrist to her elbow was hot pink and shiny. A few places had darkened and peeled back. "Any idea how this happened?"

Up to this point, Debbie had looked away from her own arm, as if not looking at it made it not exist. Finally, she looked down. Lauren felt a shudder pass through the woman's body and her mouth turned down in a grimace. But it lasted only a second. When she looked back up at Lauren, all the bad attitude was back.

"How should I know? Guess you'll have to go ask Darla," she said.

Lauren closed the file. "Normally this wouldn't raise too many alarm bells, but when we found out your daughter had the same type of seizure today it requires that we rule a few things out."

Debbie grew quiet. She folded her hands in her lap. Her whole demeanor went from pissed off to nervous in a heartbeat. "Like what? What do you need to rule out?"

Lauren flipped through her notes. "From your intake I see that there is no epilepsy in your family history. No record of previous seizures for either you or Mitzy. Correct?"

"Yeah, that's right."

"Sometimes this type of thing can be caused by

111

environmental factors. Something at the house. Do you have any construction going on? Remodeling? Anything that might be kicking up mold or spores?"

Debbie shook her head.

"Anything you both could have ingested? A strange food? A drink?"

"No, we don't usually eat together. Rick, that's my boyfriend. We ate at Piper's last night. You know that dive bar just out of town? Mitzy had frozen pizza. Probably two, knowing her."

Lauren cringed at the unkind comment but moved on. "Any overseas travel recently?"

Debbie laughed. "Yeah, we took our jet to France last weekend." She looked annoyed that Lauren didn't find her hilarious. "No travel."

"How about contact with anyone you know who traveled recently? Maybe Rick?"

"Rick? Lucky if he travels from the bedroom to the living room most days. He's on disability."

"I'm sorry to hear that," Lauren said.

Debbie waved her away. "He's just milkin' the system. Like all those blacks down in Baltimore."

Lauren squinted as if she'd just watched someone whack their head on a sharp edge. But Debbie didn't seem to notice. She leaned forward conspiratorially. "That's why I call him my sugar-nigga. Get it? Instead of sugar-daddy? Sugar-nigga?"

Debbie must have noticed Lauren's horrified expression because she stopped laughing and turned serious.

"Rick's white," Debbie said. "I don't want you to get the wrong idea."

Lauren clenched the pen in her hand. Working in ERs, she'd come into contact with all types. Junkies, pimps, racists. Sexists who demanded to see a real doctor when she showed up. *I want a doctor with a penis*, was one of the more memorable statements hurled her way. But for some reason, Debbie Berlin's racism caught her off guard. Maybe it was the casualness of it all. The certainty the woman had that her doctor would find it funny. The fact that the woman's daughter went to school with Sarah, and who was probably embedded with the same bigotry. It triggered a maternal instinct to somehow block out the unwholesome parts of the world, the dark shadows of human nature that led to hate and fear. She wondered who would look out for poor Mitzy Berlin. Certainly not Debbie. And probably not good ol' Rick either.

"Don't worry, I think I have the right idea about you," Lauren said with enough distaste that Debbie rocked back on the bed. Lauren turned on a heel and strode out of the room. "Your blood work should be back in an hour or so. Sit tight and I'll let you know whether or not you were just dehydrated or if you have some rare disease eating you from the inside out."

"Wait. Do you think that's—"

Lauren closed the door behind her and didn't hear the end of the question. She felt a little guilty for trying to scare the woman, but she wasn't feeling very charitable. Debbie hadn't asked once about her daughter.

Mitzy was just down the hall in a room where she had been kept in a semi-quarantine since her attending doc had first learned of her mother's seizure. Lauren was pleased at the precautions, happy that the seminars she'd conducted with the staff about early identification of pathogens hadn't fallen on deaf ears.

Lauren knocked on the door and let herself in. The room was similar to her mother's, but Mitzy herself was a mess. She was curled up in a ball, sobbing into her pillow. Edie Liebowitz, one of the younger nurses, sat in a chair near the window, a surgical mask covering her mouth. On seeing Lauren, she stood and crossed over to her.

"She's been like this since coming in," the nurse said. "I thought someone should sit with her. I'm sure her mother would be in here if she could be."

I wouldn't be too sure about that, Lauren thought. She patted the nurse on the arm. "Of course, thank you for doing that. You can stay or take a break if you want."

"I could use a coffee. Do you want anything?"

"No, I'm fine," Lauren said. "Before you leave, has she said anything to you?"

The nurse shook her head. "Not really. She dozed off for a while, the poor thing. I thought she might finally get some peace. But she woke up screaming. I couldn't understand what she said. Except..." the nurse looked around nervously.

"Except what?"

"Get out of my head. Get out of my head." Nurse Liebowitz whispered in a high-pitched tone, trying to replicate Mitzy Berlin's nightmare rumblings. "She was in a real panic."

Lauren looked over at Mitzy's sleeping hulk, wondering if mother and daughter hadn't ingested some of the same bad drugs. Maybe by accident, although Lauren thought if it were by accident it was because they had been carelessly left around the house, not that someone had tried to poison them. After meeting momma Berlin, Lauren was getting a clearer picture of Mitzy's home life.

"Okay, thanks. Go ahead and grab that cup of coffee. I'll see if I can talk to her a little."

Nurse Liebowitz took a step to the door, hesitated, then turned back. "I didn't tell you everything she said. I don't know why…I just…I know you have a lot on your mind with the anniversary and all…"

A pit formed in Lauren's stomach and she fought back a wave of vertigo. Nurse Liebowitz flushed red.

"What else did she say?" Lauren asked, trying to sound cold and clinical, even though her heart pounded in her chest.

"She was saying that, *Get out of my head*, you know. Over and over."

"And what else?" Lauren asked, her impatience showing through.

Nurse Liebowitz chewed on her lower lip and wrung her hands together. "It was…I might have heard her wrong…"

Lauren was about to strangle the words out of the fidgeting nurse when Mitzy Berlin rescued the poor woman from the terrible task.

The girl kicked and writhed on the bed, her legs tangled in her bedsheets. The refrain the nurse had described started, low and choked at first, more of a terrible whimper.

"…get out of my head…get out of my head…"

Lauren walked to the bedside and put her hand on Mitzy's leg. The girl's voice got louder, pleading now.

"…Oh God, please get out of my head…stop hurting me…oh God it hurts…"

"Mitzy," Lauren said in a firm voice, "wake up,

Mitzy. Can you hear me?"

Mitzy's body jerked on the bed, as if somewhere deep in a nightmare she was running from something. Something terrible. Something right on top of her. That's when she pushed herself up from the bed, eyes open but vacant, still looking at whatever hellish dream world held her prisoner, and shouted at the top of her lungs.

"SARAH TREMONT. YOU LITTLE BITCH. GET OUT OF MY HEAD! I'M GOING TO KILL YOU, SARAH TREMONT. I'M GOING TO FUCKING KILL YOU!"

Chapter 23

Lonetree and Sorenson picked their way through the rough landscape of what had been smooth valley floor only ten years ago. The massive collapse of the cave system below, brought on in no small part by several pounds of C-4 explosives the ex-SEALs had placed strategically throughout the subterranean labyrinth, had created a rugged system of pits, mounds, and escarpments across which the men slid and crawled.

It was possible to pick a twisting route through the taller features, but eventually any path would dead-end into a wall of clumpy, grey dirt marked with roots, dried grasses, and abandoned animal tunnels. It reminded Lonetree of the corn mazes he enjoyed as a kid with his brother every harvest. The best ones were the hardest to escape, the ones where the farmer had a devilish side and spent hours figuring out how best to tap into the terror of young minds at the thought of being hopelessly lost. The kind where smiles turned to concern and then finally to tears.

As Lonetree climbed through the field, he remembered the year when he and his little brother Tyke entered the maze at Old Swede's farm, a setup so confusing and frustrating that it was diabolical. The farmer was an ancient man with a thin frame and spindly arms and legs that seemed curiously unhinged, like he was one of his own scarecrows come to life. He had white hair as fine as corn silk, eyes such a pale blue that people often gave him a wide berth, assuming he was blind or at least on his way there. Of course he had a real name; it was something long and impossible to remember, so everyone just called him Old Swede. He was a widower with no kids of his own, so he labored for weeks each year creating a corn maze to which people from miles around made a pilgrimage to see what Old Swede had done.

But one year in particular stood out to Lonetree, the memory that never left him no matter how hard he tried to relegate it to the background. He was probably fourteen, making his kid brother ten. The Lonetree family was well into its long decline. Mom was dead. Dad had accomplished the almost impossible task of losing a tenured position at a small university, his drinking and crazed obsession with ancient Native American mythologies having reached a manic tenor that the Board of Trustees considered unbecoming. They lived in a trailer on the Rez, dirt poor and suspicious that their father was slowly losing his mind. But on that day, proudly putting their two bucks into the wrinkled, blotchy hands of Old Swede for a run through his maze, none of that mattered.

There was fun to be had and Joe and Tyke Lonetree were all about having it.

The first ten minutes were a mad dash down the long rows of still-green corn, all smiles and laughter, groaning in pretended frustration each time the path ended in a wall of leafy green, usually with a hand-scrawled sign tied to one of the thick stalks with a message like: "Wrong way, dummi!" or "Sukker!" or "You never get out!" Lonetree liked to imagine Old Swede sitting at his dining room table with his signs spread out in front of him, delighting in his cleverness and completely oblivious to his lack of spelling ability.

Tyke was the first to get a little concerned about the difficulty of that year's maze. His smile faded and his light jog turned more desperate. His exasperation each time they ended up back where they started became real and tinged with panic. Lonetree found it funny. It wasn't like they were going to get lost. Not for real. It was kind of eerie though. There weren't very many other people there. In fact, they'd seen only one other group of kids, four teenagers smoking cigarettes, each carrying a beer like it was a talisman. They hadn't come across them a second time. Lonetree figured that meant they'd gotten out, or maybe went back to the entrance instead.

"Can we just cut through the corn?" Tyke asked.

"If you go the wrong way you'll be wandering through a thousand acres of cornfield. Besides, there's ropes going through. It'd be a pain."

"Do you think there's a way out?" Tyke mumbled.

"Sure," Lonetree replied, "why wouldn't there be?"

"Because maybe that old farmer is fucking with us."

119

Lonetree squinted at his little brother. "Watch your mouth, Tyke."

Tyke's eyes flashed with anger. "You say it all the time. Fuck this. Fuck that."

Lonetree punched Tyke in the shoulder. Hard. In fact, a little harder than he meant. Tyke yelped in pain and grabbed his shoulder. Lonetree felt a stab of guilt but tried not to show it. He stared his little brother down like he was a dog being punished for getting into the trash. "Mom wouldn't want you cussing like that."

Tears welled in Tyke's eyes, probably as much from the pain in his arm as from the unexpected mention of their mother. It was a fresh wound, scabbed over but easily ripped back open with the slightest pressure.

"You're a prick," was all Tyke could manage. Then he turned and sprinted into the maze.

Lonetree stood there feeling...well, feeling like a prick. It was only twenty seconds. Thirty at most. But in a maze as complicated as the one Old Swede concocted that year, it was an eternity. By the time Lonetree jogged after his brother, Tyke was gone.

"Tyke, c'mon," Lonetree said. "Let's stick together." But no answer came. Lonetree hollered out. "You'll regret it once you get lost, Tyke. Last chance." He listened hard and got no answer. "Fine, suit yourself. You're on your own."

Lonetree set off by himself through the maze, doing his best to memorize the twists and turns he made, figuring out the crazy farmer's pattern. He thought he just about had it figured when he heard Tyke yell.

No, it wasn't a yell. It was a scream. High-pitched like a girl's, but Lonetree knew immediately it was Tyke. But it was only for a second, then it was gone, carried off on the wind and into the swaying stalks of twelve-foot corn.

"Tyke! Where are you?"

Lonetree listened. He stopped breathing and craned his neck. He heard nothing except the swoosh of the long corn leaves rubbing back and forth, the soft friction producing a pleasant soundtrack to the beautiful autumn evening. He wondered if he'd imagined the sound. Or if some piece of farm equipment had screeched out a sound just like his brother's scream, somehow filled it with equal parts pain and terror.

Lonetree closed his eyes as if that would make his ears somehow more powerful. "Tyke," he whispered, "where are you?"

In a burst of sound and light, Lonetree heard Tyke. Saw him. Felt him. And with horrifying clarity, knew exactly why his brother had screamed. Lonetree opened his eyes and sprinted into the maze.

He made the turns without hesitation, grunting from the exertion, driving his burning legs harder and faster.

I'm coming, Tyke. Hold on, I'm coming.

He turned the final corner, then pushed through a wall of corn. Deeper, deeper, the leaves whipping at his arms and face.

A few more steps and he found them. He wasn't surprised by what he saw. He already knew. He didn't understand how, but he'd seen everything through Tyke's eyes.

It was Old Swede, grabbing and groping, stronger than he seemed. Well-practiced at holding down squirming little boys. Tyke's shirt was on the ground, ripped and discarded. His blue jeans were around his ankles but his underwear was still half on, hitched up on one side of his hip where he held onto it with a white-knuckled fist. Old Swede pulled down on the other side, exposing Tyke's thigh and right butt cheek. Old Swede was red-faced, almost purple, with bugged-out eyes, spit hanging from his mouth in long strands like a rabid dog. In his other hand, the one not tugging at the ten-year-old boy's underwear, was a butcher's knife, enough of a threat to keep Tyke's mouth shut, but not enough to keep him from struggling.

Lonetree took this in at the speed of light, all of it in the split second between when he burst through the corn and when he slammed his fist into the side of the old man's head.

It connected with a sickening thud. Old Swede let go of Tyke and fell to the side, hand up to his ear. The butcher knife fell to the ground, weirdly sticking straight into the soft earth so that the handle pointed at the sky.

Lonetree sucked in a sharp breath, not from what he'd done to the old man, but because of what he experienced the second his fist connected. The second his skin had touched the old man's.

He saw images of everything the old man had ever done. All at once, like a thousand movies projected on a single screen. Every victim. Every pain inflicted. Every life violated and broken.

It was breathtaking, the depth of the old man's depravity. He was a predator and he'd always gotten away with it. Even now, as he groaned from the pain, there was a burgeoning certainty that he would get away with it this time too. Who was going to believe anything a couple of deadbeat Indians from the Rez said anyway?

Lonetree knew Old Swede was right.

NIGHT TERROR

So he grabbed the knife, took one step, and jammed it into the old pervert's chest.

Chapter 24

Blood poured from the wound, splashing down Lonetree's arm, forearm, and shoulder. But he didn't care. In that one instant, marking both the first and last time he experienced such an intense connection, he reveled in Old Swede's dying emotions. The old man's Catholic upbringing surged up from the pits of his dark soul with the promise of eternal damnation, hellfire, and torture. Old Swede cringed with fear and remorse and guilt.

"I'm sorry," he said to Lonetree, allowing that the fourteen-year-old Native American boy holding the knife in his chest would serve as both executioner and judge for his wicked soul.

"Go fuck yourself," Lonetree said, twisting the knife.

Old Swede's eyes bulged one final time and then the light went out of them and he fell to the ground.

Lonetree held Tyke up and helped him with his pants. He carefully gathered the torn shirt from the ground. Every piece. Then, without a single word passing between them, they walked away from the maze straight into the thousand acres of cornfield. Neither of them had the stomach to go through the turns and traps of the maze. In some way, it was Old Swede's warped mind taking form in the real world and they wanted nothing of it. They found their own way out.

As Lonetree the grown man scrambled through the torn landscape in Western Maryland, he thought fondly of the two boys hiking through the cornfield. Survivors the both of them. He wondered how it was possible he and his brother had never talked about that day. It was like a half-dream now, something mixed in with all the other horrors of his childhood. He'd never felt that same kind of unrelenting connection again. That overwhelming sense of seeing everything at once that felt like drinking through a fire hose. No, after that day he only felt an infrequent tickle of ideas in the back of his mind, suggestions, not much stronger than what passed for intuition and good luck for most people. It was like the punishment for killing Old Swede was that most of the gift Lonetree possessed was killed off. Or maybe his reward for the kindness he did the world by sending the man straight to hell had saved him from the curse of having the power.

Sorenson took a wrong step as he crawled up a ragged embankment and sent a small avalanche of dirt and rocks sliding down toward Lonetree.

"Heads up," he called.

Lonetree dodged the few midsized rocks that wouldn't have felt good bouncing off his shins and let the gravel and dirt flow around him. Once it stopped, he waved the dust away from his face.

"Thanks," Lonetree said.

"Looked like you were a thousand miles away," Sorenson said. There was concern in his voice underneath the ribbing. "I know it's not the most exciting place in the world, but…"

"I'm here," Lonetree said, tipping his head to let his partner know he'd received the message. *Pay attention. We don't know what's out here.*

It was good enough for Sorenson. He turned and continued their climb. Lonetree followed, leaving memories of his younger self and his first kill behind him.

Soon they were standing over the collapsed barn. It wasn't much more than a pile of warped lumber now, prickly with twisted rusty nails. The earthquakes during the cave-in had done what a hundred years of storms and mountain winters never managed to do, almost killing Lonetree, Sorenson, Jack, Lauren, and a wounded, bloody Sarah in the process.

They poked through the ruins, neither of them sure what they were looking for. Despite the signs posted around the area warning of unstable ground, the site had been trampled over first by law enforcement trying to wrap up loose ends to a series of missing person reports, then by scientists with their measuring devices and geological theories on what caused the collapse, and finally, once every angle had been measured and every dirt sample taken, by hundreds of gawking busybodies. The debris pile now included soda and beer cans, candy wrappers, plastic shopping bags, and all the other detritus humans tended to leave behind when they despoil a place.

But they weren't looking for anything left by humans.

"What you got?" Sorenson asked.

Lonetree shook his head. He knew Sorenson wasn't asking whether he saw anything; that would be self-evident. He was asking if Lonetree felt anything.

"No, nothing," Lonetree said. "Maybe we should go to the other entrance. See how far back it still goes."

"You think? The ground all over this place seems about as stable as a stack of leaves on a windy day. You really want to go crawl around inside that mess?"

Lonetree considered, then looked down and kicked at the pile of barn wood. "You're probably right. It's just…I thought…thought maybe…"

Lonetree swallowed hard. His throat was suddenly parched, like he'd been without water for days. His tongue felt swollen.

"Hey, you okay?" Sorenson asked.

Lonetree heard the words but they sounded all wrong, hollow, the tone unnaturally deep. He shook his head but succeeded only in adding dizziness to his growing list of bad sensations. He took a knee and tried to take a deep breath.

His lungs refused. There was pressure. More than pressure, there was a massive weight in his chest. Like a truck had just rolled a wheel onto his sternum. He clawed at his throat, the lack of air hitting him quick.

There was an explosion of pain in his head and the world turned into a flash of searing white light.

He dropped to both knees, leaned forward, and retched. His stomach convulsed in painful spasms as he

127

vomited onto a patch of bare ground.

His vision cleared enough to see that he was puking blood. Hot and red. Torrents of it.

And the rocky ground soaked it up. Too quickly for it to be anything natural.

Something pulled it underground the second it splattered against the dirt.

The Earth was drinking.

It was drinking his blood.

Chapter 25

Mama D sucked in a sharp breath and hitched over, holding her side. Felt like someone had stabbed her in the ribcage. She knew exactly how that felt, having been stabbed on more than one occasion by some clever pesh who found a shank or shard of glass they could cut her up with. The pain was almost worth bearing to see their disbelief and then horror when they realized that puncturing her body, even her lungs, just wasn't quite enough to take care of Mama D. And then when she pulled out her favorite weapon, her sword, they knew what it meant to really cut someone.

But this was different.

This pain migrated from her side right to her heart, gripped it, and held on.

What is this? A goddamned heart attack? Here? It's

gonna end here?

She looked at the wasteland around her. A gas station in Baxter, Tennessee. Off Interstate 40, halfway to their destination, the town was just a couple of old-fashioned pumps with the gallons and price spinning on a wheel inside the display. Rust covered the beat-up service garage as if it were lichen spreading across rocks in a riverbed. The black asphalt parking lot, tilted and cracked open by decades of sun and weather, was sprung with weeds precociously pushing up through the solid surface as if it were nothing more than another kind of dirt to grow in. Whatever else Baxter may once have been was long gone. There were a couple of wood buildings across the street, one with a sign that proclaimed to serve "The Best BBQ in Tennessee." Uninspired graffiti covered the walls and the windows gaped open, the few remaining shards of glass glinting in midday sun.

This is the bullshit I get to look at when I die?

But the iron clamp on her heart released its hold, slowly, like a pressure cuff losing pressure. The sensation traveled up her chest, into her throat, up into her head. Then came the burst of images, so fast and hard that she dropped to a knee. She didn't scream. No, she needed all of her energy to control her mind. To push back against this *thing* inside of her so it didn't scramble her brain like an egg in a bowl. It was that strong.

After a panicked few moments, her surprise turned to anger at the violation. She stopped playing defense and turned her full force of will against the intruder in her head. The visitor lessened its hold, but it felt too controlled for her to think she was hurting it at all. More like it was gracefully giving up ground to her. Before long they reached a kind of equilibrium in her mind they could both accept. She as the sovereign nation. The intruder as the invading army sequestered in its own camp. Occupying part of her mental landscape, impossible to kick out without a massive assault, but controlled.

Okay, you bastard. Now who the hell are you and what are you doing in my head?

As she got her answer, her anger disappeared. Slowly, a wide grin formed on Mama D's face. The intruder brought good news indeed.

Chapter 26

Lonetree rolled over onto his back. The spasms continued, the blood now bubbling out of his mouth and running down his cheeks and chin. Sorenson's face came into his field of vision. All business. The world twisted around, sky and ground exchanging places and he felt like he was floating away.

He realized Sorenson was carrying him. He focused his thoughts as hard as he could. *Get me out of here, man. Quick as you can.*

"You bet your ass we're getting out of here," came the reply. Lonetree wasn't sure if he actually heard Sorenson say those words or if his oxygen-deprived brain was filling in the blanks now. It didn't matter. He saw the ground rush by as Sorenson carried him in a fireman's hold away from the barn. Once they had made it thirty feet or so, Lonetree was able to finally take a shuddering breath. He felt Sorenson slow.

"Keep…going…" Lonetree rasped.

Sorenson didn't answer but he picked his speed back up and carried Lonetree away as fast as he could.

Lonetree took long pulls of air into his lungs, fighting to get his bearings. The image of Old Swede's bulging eyes danced in front of him and he swatted it away. Next came the sight of his own blood disappearing into the dirt.

But Lonetree knew it wasn't the Earth drinking the blood. It was something else. They'd come to this spot to find something. Well, they'd found it and they were lucky to have escaped alive.

The last thought Lonetree had before he passed out was about little Sarah Tremont. She was in more danger than he'd ever imagined.

Chapter 27

J ack and Sarah waited in the car, separated by the center
console and a chasm of brooding silence. The local
country western radio station warbled about pickup
trucks and lost love. Sarah hadn't said a word since
leaving the school. Nothing Jack did could get her to offer
up more than a shrug or a shake of her head.

She knows I lied to her.

Her question about Mama D had caught him off
guard. He immediately fell into the classic technique used
by parents since the dawn of time. Total ignorance and
obfuscation laced, for good measure, with doses of
incredulity and mockery.

*Mama D? That's a weird name. Where'd you hear that? I
have no idea what you're talking about. Hurry up now, we have to
meet Mom.*

She hadn't argued, or even asked a second time. Sarah simply nodded as if accepting the game they were meant to play where he lied and she acted as the gullible child who bought whatever her dad chose to sell her. But even though she didn't bring it up again, she also refused to talk about anything else. He got it. Silence was his punishment for treating her like a kid.

But the truth was he didn't really know who this Mama D was. And especially why she wanted to hurt Sarah. He could have admitted this to his little girl, but that would have confirmed the threat. Made it more real than maybe it needed to be just yet.

He felt a little lost. Lonetree had more answers, he had to. But he wasn't picking up his phone. Another fact Jack didn't like. Maybe the big man had been wrong and this group he was so worried about was already here. Maybe they already had Lonetree and would show up here at the school next. Or be waiting for them at home. He glanced over to Sarah and considered whether they ought to just hit the road and have Lauren catch up later. Just drive west. Or south, it didn't really matter. Just away. Right now, before anything really bad could happen to her.

Jack straightened, the thought leaving him as a black SUV pulled into the parking lot. Lauren. Finally. She pulled up next to him so that their driver's windows were next to each other.

"Hey, you okay?" Jack asked.

Lauren held up her bandaged arm. "Yeah, no big deal." She looked past Jack into the passenger seat. "Hey, baby. How are you feeling?"

Sarah shrugged and looked away. Lauren looked at Jack, but she didn't seem surprised at their daughter's reaction.

"Should we head home and regroup there?" Lauren asked.

"Why don't you take Sarah with you. Let me go to the house first and make sure everything is okay."

To Jack's surprise, Lauren simply nodded. He'd expected a dozen questions to follow his suggestion. He guessed that with Lonetree's arrival and given the trouble that usually followed the man, worrying whether their home was safe seemed a reasonable precaution.

Jack turned to Sarah but she was already opening the door.

"Love you," he called. "See you at home."

"Yep," was all the response he got.

As Sarah walked around the cars, Jack whispered, "I know this sounds crazy, but when you cut your arm…" Jack paused, sensing what he was going to say would sound twice as crazy out loud as it did in his head. "She felt it. She knew. I watched her and the very second—"

Lauren's passenger door opened and Sarah climbed in. Jack changed his voice so he sounded as normal as possible, succeeding only in making it completely obvious he'd been talking about Sarah.

She glanced at him, but didn't say anything. The look struck Jack as more sad than self-conscious. It hit him like a kick in the stomach.

Again to his surprise, Lauren's reaction was calm, almost thoughtful, like he had told her about a bad grade Sarah had received in one of her classes instead of claiming their daughter had…well…powers that enabled her to sense things happening over twenty miles away.

"We'll talk at home," Lauren said. "We should have Lonetree come over."

136

"He's not picking up his phone."

Lauren pursed her lips and he saw a flicker of fear in her eyes. He guessed she was doing the same calculations that he had done.

"Is it safe to go back home?" Lauren asked.

Jack was about to answer, but he realized she hadn't really been asking him. She was asking Sarah.

Sarah turned toward them, suddenly looking older, like a grown woman instead of a teenager. She nodded. "I think so."

Lauren let out a breath.

"Why don't I still check it out first? Stay a mile back and I'll call you, got it?"

Lauren nodded. "Be careful."

"I will. And Lauren," he added. "It's going to be all right."

She held out her hand and Jack reached for it. Her grip was strong, filled with tension. They both knew his words were hollow husks, meaningless in a world neither of them understood anymore. A world where their daughter had special powers. Where monsters were real and men fed off the life force of children. A world they thought had been destroyed when the cave collapsed.

Everything wasn't going to be all right. They both knew it. But they would cling to the lie for as long as they could.

JEFF GUNHUS

Chapter 28

S arah stared out of the window as her mom drove down the street. She was aware of her dad's car in front of them and fought down the urge to press into his mind to find out what he really thought was going on. Same with her mom. She'd only ever looked inside her parents' heads one time and that had been enough to stop her from doing it ever again. It was just curiosity that time. Trying out her new ability which was all at once terrifying and exciting. But it'd backfired when she'd stumbled on some thoughts about what they were going to do to each other once she and Becky were in bed. The rawness of those thoughts and the images that came with them made her feel dirty. After that she would no more look into their thoughts than try to sneak a look at either of them naked. It was too personal, too private.

139

That's not to say she didn't use her gift to her advantage with her parents. Sometimes they transmitted messages without even knowing it. Like her dad's panicked thoughts about Mama D. That had been like he was screaming at her. Still, with both of them acting so scared, it was tempting to dig deeper to see what was really going on.

She stared at her mom's forearm and saw a faint streak of red where the blood had nearly soaked through.

"Did it hurt?"

Her mom looked startled, then looked at the wound. "Yeah, but we Tremont women are tough, right?"

Sarah nodded. "Right."

She could tell her mom was gearing up to ask her something. She just hoped it wasn't going to be whether she actually remembered being abducted. Remembered everything that happened back in the cave. With everything that was going on, it didn't seem like a big deal that she knew. But somehow having to admit to the years of lying about it seemed overwhelming to her. She wondered whether it would just be easier to keep telling the lie than it was to come clean.

Her mom cleared her throat and Sarah didn't need any special gift to know that she was nervous. "I want to ask you about Mitzy Berlin."

Sarah looked away and brought a thick strand of long blond hair to her mouth to chew on. That was worse than being asked about the lie. She didn't want to think about it. She wanted to pretend it never happened. That it was just some bad dream.

"I saw her in the hospital. Her mom too."

Sarah cocked her head. She didn't know anything about the mom. Other than what she'd seen in Mitzy's mind anyway. Sarah remembered feeling so angry at the mother for letting it happen. She felt Mitzy's rage at the betrayal and wanted to hurt the mother. For a few seconds, she knew what it was like to be Mitzy. That crazy girl wanted to light her mom's Goddamn bed on fire and lock the door. She wanted to cover her mom's naked body with maple syrup and tie her down in the alley behind their apartment where the rats could tear at her flesh while she kicked and screamed. She wanted to cover the bitch's face with a pillow and laugh when she struggled to breathe.

"Sarah!" her mother called out.

Sarah looked around. The car was parked on the side of the road, but she didn't remember that happening. Her mom had her hand on her shoulder. She didn't remember that either.

"Are you okay?" her mom asked. "You were staring out the window, mumbling to yourself. I couldn't get you to stop."

"Sorry. I'm fine. I was just…I don't know…"

"It was more than that, honey." Her mom squeezed her shoulder tenderly. "It's okay. We can talk about this."

"Talk about what?" Sarah asked.

Her mom shifted uneasily. "Honey, did you…I mean…did you hurt Mitzy?"

Sarah thought she might throw up again. Right there in the car. She didn't want to think about it. Trying to deflect, she asked, "What happened to Mitzy's mom? Is she okay?"

"She had a seizure just like Mitzy's. She's okay now though."

"Any burns?" Sarah asked.

141

Color drained from her mother's face. She nodded, unable to hide the quaver in her voice. "Her arms. They're not sure how it happened. How did you—"

"And Mitzy? She's all right?"

"She's okay."

Sarah turned away again and fixed her eyes on a tree standing alone in the distance. That was her. Strong, able to bend to the wind, but alone. "Then I didn't really hurt her. Or her worthless mother."

"Sarah Lynn Tremont. Why would you say something like that?"

Sarah shrugged.

"I just asked you a question. Why would you say that about an adult you don't even know?"

Sarah spun in her chair, her mom's shocked expression barely registering with her. "Because I do *know* her. And she's a worthless piece of shit." The words came out as a hiss. She felt her face screw into a grimace, her lips curled back over her teeth like an animal. "And you know what else? I wish I had hurt her more. Hurt her so bad that she couldn't walk again. Not ever. I wish I'd burned her crispy. What do you think of that, bitch?"

The thoughts roared through her mind like a steam engine, hissing and fuming, a clatter of mechanical power—and then they were gone. She slumped in her chair and shuddered, gooseflesh covering her skin. The thoughts left her feeling sick again. Just like after Mitzy fell to the ground. She felt so bad for what she'd done, knowing that with just a little more effort she might have killed the girl. And now Mitzy's mother too. Miles away? What was happening to her?

Tears filled her eyes and poured down her cheeks. She sobbed, crossing her arms over her chest, rocking back and forth. But soon another set of arms wrapped around her and she leaned into her mom's embrace.

"I'm sorry. I didn't mean it. I don't want to hurt anyone. I didn't mean to call you that. I'm so sorry, Mom. I'm so sorry."

Her mom hugged her tight.

"I don't want to go back to the cave," Sarah whimpered. "I can't do that again."

The arms around her tightened until it hurt. Then her mom told her the same lie she'd heard from her father before he pulled away.

"Everything's going to be all right, Sarah," her mom whispered into her ear without a shred of conviction in the words. "Everything's going to be all right."

The boy's voice Sarah heard earlier that day whispered in her head, the sadness in his tone leaving her cold. *I'm not so sure about that.*

Chapter 29

Jack pulled up to the house slowly. It was a two-story home built to their specifications, the light and airy feel a throwback to their Californian roots. The house was set well off any road and the long driveway wound through the forest surrounding their property. A fleet of cars could have been parked by their front door without him knowing it until he was three hundred yards from the road. As he turned the final bend, he was relieved to see Sorenson and Lonetree sitting on the lowered tailgate of Lonetree's Expedition, waiting for them. He knew they were more adept at surveying the area for danger than he would ever be, so he texted Lauren to come to the house.

By the time he parked the car and got out, the two men had already crossed the short distance over to him.

Jack reached out and shook hands with Sorenson. "Welcome back."

"I wish it was a social visit," Sorenson said.

"Me too," Jack replied. He noticed blood on Lonetree's shirt. He nodded to it. "Everything all right?"

"Yeah, sure. Just peachy," Lonetree grumbled. "Where's Sarah? I thought she was with you."

"Lauren has her." Jack tried to read anything off of Sorenson but got nothing. "I came here first. As a precaution."

"So you believe me now. That there's a problem?"

Jack nodded. "You were right. About Sarah, that is. She still has…you know…still has…"

"Powers?" Lonetree asked. "Jesus, Jack. You probably sucked at the birds and the bees talk, didn't you?"

"Her mother did…" Jack cleared his throat. "Some things happened today."

"Some things happened to us too. Why don't you go first?"

Jack went over everything he knew. He spoke quickly, eager to get done before Lauren and Sarah arrived. He told them about what had happened at the school. How Sarah had felt Lauren's injury.

"I think somehow Sarah sent that kid to the hospital," he whispered. "Just from using her mind," Jack said, still only half-believing it. "The thing with Lauren pretty much proves she still has the gift, right?"

Lonetree and Sorenson took the story in stride. Jack wondered at the things these two had endured over the past ten years that they didn't even flinch at the idea that his daughter was a psychic phenom with the ability and desire to hurt people.

145

"We had an interesting morning too," Lonetree said. "Nick here saved my life."

"You make it easy," Sorenson said. "You keep putting yourself in danger and making a mess of things. Eventually I have to jump in there and help out."

"Lucky me," Lonetree deadpanned. He turned to Jack. "I won't bore you with the details, but we went out to the old mine shaft site. Seems something we buried out there isn't as dead as we hoped."

Jack felt his stomach fold over on itself. An acidic taste rose in the back of his mouth as a shudder passed through his body. "The Source?" Jack asked. "Th...that's not possible. The shaman was buried under a mountain of rock." He tried to look strong in front of Lonetree and Sorenson, but it took all of his concentration to keep his voice from shaking.

A burst of images of the grotesque creature flashed in his mind from the night in the cave. Jack had come within inches of death in the final fight with the shaman, a fact that his subconscious was nice enough to play out for him over and over again in his nightmares.

"Maybe," Lonetree replied. "Probably. Huckley wasn't strong enough, I don't think. And he was the strongest of the group. The kind of strong we're talking about anyway. This is bad, Jack. Real bad."

"But it's still buried, right?" Jack said, his eyes flashing up the driveway as Lauren's SUV made its way toward them. "How dangerous can it be?"

"It's pretty strong," Sorenson said. He motioned to Lonetree. "Tell him."

"Tell me what?" Jack asked.

"I think I made it a little stronger," Lonetree said.

When he was done explaining what had happened at the cave-in site, Jack felt like he might get sick himself. His legs wobbled beneath him and he leaned against his car for support. Lauren walked up to them by herself, leaving Sarah in the car behind them. Based on her reaction, he knew he looked as shaken up as he felt.

Lauren hugged both Lonetree and Sorenson, all of them mumbling hellos. But her face was stricken. She stood next to Jack and slipped her hand into his and faced Lonetree.

"Jack told me what you told him," Lauren said. "About this Mama D person coming after Sarah."

Lonetree said, "Look, I know you don't like to believe in this stuff, but—"

Lauren held up her hand. "I'm more open-minded right now than you might think."

Jack noticed the edge in her voice. He glanced to the car and wondered what might have happened on the way to the house. "Did something—"

"I'll tell you later," Lauren said. "This…person…what does she want with Sarah? No bullshit."

There was a flicker of surprise on Lonetree's face, then a nod of satisfaction. "Okay, no bullshit. Mama D wants Sarah because of her psychic powers. She'll be able to consume Sarah's gift, making her stronger than ever."

Lauren wore her professional expression, a doctor listening unemotionally to facts in an effort to discern a diagnosis and decide on treatment. Jack knew the look and knew it masked Lauren's considerable intellect churning in full problem-solving mode. Still, her grip on his hand nearly crushed his knuckles.

"So, we either run or stop her somehow," Lauren

147

said.

"There's a third option," Sorenson added.

Lonetree shot his partner a look, clearly unhappy with the interjection.

"What?" Jack asked. "What's the third option?"

Lonetree looked away, kicking at the ground.

"Eliminate the prize she's after," Lauren whispered. Lonetree looked up. His face showed that she'd guessed it. "Is that even possible?" she asked.

"Wait, wait a second," said Jack, feeling like he was chronically three steps behind the conversation. "I don't understand what you're saying. Sarah's the prize, right? You want to eliminate her?"

"The prize isn't Sarah," Lauren whispered. "It's her powers."

"If we can remove her gift, there's no reason for Mama D to chase her down," Sorenson said. "It won't help the next victim she targets, but it'll keep Sarah safe and…"

"…and let her lead a normal life," Lauren finished for him.

"But is it even possible?" Jack asked. "To get rid of her powers, I mean?"

"Probably not," Lonetree said, glaring at Sorenson. "But maybe." Jack and Lauren stared him down until he gave in. "There's this guy. A medicine man my dad used to visit to record the old stories. He used to force me to come along. Native American guy. Lives in West Virginia, about two hours from here."

"Can he help?" Jack asked.

"I've heard stories." He nodded toward Sorenson. "Guess I shared some of them with big mouth over here." Lonetree shrugged. "I don't even know if he's still alive. He was old as dirt when I was a kid, but I guess it's a shot."

"Let's do it," Lauren said stiffly. "Right now if we can."

Jack and the other two men looked at her, surprised. Jack had expected her to argue for involving the police, or to try to rationalize away the phenomenon they'd witnessed with Sarah that day. While she said she believed him about what happened in the caves, she never saw any of it directly. Jack always felt part of her still held onto the hope that there was a scientific explanation for everything they'd been through. But her posture now left no doubt that she believed Sarah had a gift of some kind. Something so unexplainable that going to a Native American medicine man seemed like a rational step to take.

He leaned in close to her. "What happened in the car with Sarah?"

Lauren shook her head, in full doctor mode. In control. Decisive. Her sweaty hand clutching Jack's her only outlet for the stress she was internalizing. "She hurt someone in her school today. A bully that was picking on her friend. She used her powers. On her. And on the girl's mom who was miles away. She sent her into a seizure and burned the skin on her arms."

Lonetree shifted his weight uncomfortably.

"It's like she's losing control," Lauren whispered. "She's not who we think she is."

"Lauren, that's not fair," Jack said.

"She remembers everything from the cave, Jack. Every detail," she said. "And she always has."

"I don't understand," he said.

"She hid it from us all these years. To make us feel

149

better, is what she said. But she lied to us. She admitted it to me on the way over here."

Jack squeezed her hand tighter. He was having a hard time reconciling his image of his little girl and this new information. Lauren saved him from having to say something.

"She needs help. And she's not going to find it at a hospital." She looked at Lonetree. "We've trusted you with our lives before. Do you trust this person? This medicine man?"

Lonetree thought the question through, weighing it. Finally he said, "No. No, I don't."

The answer deflated the momentum of the small group.

"Why? Could he somehow hurt Sarah?" Jack asked, images of a Catholic priest conducting an exorcism jumping into his head.

"No way, I wouldn't let him," Lonetree said in such a voice that they all believed him. "When I say I don't trust him, I mean I don't trust that he's anything more than a sham. There was always something off about him. Usually I can tell if someone is...you know, like Sarah. I can sense she has the gift. I never felt that from this guy. But his reputation has traveled a long way. In Native American circles anyway."

"Low probability of success with negligible risk. A positive outcome saves Sarah from having to deal with this...this...monster coming for her," Lauren said. "If this were a medical treatment, it's a no-brainer to try it."

Lonetree seemed to think it through. "Given everything in play..." he paused, then gave in reluctantly, "It's probably our best bet."

Lauren looked to Jack and their eyes met. In the way that only married couples can communicate, an entire conversation took place with the barest changes of facial expressions. A question, an answer, a question back, approval, concern, comfort, final confirmation, and then mutual resolve. All in a few seconds and without a word between them.

Jack turned to Lonetree and nodded. "Okay, I'll drive. Last I remember, you're not very good at it."

Sorenson laughed. "See, I'm not the only one who thinks so."

"C'mon," Lonetree growled. "Like I said, it's about two hours. When we get there, let me do the talking."

"Should we call ahead?" Lauren asked.

"No, if he knows we're coming, he'll leave. One thing I do remember is that he doesn't really like white people."

Jack and Lauren exchanged a look as they climbed into the SUV. "Sounds like a real charmer," said Jack, firing up the engine. He spun gravel under the heavy tires and roared off his property. Never in a million years when he left the sun-drenched shores of California for Western Maryland did he think he'd be on the road with his wife and two ex-Navy SEALs on the way to see a Native American medicine man who could hopefully remove his daughter's psychic powers before a psychotic cultist could arrive to chase her down.

And people thought California was strange.

He gripped the wheel and headed west, already wondering about their next move if the medicine man failed. Every alternative either got messy in a hurry or involved them going on the lamb for weeks, maybe years.

He just prayed that this medicine man was better than Lonetree gave him credit for.

He looked into the rearview mirror and caught Sarah's too-serious face staring back. Jack gave her a wink and was rewarded with a smile. Then she looked back out the window and the serious look returned. As he sped down the road, he grabbed onto the only certainty he could find in the midst of all the strangeness and doubt.

He loved his little girl. And he and Lauren would do anything to save her.

Chapter 30

The last half hour of the drive took them up a twisting road deep into the Appalachians. Two well-kept lanes of asphalt with a wide shoulder turned first into a narrow, potholed road and then eventually into a gravel lane, not much more than an old logging trail. They only had to face a single oncoming car and Jack was forced to pull into a small opening in the forest to let it pass. The car carried two men wearing work jackets, long black hair pulled back in ponytails. Native American faces scowled at them as they passed by.

Lonetree may not have been up there in the last twenty years but he knew the directions well enough. He didn't hesitate as they came to the various forks in the road and turns down what looked like deserted dirt trails. Finally, a crooked old shack perched on a rock

153

outcropping came into view. It looked to be built with scrap bits of wood, metal, really anything that might keep out the chilled mountain air. Irregular-shaped windows dotted the wall in odd places. Small, almost like portholes on a ship. A stove-pipe chimney clung to the roof, tilted to one side, spouting a steady cloud of smoke.

Jack stopped the car about twenty yards short of the building. "You're sure this is the place?"

Lonetree nodded gravely. "That's it."

Jack picked up on the strange tone in the big man's voice. He remembered how Lonetree had said his father used to bring him here as a kid. He wondered what ghosts Lonetree was seeing as the place triggered old memories. What little he knew about his father, he was pretty sure they weren't happy ones.

"At least it looks like someone's home," Lauren pointed out.

Lonetree popped open his door. "You guys stay here. Sorenson."

"Got it," Sorenson replied, crawling out from the third row of seats in the back of the SUV and following Lonetree out.

Jack watched as the two men spread out and approached the shack with care.

"Look over there. At the trees," Sarah said.

Jack followed her line of sight and saw what she was talking about. Strung up from the trees were bizarre little structures, most no more than a few feet tall. They were a combination of branches and twine, tied and bent into geometric shapes, three-dimensional trapezoids and cylinders. Some with feathers. Others with antlers or animal pelts. They all hung down on a thin string so that they swayed and turned on their axes with the barest breeze drifting through the trees. They appeared at once amazingly fragile and yet somehow projected strength and power.

"They circle the property," Sarah said, a pointed finger playing long distance connect-the-dots through her window.

"I wonder what they are," Lauren said. "Maybe they're—"

Any conversation they might have had about the weird little structures was interrupted by the first shotgun blast coming from the house.

Even in the car, it shook the air.

"Jesus," Jack called out. "Sarah, get down."

Sarah cried out and ducked down in her seat.

Jack had his foot on the gas, ready to drive up to Lonetree and Sorenson, but the two men hadn't moved. In fact, Lonetree held a hand up toward Jack, telling him to stay put.

"Wait a second," Lauren said.

Another shotgun blast erupted from the shack. A shower of dirt and leaves sprayed up right in front of Lonetree's feet, but he didn't even flinch. Lonetree and Sorenson stood with their open hands held to their sides.

The front door opened and an ancient man hobbled out, shotgun wobbling more or less in Lonetree's direction. Judging by how unsteady the old man was, Jack wasn't certain the first two shots had been warnings or just misses. As he stepped out of the shadows of the porch covering the front of the shack, Jack got a better look at him. He wore his hair just like the men in the car they'd passed, only his was shock white. His hairline was receded to reveal a pocked and sun-damaged landscape that went back nearly mid-scalp. His nose was wide and

155

hooked. Though stooped and favoring one side, he carried himself with a proud bearing. This was his property and he planned to defend it.

Jack and Lauren watched as Lonetree approached the old man. He was talking to him, periodically pointing to their car. Suddenly, something Lonetree said broke through to him and the old man lowered the shotgun, gripped Lonetree's arms, and looked him over, grinning madly.

"Looks like he remembers him," Jack said. "That's a good sign."

The old man called over his shoulder and a woman appeared in the door, the other half of an ancient pair. A nearly matching set with white hair pulled back into a braid, a wrinkled, craggy face that showed a lifetime in the sun, and a diminutive frame that seemed likely to drift and turn in the same gentle breeze as the twig-and-rope structures dangling from the trees. She smiled on seeing Lonetree, but then looked up sharply at the SUV. She frowned, said something to the old man, then disappeared back inside.

Lonetree turned to Jack and Lauren and waved for them to come out.

"Here we go," Jack said.

"I'm scared," Sarah said from the backseat.

Lauren turned in her chair. "We're not going to let anything happen to you, okay? Like we talked about, we're just here to talk."

"But that man has a gun," Sarah said.

Jack reached back and took her hand in his. "We're not going to leave you by yourself with him. Not for one second, understand?" Sarah nodded. "But he might be able to help you. Get rid of your…you know…superpowers."

In spite of the situation, Sarah grinned. Then she stifled a laugh. The reaction took Jack by surprise. He looked over to Lauren and found that she was holding back a smile too.

"Superpowers?" Sarah said. "Like in the movies?" She laughed.

It was infectious. Soon Lauren burst out laughing which sent Sarah off even more. Jack followed right after them, the tension pouring out as a high-pitched chuckle.

They all shared a good laugh together, a little from how ridiculous it all sounded, a little from the way Jack had said the words so miserably, and a little because they just needed to release their tension. They took a minute and remembered what it felt like to be normal again. But just as fast as it had come, the moment passed them by. An awkward silence fell over the car, no one wanting to be the first to move on to what lay ahead of them.

"I wish Becky was here," Sarah said softly.

"I know, honey," Lauren said. "We'll go see her soon, I promise."

Sarah studied her hands, clasped together on her lap. She nodded without looking up. "Okay, let's go." She opened her door and stepped out of the car before either of her parents could react. Jack wondered at his daughter's strength and, not for the first time, felt enormous pride in her courage.

Jack and Lauren opened their doors and followed Sarah toward the medicine man's shack, hoping beyond hope that he would be able to help their little girl.

JEFF GUNHUS

Chapter 31

The inside of the shack took Jack by surprise. With the dingy, ramshackle exterior it seemed a safe bet that the interior would look much the same. Instead the old man directed them into a well-lit, tastefully decorated room that suggested the inhabitants enjoyed both order and comfort. The floors were polished hardwood with woven rugs strategically placed in high-traffic areas. Bookshelves lined the walls with old tomes facing spine out in an organized manner. An old-fashioned woodstove squatted in the corner of the room like an armor-plated insect, producing just the right amount of heat to make the room cozy. One side of the room was a small kitchen. Even there, everything was in perfect order. Knives in their proper place in a wood block. Pots hanging from an overhead rack all turned in the same direction.

Only one place stood out amid the smooth consistency of the kept home. A worn recliner occupied a corner of the room. Next to this was a side table covered with a cluttering of junk. Old soda cans, peanut shells, half-done crosswords, piles of newspapers and magazines that threatened to spill over into the rest of the neatly made room. The old medicine man walked to his chair, knocked the table with his legs, and sent a tiny avalanche of debris to the floor. He looked up at the woman with an exaggerated expression of guilt, then lowered himself carefully into the armchair. The others took seats on the sofas nearby. The old man's wife, shy in front of them, retreated to the kitchen and busied herself making a plate of food for the guests.

The old man dug through the junk covering his table until he found a pair of reading glasses. These he placed on his face, balancing them on the end of his nose. "Little Joey Lonetree," he said in a deep, resonant voice, heavy with a Native American accent, "it is good to see a familiar face."

Lonetree nodded. "Thank you for seeing us, Powatan. But I'm not certain how familiar my face is. It's been many years."

"One year. Many years. I can still see the young boy in your face." He leaned closer. "But not in your eyes. They are dark and cold. Tell me, what has the white man's military done to you during these long years to make your eyes look that way?"

Lonetree shrugged. "My commander-in-chief was a black man."

Powatan waved the comment away like it was a fly buzzing near his face. "But it's still a white man's army and white man's world."

Lonetree grinned. "I have no complaints. The recruiters told me I'd see the world and get to kill bad guys. They kept their promise on both counts."

"And they told you that you could come home and rest in peace when you were done, didn't they?" Powatan pointed a gnarled crooked finger at Lonetree's chest. "Was that the truth too? Have you been able to come home? Because I think maybe you have not. And maybe you never will."

Lonetree shook his head, clearly uncomfortable with the line of questioning. "We're not here because of me," he said gruffly. "And we would not have bothered you at your home unless it was urgent."

The old man nodded regally, as if accepting penance from an unruly subject. "I know why you are here. I saw a vision of your arrival," he said, "but it was unclear when and how many would be with you." A clatter of dishes from the kitchen made them all spin around to look at the old woman. She waved a hand their direction without looking up. The old man looked irritated. "I'm sorry, Ichote is a good wife but fumbles now that she's older."

Jack looked down at the ground, embarrassed by the man's rude remark. Lonetree hardly seemed to notice.

"You met Nick Sorenson outside. This is Jack and Lauren Tremont." Lonetree turned a nod toward Sarah sitting on the couch next to Lauren, claiming the spot farthest from the old man. "And this is their daughter, Sarah. The one we have a question about."

Powatan squinted at Sarah. He pursed his lips and

stared. The room seemed frozen in a vacuum as all sound disappeared. Sarah looked down at the floor, avoiding his eyes.

The old man turned to Jack. "You want to take away her ability to feel the true world. Why would a parent want this? Why do you live in fear of her?"

Jack wasn't sure how to answer. He glanced left and right, first at Lauren and then at Lonetree. His voice came out a whisper. "I don't live in fear *of* her. I live in fear *for* her."

Jack startled as Ichote stepped in front of him and held out a plate of crackers, sliced meats, and vegetables. He smiled at her but shook his head. "No, thank you though."

She leaned in and whispered, "Maybe I should take the child and wait on the porch."

The woman's soft voice trickled into his ear like sweet music and he found himself nodding. He looked to Lauren. They had agreed not to let Sarah be alone, but that was with the medicine man. This old woman certainly couldn't hurt her. And maybe it was better to let the old man speak freely about what, if any, solution he could offer them. Judging from the little he'd said so far, Jack was guessing Powatan wasn't known for his soothing bedside manner. He looked to Lauren to gauge her feelings about it.

Ichote also turned to her with a soft smile and said the most powerful words she could have come up with. "I am also a mother. I will care for her as my own." When Lauren still hesitated, Ichote added, "You will be able to see us the entire time through the window." She turned to Sarah. "If it is all right with you, Sarah."

Sarah nodded. Her eyes were locked on Ichote's and she slowly stood. "Yeah, you adults can talk. We'll be right outside."

Chapter 32

Powatan watched silently as Ichote and Sarah walked across the room, opened the door, and left. The adults turned back to him expectantly. He knew what his role was now and began a long, dry explanation of Native American shamanism, insisting that the Tremonts hear him out in order to bring context to the discussion about their daughter.

He regaled them with a rich detailed history, purposefully leaving out the fact that the most powerful shamans were actually women. He didn't want to put anything in their minds that might key them into what was really going on. Especially Lonetree. He remembered being told that the boy had the gift when he was younger and had to assume there might still be something there.

As he often did, Powatan wondered what it would be like to have the gift. No matter how much Ichote described it to him as a nearly unbearable curse, he wished he could experience it for himself, if only to remove the burden from her shoulders and place it on his own.

But until that day, he had his own job to do. Ichote had made it clear that this was an important one and he intended to give her as much time alone with Sarah Tremont as she wanted.

Chapter 33

S arah watched the old woman's back as she followed her off the porch and into the front yard. Ichote carried a pitcher of lemonade and two glasses. Sarah guessed they were heading for the picnic table set against a row of apple trees close to the small stream that tumbled through the property.

Most of the apples had already been picked, either by humans and animals in the area, or lay on the ground, half-dissolved back into the earth. There were a few apples that still clung to the high branches, too ornery to let go of their tree home. But the weather had been cold at nights and so the once round, shiny apples were shriveled and malformed. They were not the last, best prizes of the year, but the unwanted refuse, trapped by their own stubbornness to cling to what they already knew. Sarah wondered if the woman she followed was like one of those apples. Or if she was the tree.

Ichote glanced over her shoulder with an amused expression on her face. She stared up at the leftover apples on the tree, the same ones that Sarah had just been looking at, and gave a low laugh. Sarah sucked in her breath and felt a rush of heat in her cheeks as she realized the woman must have read her thoughts. She tried to clear her mind of anything that might be embarrassing, but the harder she tried not to think about something, the more quickly inappropriate images came to her mind.

She saw Ichote dressed in a clown costume. She pictured her squatting on the toilet, going to the bathroom. There was an image of her riding a bicycle with a pointy hat like the witch in the Wizard of Oz.

"Is that how you think of me?" Ichote said quietly. "As a witch?"

Sarah stopped in her tracks and considered running back inside. It wasn't that she was scared, okay maybe just a little, but she was so embarrassed she thought she might die right there on the old woman's front yard. Shrivel up like one of the apples and melt into the ground.

"Please don't," Sarah said. "It's not polite to go into someone's head."

Ichote swiped her hand across the surface of the picnic bench, removing the dried leaves that covered it. "I agree," she said. "But I'm not in your head and will not go there. Without your permission anyway."

"But how can you…"

"How can you hear a radio turned up to full volume?" Ichote asked. "Do you need to go inside the speaker? Crawl into the electronics?"

167

"I don't understand."

"To me, and to others like me, like us, your thoughts seem like shouting. Even now, I'm actively shutting them out and they are still loud. Like closing a thin curtain to block out the sounds of a room full of people. You must learn to control it."

Ichote sat at the table, folded her hands in front of her, and waited. Sarah brushed away the leaves from the bench on her side. The wood was rough and grainy and looked like a thing of the forest that had been found instead of made. She carefully stepped over the bench and slid her legs under the table. Mirroring the old woman, she folded her arms in front of her on the table.

"I hear people's thoughts sometimes without trying," Sarah said. "But it's never loud."

"You likely have not met people who have our kind of power," Ichote said.

Our kind of power, Sarah thought to herself, noting the confidence in the old woman's voice. "Your husband," Sarah said. "He's not like us, is he?"

Ichote shook her head.

"He tricks people into thinking he is. That's not very nice."

Ichote remained expressionless. "He does what he does because I ask him to. And to protect me. He's a good man. A good husband."

"But he's tricking them right now, isn't he? Because you wanted to talk to me alone and you knew my mother wouldn't let you."

Ichote nodded. "It's not polite to go into someone's head."

"I didn't," Sarah said. "I just figured it out is all."

The old woman unfolded her arms and touched her fingers together, forming a little point with them. "Would you like to know how to turn down that bullhorn you have there?"

"Can I turn it off?"

"Is that what you want?"

"Yes," Sarah said, but then she thought about it. "But would I be able to turn it back on again?"

"Let's work on turning it down first," Ichote said. "Close your eyes."

Sarah hesitated. Even when she finally did it, she peeked a couple of times to see what the old woman was doing. She just sat there, not moving, so she closed them completely.

"Right now, your thoughts are spraying out in the world the way a sneeze gets sent out in a thousand particles when you don't cover your mouth. Do you cover your mouth when you sneeze?"

"Of course."

"That's right. Because you don't want all of that spit and boogers flying around and getting germs everywhere."

Sarah giggled. Something about the old woman saying boogers cracked her up. She felt herself relax a little more.

"We're going to picture a barrier that you can put up to block your thoughts from spraying out in the world, okay?"

"Okay."

"Just visualize a wall. Doesn't matter right now what it's made of. Wood, rock, steel. Pick whatever you can see the best. And focus on it. Can you see it?"

Sarah could see it. She chose a heavy-duty door to

a safe just like she'd seen in a cartoon somewhere. It was thick, with metal bands crisscrossing over it and covered with rivets that made it look tough and imposing.

"Yeah, I have one."

"Now you have to make it big. As big as the sky. Stretch it out in every direction as far as you can see," Ichote said. "If you do it right, then…"

Sarah peeked through her closed eyes and saw the old woman with a surprised grin on her face.

"If I do it right, then what?" Sarah asked.

"Then I can't hear anything," Ichote said. "Not even a murmur. That must be a thick wall indeed." She leaned forward and looked Sarah over as if just really seeing her for the first time. "This usually takes a lot of practice and time to learn. Especially for one so young."

Sarah was surprised at the comment. "You've met other kids like me?"

Ichote nodded her head, but then stopped herself. "Similar, but not like you. At least I don't think so."

Sarah didn't like the sound of that so she turned her attention back to the wall. "How does it work? Is this an actual wall?"

"The mind is an amazing thing. It can be both wonderful and terrifying at the same time. Even with a dozen lifetimes of study we would only touch the surface of how it works."

"But we studied it in school. Synapses, neurons, all that stuff. Scientists know all about it."

"Bah, scientists. With them it's always how, how, how. And never a thought to why. They try to rationalize a world based on rules and limitations. But there are no such things. They leave blank spots in their descriptions of the natural world and hope no one asks a question."

Ichote drew in a breath and slowed down. "Think of a seed. It can lie in a desert for years. A dry, dead husk. Add water and sunlight and it grows. Science describes this perfectly, the germination of the seed, the replication of cells. Except for how life sprung from a dead thing. Except for why this happens. And who caused it to be so. Don't ask those questions because they aren't convenient and no one knows the answers."

"So this wall you had me think of, you don't know why it works?" Sarah asked.

"I have ideas. I don't think it's the wall itself, but the image communicates your intention to your mind. With a mind like yours, that intention becomes real." Ichote turned deadly serious. "But I'm guessing you know that already."

Sarah froze. This woman knew about Mitzy and her mom. She'd lied to her and been in her mind without permission. She added another layer to her wall just to be safe, coating the entire thing with endless miles of soundproofing tiles just like the ones in her band room at school.

"I don't know what you're talking about."

Ichote pursed her lips and her eyes flashed with anger. "Liar."

Sarah tried to swallow hard, and found that she couldn't. Her throat was too dry. She considered sticking with her lie. She even thought about standing up from the picnic bench, marching back into the house, and telling all the adults they'd been tricked and made fools of. That the man they were talking to was just a puppet.

But the old woman had taught her about the wall. That was a gift freely given and a lesson she doubted anyone else could have taught her. Maybe she could help.

Not sure how it would work, she closed her eyes and thought of what had happened with Mitzy and sent it out through her wall.

To her surprise, Ichote sucked in a sharp breath and slammed her hands to the table. She gripped it as if a brutal wind had come from nowhere and threatened to blow her away unless she held on tight. It took Sarah a second to realize she might be the one causing the old woman's reaction. She stopped sending the images to her. The moment she did, Ichote slumped forward, panting for air.

"Are you okay?" Sarah asked. "I didn't mean to. I was just trying to—"

Ichote held up a hand. "Shhh, it's fine. I've never…it just caught me by surprise…" The old woman steadied herself and sat up straight again. "You're like a grizzly bear playing with a squirrel. You don't know your own strength."

"Isn't that dangerous for the squirrel?" Sarah asked.

Ichote chuckled. "I suppose it is." Then she turned serious. "Thank you for sharing that with me. I know it was hard for you to do."

Sarah nodded. "But you already knew, right? Even before I sent it?"

Ichote shook her head. "Just pieces. A guilty conscience projects information without trying. What you shared with me was pure and unfiltered. The ability to do this is very rare."

Sarah felt ashamed now that someone else knew what she'd done to Mitzy and her mother. Her eyes welled with tears.

Ichote made a move as if to reach out for Sarah's hands, but decided against it. Sarah thought she saw a flash of fear in the old woman's eyes. Ichote seemed unsure what to do with her hands, having been caught in the middle of the act. She crossed them once again on the table in front of her.

"I saw the images, but I also felt the remorse you felt afterward," Ichote said kindly. "You are not a bad person, Sarah. You need to know that. No matter what happens."

Sarah had felt comfort in the old woman's words until the last sentence. Those four words felt like knives in her flesh. "What do you mean, no matter what happens?"

"Honey, there was something else in what you sent me. No, it was more like there was some*one* else."

Sarah wrapped her own arms around her shoulders, fighting back a sudden chill. She felt her stomach hollow out and her mouth watered the way it did before she threw up when she was sick. She wanted her parents. She wanted them right away.

"This someone wanted to hurt her. This someone wanted to kill that girl. Burn her mother. You felt it, didn't you? You know what I'm talking about."

Sarah wanted to scream no and run back into the house. But she knew if she did, nothing would change. Her powers that she didn't even understand would still be there. She might hurt other people. And she would have no idea what to do about any of it.

Can you get it out of me? Sarah sent the message with her mind, using the controls Ichote had taught her.

"I don't know," Ichote said. "I have to see what it is. I have to come in and look for myself. Will you let me do that?"

173

Will it hurt?

"I don't know," Ichote replied. "I don't think it will, but I can't be sure."

"You should have just told me it wouldn't hurt."

"I will never lie to you, Sarah. Not ever."

Sarah looked over her shoulder to the shack behind her. She imagined her parents sitting comfortably on the leather couches, listening to the man drone on with his stories, warmed by the woodstove glowing in the corner. They probably had a view of the picnic table through one of the windows so they wouldn't worry about her. All they saw was her sitting at the table with the fragile old woman. They couldn't know what the woman had just asked of their daughter. Or that their daughter had already made her decision.

"Okay, you have my permission," Sarah said.

Ichote nodded and Sarah noticed a hesitation. A deep breath as if the old woman were girding herself for a particularly hard, unpleasant task. She reached out across the table, her hands outstretched, weathered, cracked palms facing the sky.

"Take my hands and relax. This shouldn't take long."

Ichote, shaman and medicine-woman, whose powers were considerable in their own right, was correct.

The screaming started only a matter of seconds after Sarah placed her hands on top of the old woman's. But it took a lot longer than that for the screaming to stop.

Chapter 34

Jack was off the couch and halfway across the room the second the scream reached them. But Lonetree and Sorenson were faster and they barreled through the door ahead of him. He followed right behind them, crashing into their backs before he realized they had stopped in their tracks before they stepped off of the porch. He shoved them aside and it was his turn to freeze.

Sarah sat at the picnic table, her back to them. From Jack's vantage point, he could only see the back of her head and that her arms were stretched out on the table in front of her. But her posture was relaxed. She didn't appear to be in any kind of distress. The screaming wasn't coming from her.

Ichote sat across from Sarah, her body ramrod straight and jerking violently. Her eyes were wide open, but they were rolled back in her head so that only a pale yellow showed there. Her lips were curled back over her teeth in a snarl. Every muscle in her face contorted into a hideous mask, pulled so tight that small tears appeared in her paper-thin skin and tiny rivulets of blood dripped down her cheeks. Everything in her face made her look menacing, like a dark creature ready to devour the little girl in front of her. But the sound coming from the old woman's throat was unlike anything Jack had heard before.

It was high-pitched, almost to the point of being painful to the ears, and it didn't match the face at all. It wasn't mean or aggressive, but rather a piteous whine filled with pain and begging. She sounded like an animal caught in a trap, metal cut down into the bone, ready to gnaw off its own leg to escape.

Sorenson pointed up to the trees and they all looked. The twig-and-rope structures hanging around the property all strained against the strings tying them to the trees, pushed outward by an unseen wind. They twisted and rattled, pieces of them peeling off and flying out into the forest. Jack turned to his left and saw more of the structures there, but these were pushed outward in the opposite direction. He looked back to the picnic table and realized whatever force was hitting the bizarre mobiles, ground zero was Sarah and the old woman holding her hands.

"Sarah!" Lauren cried next to Jack's ear, shocking him into action.

They all ran down toward the picnic table. But just as they reached it, a shotgun blast ripped through the air. Even with Ichote's continued screaming, the gunshot made them involuntarily duck and then freeze. They turned to see Powatan stepping down the porch steps, the gun waving them away from Sarah and Ichote. None of them moved away, but none of them moved closer either.

"You damn fools," Powatan said. "You'll kill her if you're not careful."

The old man carefully walked closer to his screaming wife, looking her over carefully as if for clues. Jack wondered how long she would be able to go before the tissue in her throat sloughed off like dead skin and stripped her vocal cords bare and unusable.

His bigger concern was Sarah. He moved closer so he could see her and was surprised to find her face totally calm. Relaxed even. While every piece of body language said she was fine and not under distress, her eyes told a different story. She was terrified. Her eyes rolled in their sockets until they were looking directly at him, pleading for his help. And that's when he understood. She was frozen, locked in a death grip with the howling old woman.

"Separate them!" Jack yelled.

"No, not yet," Powatan shouted back, swinging the shotgun around recklessly.

Lonetree reached out and in the blink of an eye had the shotgun out of the old man's hands, the shell ejected from the chamber and the barrel broken open so it no longer posed a threat.

Jack wasted no time. He reached out for Sarah. As he did, Powatan gripped his arm. He couldn't hear the old man over the screaming, but the body language was universal.

Please. Let me do this. I beg you.

Jack looked at Ichote, blood flowing freely from fissures across her forehead. Then at Sarah with her panicked eyes. Whatever was happening, the old woman seemed to be bearing the brunt of it. Jack pulled his hands back from Sarah's. The second he did so, Powatan lurched past the table, unsteady on his old legs, and reached behind a bush.

"What are you doing?" Lauren cried. "Stop this."

"Wait," Jack shouted. "Give him a chance."

Powatan staggered back toward them, carrying one of the twig-and-rope structures. It was bent into the shape of a pyramid and trussed up with twine. He brought it back to the table, lifted it over his head, and then thrust it onto the table where they held hands.

Jack felt his ears pop, the way they did in a fast elevator. Something changed because all of the other structures lost the invisible force pushing them and they swung back into position. Sarah and Ichote pulled their hands from one another.

And, thank God, the old woman stopped screaming.

Jack and Sarah ran to grab Sarah as she tipped to her right, her body rigid. Lauren gathered her up in her arms.

"You're cold, baby." She looked at Jack. "She's freezing."

Jack didn't need to be told. He was already reaching out to her, making sure she was real, making sure she was okay. But she wasn't okay. Her lips were blue and her teeth chattered. Her face was drained of color.

"Let's get her inside," Jack said. He looked across the table and saw Powatan had Ichote wrapped in his arms, tenderly kissing her blood-covered face, whispering words Jack didn't understand to her. Her eyes were wide open, no longer rolled in the back of her head, but locked in a thousand-yard stare, not registering them at all. "Lonetree, bring her."

Lonetree stepped in and Powatan let the big man gather his wife up in his arms. Jack did the same with Sarah and they ran back to the shack and the warm fire there.

Once inside, Powatan produced heavy blankets from a closet and Sorenson stoked the fire with new wood. Within a few minutes, the inside of the shack was hot enough that Jack felt sweat on his brow. Lauren sat on the floor next to the stove, holding Sarah to her chest as if she were a newborn. Before long, Sarah looked up at Lauren holding her and smiled.

"Hi, Mom," she said with a soft, raspy voice, as if she'd been the one screaming. "How'd I get in here?"

Lauren choked back a sob and smiled. "Are you warm enough, baby?"

"Yeah, feels good. It was so cold outside that I…" She froze and turned to look around the room in a panic. She calmed down when she saw Ichote, sitting in the leather recliner, a blanket pulled up to her chin, staring into the fire.

"She's all right, little one," Powatan said, dabbing his wife's face with a wet towel to clean the blood from it. "I've seen this before. It will pass."

Jack felt relief as he saw Ichote blink once, then break contact with the fire to turn her eyes on Sarah. But the sensation passed when he saw the old woman's expression. It was as if the fire from the stove still burned in her eyes. And they burned with pure hate.

Jack felt Sarah stiffen next to him. Lauren must have felt it too.

Sarah turned away from Ichote, a shudder passing

through her body. "Can we go? I want to go. Right now."

Lauren pulled the blanket tighter around her daughter. "I think we should warm you up a little more first, honey. And we need to find out whether your powers can be…" her voice trailed off as she also saw the look on Ichote's face. She looked like she might at any second lunge from her chair and attack Sarah.

"No, I want to leave now," Sarah said.

"Okay, maybe you're right." Lauren stood.

Jack stepped between Sarah and Ichote. He didn't know what had happened outside or what the look of pure hatred was about, but he knew he didn't trust the old woman and what she might do. He guided Lauren and Sarah to the door, keeping his eye on Ichote. The old woman stared Sarah down the entire time.

Jack gave Lauren the key and said he'd be right behind them. Once they left, he turned back to the room.

"So, what the hell is going on?" Jack demanded.

Powatan, picking up on his wife's signals, had turned on them too. He shook his head at Jack and pointed to the door, speaking quickly in a Native American tongue. Jack didn't understand the words, but the meaning was clear. *Get the hell off my property.*

Lonetree leaned in and whispered, "Give me a few minutes alone with them. You too, Sorenson."

Jack wanted to protest. He wanted to demand from the old woman exactly what she'd done to his daughter. But part of him knew that somehow his daughter had done something to her. And he wasn't completely sure if he wanted to know what it was. He knew that Lonetree talking to them alone was probably their best chance to get information from them. Besides, he admitted he'd be more than happy to escape the old woman's piercing stare.

Without a word, he turned and left the shack, Sorenson right behind him. As the door shut, he heard the old woman say five words that filled him with dread. They were in English, and came across the room too neatly for it to be an accident. She'd wanted him to hear it, somehow he felt sure of it. As he walked back to the car, he rolled the words back and forth in his mind, trying to reinterpret them in the best possible way. But the five words defied rationalization. They held up against any chance of wishing them away, especially given everything he knew and everything he'd seen. They were five words he wished had never been spoken and that, if they had to be spoken, that he had never heard.

The old woman's voice echoed in his head, over and over.

"The devil's already inside her."

Chapter 35

J ack and Sorenson leaned against the hood of the car, waiting for Lonetree. A front was moving in, the kind where a line of black clouds marches out of the west like an army on the march. A chill filled the air as the temperature dropped with the sinking sun. Sorenson lit a cigarette and took a long pull. Jack regarded him with surprise.

"I thought you guys were fitness freaks," Jack said.

Sorenson shrugged and took another draw. "A couple a day. Not the end of the world."

"Those things will kill you."

That got a chuckle out of Sorenson.

"What?" Jack asked.

"Given the things we're dealing with, I don't think it's going to be tobacco that ends up getting me," Sorenson said.

Jack considered that, took a quick look into the car behind him, and saw that Lauren and Sarah were in the backseat together, talking. "Hand me one of those, will you?"

Sorenson didn't seem too surprised. He tossed Jack the pack and his lighter. Jack took out a cigarette and balanced it in the palm of his hand for a couple of seconds before putting it in his mouth and lighting up.

He breathed in deep and long, exhaling through his mouth and nostrils. Sorenson nodded.

"I figured by the way you eyed the pack when I took it out that you were a reformed sinner."

"Stopped when the kids were born. My first company I started was built on caffeine and nicotine." He took another pull from the cigarette and sighed with satisfaction. "And a little bud now and then when things got tense," he added with a laugh.

"Nothing wrong with that," Sorenson said, catching the pack that Jack tossed back to him. He pulled out another cigarette. "Nothing wrong at all."

A comfortable silence fell between them, the only sound the wind picking up in the trees above them, rattling the dried leaves, sending a handful of them on a twisting suicide dive with each gust. They smoked their cigarettes and enjoyed the communal experience lost on non-smokers. What they didn't understand was that it wasn't only the nice buzz, the heightened senses, the mellow satisfaction. It was the social feel of sharing a smoke with a friend or even a stranger. It wasn't unlike gathering around a campfire, a trigger that stories were meant to be traded and observations about life to be made.

"You've seen a lot," Jack said. "Ever see anything like that before?" He nodded over to the picnic table, feeling foolish as he did. What else could possibly be on either of their minds?

Sorenson shook his head. "Nope. New territory for all of us."

"Are these people coming after Sarah…" Jack stumbled on the words and had to take another drag to steady himself. "Are they, you know, as bad as all that?"

"Whatever you're thinking, whatever you're imagining," Sorenson said, "it's worse." He nodded toward the shack where Lonetree was still holed up. "I've been in some shit with that man, I mean, really bad shit. And I've never seen him show any fear. I'm sure he feels it, he's human like the rest of us, but I've never seen any sign of it." The door to the shack opened and Lonetree walked through the front door by himself. Sorenson took one last drag, then flicked the half-smoked cigarette away. "Until now. This has him scared. And that ain't good."

Jack felt a pinch in his stomach, both from Sorenson's words and from the drained look on Lonetree's face as the big man paused on the porch to collect himself. Jack didn't like the look. He stamped out his own cigarette and walked toward Lonetree, meeting him halfway between the car and the shack.

"So? Can she remove Sarah's powers?" Jack asked.

Lonetree shook his head.

"What did she say?" Jack asked, more insistent.

Lonetree shrugged. "Nothing, really. Let's get out of here."

Jack put a hand on Lonetree's chest and stopped him. "Bullshit. You were in there for a while. She said something."

Lonetree looked down at Jack's hand still on his chest and then back up. "Nothing you want to hear."

Jack pulled his hand back. *Too late for that.* "I heard her. When I walked out the door. She said Sarah has the devil inside. What did she mean by that?"

Lonetree looked past him, staring at the car. "I don't know," he finally said. "Hell, Jack, I didn't even know the old woman was the one with the gift. All those years I thought it was the husband. Honestly, I'm not sure about a lot of things right now."

Jack felt the honesty in the big man's words. It was unlike Lonetree to admit to uncertainty, or to any weakness for that matter. Self-doubt had been sweat and bled out of him in the SEALs. So hearing him so openly admit it now filled Jack with a growing sense of dread. But, for now, that emotion had to compete with the anger that welled up inside him at Lonetree's stonewalling.

"Okay," Jack said, his voice rising. "I'll buy that you're not sure of things right now. But Ichote still told you something. I deserve to know. She's my daughter for Chrissake. Not yours."

Jack half-expected Lonetree to match his growing temper and shout back at him. But he didn't. He just stared Jack down, immoveable.

"Are we done here?" Lonetree asked, his voice too calm for Jack's liking.

Sprinkles of rain appeared, dotting both men's shoulders with drops. Neither of them took notice as they locked eyes. A car door slammed behind them and Sorenson jogged over.

"Hey, you're freaking the girls out," he said. "You guys can stare at each other in the car. C'mon, let's get out of here."

Lonetree stepped toward the car but Jack grabbed his arm. "You're going to tell me everything she said. Understand?" Then he marched off to the car.

Lonetree watched him go, ignoring the increasing rain. He didn't blame Jack. The guy was under a lot of pressure and there just wasn't a lot of good news to go around. If the bond Lonetree felt toward Sarah was any indication of what it must be like to be a father, then he couldn't imagine how Jack was handling the stress, especially given all he'd been through over the last ten years. Still, he didn't appreciate any man getting in his face. He slowly let go of the edge of his jacket he held in his fist.

"What was that all about?" Sorenson asked.

"He wants me to tell him what the old woman said."

"And…" Sorenson said.

"And I'm not going to tell him."

Sorenson gave him a look. "Why the hell not?"

Lonetree lowered his voice. "Because what she told me makes this a hundred times worse than anything I could have imagined."

"What could be that bad?"

Lonetree gave him a hard look. Sorenson's mouth fell open. He looked back to the car, and then to Lonetree.

"You can't be serious," Sorenson hissed. "This is bullshit."

Lonetree put a hand on the younger man's shoulder. "We play it out. The old woman might be wrong."

"Do you think she is?"

Lonetree couldn't look at him. He didn't want Sorenson to see the truth in his eyes. He just walked to the car, muttering under his breath. "Let's pray to God she is," Lonetree said. "And hope He listens for a change."

Chapter 36

The ride home took longer than the ride out. And the first half of it was mostly silent. The weather had only gotten worse. Rain pelted the windshield in heavy, windblown drops, making the world outside a blurred smudge of grey shapes and headlights. The bleakness matched the mood of the SUV's occupants, all brooding in their own thoughts as they watched the landscape slide by. Jack drove with Lonetree in the passenger seat, Sorenson in one of the captain's chairs in the second row, and Lauren sitting next to Sarah in the far back.

Exhausted from her ordeal, Sarah snored quietly, cuddled up with her mom like when she was a toddler. Lauren had her arms wrapped around her as if the embrace were the only thing keeping her little girl from floating up through the roof of the car to be lost in the night sky.

Jack adjusted the rearview mirror so that the image of Lauren and Sarah together filled the frame. He found it hard to keep from looking back at them, wondering how his little girl had grown up so quickly, and thankful her mother was so strong in the face of this second dose of insanity. For all the darkness surrounding them, this picture of mother and daughter was a needed reminder of what was good about the world.

But Jack knew it was a false reality, a shadow of a thing remembered but that was gone forever. He wanted to see an innocent child sleeping in the safe love of a mother's arms. But he knew it for what it really was. A little girl with powers she didn't understand, powers that could cause physical pain in others, even across distances. And Lauren was a mother clinging with panicked desperation to a child in terrible and immediate danger.

He wondered if things would ever go back to how they'd once been, or if this was the new normal for them. His maudlin thoughts were broken apart when Lauren spoke up from the back row.

"Wait a minute," she whispered, her voice like breaking glass in a quiet room. "Why are we going back home? What if these people are already there?"

The SUV slowed as Jack instinctively eased off the gas. He looked at Lonetree. "She has a point. We could be walking back into a trap, right?"

Lonetree shook his head. "They're not there yet. Mama D isn't anyway. And she's the one to look out for."

Lauren checked to make sure Sarah was still asleep. She was, a little line of drool hanging from the side of her mouth. "How can you be sure?" she asked.

189

JEFF GUNHUS

"I remember you told me the guy you caught had instructions not to come to town early to reduce the chances of raising suspicion," Jack said. "But that's the rank-and-file bad guy. How do we know Mama D's not here?"

"Mama D told them that she was on the trail of a special treat for them, not that she had it yet. Every time Sarah uses her powers in a big way it adds to the trail leading Mama D to her. It's like a shot being fired in a valley."

"Mama D is pinpointing Sarah's location through triangulation," Sorenson explained.

"I don't get it," Jack said.

"Ever try to find a sniper in the mountains?" Lonetree asked.

"Yeah, just last week," Jack replied. He was still pissed at Lonetree and didn't mind showing it.

"On the first shot," Sorenson jumped in, picking up the example, "no one has any idea where the shooter is. Everyone is surprised but now they're sure as hell wide awake. Even so, no one has a bead on where it came from. Second shot, everyone is waiting for it. Tuned in to try to figure out what direction it came from. Still, I've seen five SEALs point in five different directions on the second shot. But by the third and fourth shot, you can pin the location down pretty good."

"That's why any half-decent sniper moves location after two shots," Lonetree said. "So they don't risk tipping off their location."

"And you think these people trying to find Sarah are tracking her each time she uses her powers?" Jack asked.

"Ichote said she felt Sarah when she used her powers," Lonetree said. "Like a punch in the throat, is how she described it. That was the second shot for her."

"Second?" Sorenson said. "What was the first? Has she used her powers recently?"

Jack shook his head. "We thought they were gone."

"The first was almost exactly ten years ago," Lonetree said, and they all knew what he was talking about. Lauren and Sorenson had heard details about it, but Jack and Lonetree had witnessed it firsthand. A cave of skeletons trapped in rock cages coming to life, bones rattling against ancient confinement. The stone prison holding the creature Huckley and his men called the Source exploding as if a bomb had gone off. All things brought on by Sarah's psychic powers.

"If yesterday felt like a punch to the throat, what Sarah did in the cave probably didn't feel very good," Jack said.

"Ichote said she was in bed for two days after that one," Lonetree said. "She said it was like getting hit by a car you didn't see or hear coming. She was in her garden and then it was two days later and Powatan was trying to feed her soup in bed, threatening to take her to a white man's hospital."

"Then he must have been scared," Sorenson chimed in.

"But how can we be sure this Mama D person isn't more powerful?" Lauren asked. "That she couldn't put a bead on Sarah after only one time?"

"Don't underestimate how powerful Ichote is. I have a pretty keen sense of these things and I didn't pick her up at all."

191

"I don't get it," Jack said.

"She was blocking you," Sorenson said. "So you couldn't see her."

"Wait, so could Sarah learn how to do that?" Jack asked.

Lonetree nodded. "Eventually she'll need to. There are more people in the world than you'd expect that have some of the gift. Most people bury it deep inside when they're young and it withers without use. But others nurture it and use it."

"That would solve it then," Lauren said excitedly. If she just learns how to shelter her powers and not use them again, then they'll never find her, right?"

Jack looked at Lonetree but immediately saw from his expression that he was about to rob Lauren of her solution.

"It will take years for her to develop the skill. Even if she could master it faster, power always finds a way to be used. Especially when it's something as strong as what's in her. Sometimes for good. Sometimes not."

This last comment sucked the air out of the car. Jack imagined Mitzy Berlin and her mother, both on the ground, convulsing, eyes rolled back in their heads, spittle frothing at the corners of their mouths. He looked at Lauren and could see she was having the same thoughts.

"So what do you suggest we do?" Lauren asked.

"We go back to your house. Sorensen and I do a sweep of the place as a precaution before we go in. We get a good night's sleep and then in the morning…" Lonetree paused, girding up to deliver bad news. "We have Sarah call Mama D and invite her over."

Jack twisted in his seat to glare at Lonetree, causing the SUV to swerve to the right. The car next to them blared its horn as it swung wide to the shoulder to miss them. Jack corrected, the adrenaline pumping both from the near accident and from Lonetree's suggestion. "You want to use her as bait? Are you crazy?"

"Think about it," Lonetree said. "It makes sense. Every other option gives you nothing but uncertainty. If you run, you'll spend every waking minute looking over your shoulder. To buy yourself what? A few weeks? A couple of months? Because Sarah will use her powers again and Mama D will find her."

"We can go to the police," Lauren said. "It's what we should have done from the beginning."

Sorenson spoke up, his voice smooth and calm, obviously trying to slow down the rising emotions in the car. "And tell them what? That your daughter with psychic powers is being hunted by a horde of semi-immortal supernatural cannibals who you haven't seen yet, but who you know are coming for her because known-fugitive-from-the-law Joseph Lonetree told you so? The only agency that will take any interest in that story is Child Protective Services."

"Maybe she could demonstrate her powers to them. Make them believe," Lauren said.

"What kind of life would that leave her with?" Jack replied.

"Do you really want the government to take custody of her?" Lonetree asked.

"Better that than these people getting a hold of her," Lauren said.

They were talking over one another now, refuting each other's points before the words were all the way out. So when Lonetree winced in pain and held his hand to his temple, Jack didn't even notice. Had he noticed, he might have thought the big man just had a headache, or some kind of nerve pain from a wound from some long-forgotten fight. Even with the experiences of the last few years, he never would have suspected what was really going on in the head of Joseph Lonetree. Because, if he had, he would have pulled the car over right away and put an end to it. But he had no such insight, so he kept driving and the argument about what to do next kept rolling right along, although, for the most part, without Lonetree's participation.

He was otherwise occupied.

Chapter 37

*L*ONETREE! Sarah shouted. *CAN YOU HEAR ME?*

Lonetree flinched, his hand flying to his head like she'd just thrown a dart at him and scored a direct hit.

Jesus, kid, Lonetree thought silently, holding his head as if it might burst open. *Take it down a notch; you're going to fry my brain yelling like that.*

Sarah suppressed a giggle. She didn't want to tip off her mom that she was awake and listening to the conversation in the car. While she felt a smidge of guilt for pretending—she thought the drool on her mouth was a particularly nice touch—she knew it was the only way the adults were going to talk about the good stuff while she was in the car.

She hadn't been sure if she could reach Lonetree or not, but something about him told her she would be able to if she tried hard enough. She imagined a big round dial on a radio, the old kind they saw at garage sales sometimes, with the numbers one through ten positioned around it. Her dad always made a joke about turning it up to eleven but, like most of her dad's jokes, she never got why it was funny. But just for him, she reimagined the dial and the numbers transformed so that the top number, the place where the indicator arrow pointed, was a fancy-looking number eleven. She twisted the knob down to a two.

Is this better? she asked, sending the thought toward the front seat. She could hear the other adults still talking, but they sounded muffled now, like they were underwater. She focused on hearing Lonetree's voice.

Yeah, that's fine. Pretty neat trick you've got there.

I gotta admit, it is pretty cool. Ichote taught me. Like Professor Xavier in the X-Men movies. She experimented and sent Lonetree an image of the bald actor who played Professor X, the wheelchair-bound leader of the superhero mutants. For fun, she imagined Ichote's face on the man's body. It struck her as funny for a second, but then she decided she didn't like the image of the woman in a wheelchair so she dissolved it into a puff of smoke.

I love those movies, Lonetree said. *But I'm guessing that's not the reason you nearly scrambled my grey matter to get my attention.*

Grey matter?

Lonetree's voice came back with an amused tone. *Another way of saying brain.* There was a pause. *Have you been listening the whole time?*

Yes.

So you know you're in danger?

Yes. But I knew that before you told me. I think I knew from my dad, but I can't be sure. It just feels like I've always known about her. But how can that be? I don't understand it.

All the play was gone from Lonetree's voice this time. *You're just getting used to…wait a second.*

In the world outside of her mind, Sarah heard Lonetree's real voice, the one that needed air passing over vocal cords to work, fill the car.

"I'm sorry, I was lost in a thought," he said. "What was the question?"

Her mom spoke up. Sarah heard the words but also felt them as she snuggled into her mom's chest.

"I said, did Ichote tell you anything that might be useful? You were in there for a while."

"I already told Jack, nothing that would help us."

Tell them it was about your dad and brother.

Sarah felt a red flash of anger from Lonetree.

We did talk about them. Stay out of my mind without permission.

Sorry, she replied, meaning it. *Just trying to help.* She heard his voice in the car.

"We talked about the way my dad and my brother died. Nothing to do with Sarah that you haven't already heard," Lonetree said.

The comment had the desired effect. It stole the emotion away and reminded everyone in the car that Lonetree had sacrificed much in the battle against evil. Everyone fell silent.

That was pretty smart, Lonetree said.

Kids are the best manipulators, Sarah replied, hiding her excitement over the compliment. *Besides, it was true, wasn't it? I didn't really peek, I promise. It was just there. Like seeing a sign on a road when you drive by. I didn't mean to see it. It was just kind of hard to miss.*

Settle down, kid. It's fine. Just…stay out of my head, okay? Plenty of stuff you don't want to see in there. Promise?

Okay.

No, I want you to promise. It's important. Say it out loud that you promise not to go into my head without permission. Lonetree's voice was strained. Urgent.

I said okay.

Promise me!

The thought roared through her head like a storm. She jerked backward and felt her mom's arms wrap tighter around her, her hands patting her shoulder.

"Shhhh…it's all right," her mom whispered. "Go back to sleep."

Sarah relaxed her tense body, thinking it would feel like she was falling back asleep. She felt her mom's grip ease as she thought her daughter drifted off again.

I'm sorry, Lonetree said. *But it's important. I need you to promise.*

I promise, she said. *Geez.*

There was silence between them, matching the silence in the car.

So…you wanted something? Lonetree asked.

They're not going to let me be used as bait. You know that right?

Lonetree nodded, only she felt him do it rather than saw it. Or rather, she felt a sense of agreement and somehow knew that if she opened her eyes she would see the big man nod his head.

But she has to be stopped, she said. *Just like Huckley and the Source had to be stopped or…or…they…*

Or they'll keep killing kids.

Yeah, or they'll keep killing kids. There was a quaver in her voice. She knew it didn't make any sense because the voice she heard only existed in her head. Still, it reflected how she expected her voice would sound if she spoke out loud, choked with emotion and struggling to get out. *I see them sometimes, you know. The kids Huckley and the others kidnapped and took to the Source. I don't know how that's possible, but I can see it like I was there. Like I lived it. I can…I can hear them scream. Hear them beg to die.*

It's not real, Lonetree said. *You have to keep reminding yourself of that.*

But that's the problem, don't you see? It was real. They're actual memories, not something I made up. Like this one kid, Charlie. He's always right in my face whenever I close my eyes. He keeps asking me to promise I'll see it through. That I'll stop them no matter what it takes. I tell him I'll try, but I don't know how.

Are you talking about Charlie Winters? Lonetree's voice sounded thick and slow.

Yeah, how do you know his name?

Lonetree looked reluctant to answer. When he did, his voice was stone-cold. *He wasn't killed by the Source. It was Mama D who did it.*

No, I see him in with all the others, Sarah insisted.

Trust me. I put him out of his misery myself when I found him. It was Mama D and it was only two days ago.

Sarah nodded, processing this information. *His voice is stronger than the others. I think he's still in pain. That's not possible, is it? I mean, they're dead, right?*

Yes, they're all dead.

There was another awkward silence. Then Sarah asked, *Was there something special about Charlie?*

The answer came back slow and forced, like

Lonetree was trying hard not to reveal any emotion in his thought. *There was probably something special about all of them, don't you think?*

She signaled a sense of agreement and felt the same feeling come back to her. But there was some other feeling on the edge of what she could sense. It took a few seconds to isolate and identify what it was and she blushed when she figured it out. Lonetree had a growing desire that Sarah would just shut the hell up.

But she had questions for him. Questions she knew she couldn't ask her parents and expect to get a straight answer. They still thought she was just a little kid. Lonetree knew that wasn't true.

You're going to tell me everything you know about Mama D.

And why am I going to do that?

Because I need to decide whether or not I'm going to disobey my parents and help you kill her.

Silence.

Long and tense. Sarah risked being seen to barely open her eyes to look at Lonetree. From the backseat, all she could see was the outline of his head. His face was quartered away from her, staring out the window, thinking hard about her proposition. Finally, his voice reappeared in her head.

Okay, here's what I know. I'm sorry for showing you this, but I think you have to understand the truth.

Sarah was about to reply when a torrent of images burst into her mind. Bodies. Bloodied and mangled. Flesh torn away in strips. Bones gnawed, marrow sucked from them. A dozen of them. Two dozen. Then a boy she recognized, even worse than the rest. Half-eaten, entrails spilling out of the gaping holes ripped in his abdomen.

His privates chewed up like gristle on a steak. Cheeks flailed from his skull. One eye socket staring up at the ceiling, empty except for the puddle of blood trapped there and spilling out, like he was weeping. But the worst of it all was that he was still alive. Impossible as it was, he was still alive, his destroyed face still yawning open and snapping shut like some kind of mechanical automaton at a carnival. Only this wasn't some kind of robot, this was Charlie Winters. And he was screaming from the pain. Screaming. Screaming.

Screaming, Sarah bolted upright, knocking the back of her head against the underside of her mom's chin so hard that it almost knocked her out.

Sarah tried to scramble to the far side of the bench seat. The seatbelt that had been loosely draped across her snapped tight and held her in place as effectively as a pair of orderlies at a mental hospital.

"No!" she screamed, clawing at her own head. "Get it out. Get it out of there."

She lurched to one side as the car swerved violently. Then pressure across her chest as the seatbelt held her back when the SUV screeched to a stop.

Then hands were on her. She fought them. These were the same hands that got Charlie. If they got her, then she would end up with the peeled-off skin, the vacant eye socket with ripped edges, the white ribs sticking out of a half-devoured torso.

You have to kill them before they kill you, said a voice in her head she didn't recognize, calm and reasonable, like it was stating a fact as clear as rain is wet or the sun is hot. The voice was right. She had to stop them before they got her.

"Get off me!" she screamed.

There was a shattering of glass and then the hands were gone. Her seatbelt unbuckled even though her hands were up, covering her face. She was halfway out of the car, through a door she had no memory of opening, before Lonetree's voice broke through to her.

Sarah. Stop. No one is going to hurt you. Stop or you'll hurt yourself. You'll hurt your mom and dad.

She froze in place.

That's right. Open your eyes and look. It's just us. No one's going to hurt you.

Sarah opened her eyes. The dome light was on, which cast everything in stark shadows. Sorenson was next to her, out of his seat, one knee on the console in between the two chairs in the second row, ready to grab her. Her mom was behind her, face white. To Sarah, it looked like her mom couldn't decide if she meant to grab her or just protect herself. But why was she behind her? That's when Sarah realized that somehow she'd crawled into the second row. She saw movement outside and she twisted that way. It was her dad looking at her through the smashed window of the rear door. The metal door itself was crumpled, as if it were made of tinfoil.

"It's okay, baby," her dad said from outside. "It was just a bad dream."

She sagged forward and sobbed. Cried harder than she ever had. Then his strong hands held on to her, only this time she didn't try to get away. This time she leaned into them and felt her dad hold her tightly and rock her.

"It was just a bad dream," he whispered in her ear.

Only she knew it wasn't a bad dream. Lonetree had shown her what she needed to see. He'd treated her like an adult and shown her the truth and she'd bawled like a baby.

I'm sorry, came Lonetree's voice, filled with guilt. *I shouldn't have—*

No, Sarah snapped back. *I needed to see that. I needed to understand.*

A pause.

So, what's it going to be? Lonetree's voice came back, now rid of its guilt and softness. This was Lonetree the soldier talking to her. *You giving up? Or are you going to take it to the enemy?*

Sarah leaned back in her dad's arms until she could look him in the eye. She wiped her tears away and said, "I'm sorry about the car door, Dad."

He barked out a tension-releasing laugh, tears welling in his own eyes. "Don't worry, honey. We can get a new door."

She let him hug her again, let him feel confident that his little girl was all right. As she hugged him back, she mustered as much anger and strength as she could and used them to make sure Lonetree knew she meant what she said next.

Now we go after Mama D, Sarah replied. *And we make her pay for what she's done.*

Chapter 38

Mama D glanced up from her booth at the Waffle House in West Virginia. The sensation didn't pack the same punch as the one before, but she immediately recognized it was the little girl. Sarah. She whispered the name and found it hard to get used to after a decade of thinking of her as an idea of a person instead of a specific name. Sarah. She liked the sound of it. Yes, it was her she felt. She was sure of it.

Mama D had a true gift of taste. In the same way a great sommelier could identify the appellation of a Cabernet with a simple roll of wine across the tongue, or a drunk can call out a cigarette brand from only the last suck off a discarded butt, Mama D could sort through the minds projecting their gift out into the world and lock on to one. To her, it was a signature. A DNA built into the way the power was shaped and colored.

Not everyone who took part in the ritual shared this ability and when any developed the skill, Mama D made sure they met an unfortunate accident. Like the woman in New York City, who may have proven to be stronger than Mama D if she was given enough time, who fell off the subway platform as she stood in front of Mama D, smacking head-first into a train at full-speed. Or the teenager who had enough natural skill at tracking that others in the group had insisted she be brought in to be one of them. Mama D did as she was asked. Brought the pretty blond-haired teenager on board…and then served her heart for dinner with a side of shoestring fries and some broccolini that same night.

Nobody but nobody messed with Mama D. Sometimes the new generation just needed to be reminded exactly why that was.

"Was it her?" Jimmy asked. "I saw you look up. Like when you get somethin'."

Mama D nodded. "Yawp, that was her all right. Let's see the map."

Jimmy pulled a map out of a backpack. An old, folded-up number. The kind responsible for countless fights among road-tripping married couples, and undoubtedly as many divorces. But if there was anything Jimmy was good at, it was maps. Well, that and luring attractive young girls away from their families for a ride in the trunk of Jimmy's car. It was the reason Mama D had kept him when she sacrificed those others to Lonetree, that Goddamn Indian. She had already gotten what she wanted out of the Winters boy before she left, but it still made her seethe when she thought about sneaking out of town the way she did. But Lonetree and his friend were scores to settle on a different day.

Jimmy unfolded the creased, raggedly thin map with expert precision and smoothed it flat on the tabletop between them. There, for all to behold, was the entire Mid-Atlantic, encompassing a swath of the Eastern seaboard from New York down to Virginia.

The map was covered with pencil marks and little notations in tiny writing. Jimmy didn't bother hiding anything from the other customers that passed their table. First, everything on there was written in a code only he understood. Second, it seemed highly unlikely that anyone in a Waffle House in West Virginia could have made any sense of what the map meant.

Mama D studied the pie-shaped areas Jimmy had colored onto it, each one a different color. They each started from whatever city she had been in when she sensed Sarah. A decade ago, they were in Austin, Texas when the little bitch had literally knocked her off her feet with a nuclear blast of power. All she could remember when she came to the next day was a vague sense that it had come from a generally Northeast direction. Jimmy had dutifully drawn two heavy lines on the map, both starting in Austin. One line cut through Northeast Texas, through Arkansas, Missouri, making a bead up through Michigan and Quebec. The other headed out of East Texas cutting through Louisiana, Mississippi and ending in South Carolina. Somewhere in this cone was the promised land. A pesh more powerful than anything they'd ever experienced. Maybe even powerful enough to solve the problem that haunted her most of all.

The challenge was that the cone encompassed nearly a third of the country. Mama D spent the next six months hunting only inside that cone, waiting for a second shot to pinpoint the girl's location. But nothing came, which was unusual for a pesh. It was hard to imagine any kid discovering they had the gift to affect things with their mind, to read the thoughts of others, and not use that power as soon and as often as possible. In her experience, they were worse than teenagers discovering the joys of a good masturbation session. They couldn't keep their hands off their new powers.

But this one was different. She just disappeared. It was so unusual that she reached the only reasonable conclusion. The nuclear blast Mama D had felt must have been the moth sparking in the fire, just the heat signature of the little girl's death. Nothing else made any sense. So, disappointed, she turned her people back to the open highways and back roads of flyover country where the hunting was easier and the risks lower. There was talent to be found—and devoured—but nothing like the promise the little girl held. That was a once-in-a-century opportunity and it was gone.

Or so she'd thought. Until the visitor came to her, and changed everything.

"What you think?" Jimmy said, tapping the map on the table.

Mama D shirked aside the irritation she felt at Jimmy's tone. It was too familiar, bordering on bossy. Long-term, right-hand man or not, that wasn't going to fly. But she didn't need the distraction now. She needed to focus on the map.

There was Prescott City, roughly circled with a red pen. This was where the voice had instructed her to go, giving her a date and time. But she wanted to find the girl without its help. She wanted to possess her on her own.

So, even as they traveled to the location given them by the voice, the search continued.

The other hits had created a narrowing prospect field, an area over West Virginia, Virginia, Western Maryland and Pennsylvania where the cones from the other hits overlapped. As a percentage of the country, it felt like progress. But it was still hundreds of square miles, not narrow enough for a good hunt.

Mama D closed her eyes and tried to remember what she had felt coming from Sarah. Fear, a need to escape, power. She wondered if someone else was already after her. Maybe she wasn't the only one in front of whom the visitor had dangled this particular piece of candy.

She dug her hand into her leg until she felt a pinch of pain and used it to clear her head. Usually she was able to focus and block everything out, but she'd been having trouble recently. She wondered whether it was because she hadn't fed very well for a while. Or if it was…

"Damn!" she said, loud enough that the couple in the table next to them looked up from their artery-clogging plates of biscuits and gravy. She shot them a withering look and they got back to shoveling food into their mouths.

"What's wrong?" Jimmy asked.

"Shut it," Mama D snapped, not wanting to admit the trouble she was having concentrating for even a small span of time.

Jimmy lowered his head in the animal kingdom's universal sign of subservience. He knew he'd offended her somehow and he feared the price tag that came with the offense. This made Mama D feel a little better.

She closed her eyes again and tried to recreate the feeling of Sarah's mind.

It was powerful, but didn't hurt her this time. Mama D had taken precautions. Sarah had knocked her flat once but that would never happen again. She sought out direction in the memory of the psychic burst, her hand hovering over the map. Finally, when it felt right, she put her palm down. When she looked up, she was surprised. Her hand covered an area mostly outside of their prospect field.

Jimmy screwed his mouth into a little pucker, but didn't say what she knew he wanted to. She watched him closely, wondering if he was going to do a deeper dive into the pile of shit he was already in. He knew he was already in trouble with her. Challenging her ability would only make it worse. He just nodded and used the hard edge of the grease-stained plastic Waffle House menu to draw two new lines on his map. Done, he leaned back and studied it.

"Maybe they're traveling," he said. "You know, gettin' outta Dodge."

Smart, she thought. A way to acknowledge that the spot was out of the area they'd been honing in on without coming right out and saying it. Not only that, but she considered that he might be right. Someone that strong might have sensed they were coming for her. She doubted it though. The defenses she'd erected around her mind were stronger than anything she'd built before. She had no intention of letting the little bitch-darling knock her on her ass again.

"This fella, the guy you were talking about," Jimmy said softly.

"The visitor," Mama D said, hating the sound of

reverence in her own voice.

"Yeah, the visitor," Jimmy said, not making eye contact. "Why do you think he's slow-playing us? I mean, if he knows where she is, why doesn't he just tell us? Why is this date so important?"

Mama D scowled. Not because it wasn't a fair question, it was. In fact, it was the same question that kept churning in her head. It was the reason she was still trying to locate the girl without the visitor's help. But coming from Jimmy, it sounded like another challenge to her authority. Worse, to her intelligence. She sent him a mental image of her snatching up the fork on the table and jamming it into his eye, twisting it violently to scramble his brain. Jimmy got the image and jerked backward, hitting his head on the cheap laminate wall behind him. And he got the point. He grabbed the check and headed to the counter with it.

Mama D watched him go. Jimmy was part of the old crew and she needed him on this trip. Hell, she'd called them all in for this. The old guard. The hired guns she'd cultivated over years, handpicked veterans from the nation's wars. The new recruits. All converging on one point on the map from around the country. But once it was done, Jimmy would have to be dealt with.

It was a shame. There weren't many of the old ones left. But there were always new people ready to take their place, unspoiled by time and lacking the moody, taciturn ways people tended to develop after taking the gift for too long. The new followers she'd recently acquired from Texas were so easy to handle and eager to please. They were gun-toting, ex-military types who hopefully could handle Lonetree once and for all. They were the future, not Jimmy.

But she would deal with that later.

She looked over and saw a ten-year-old, dark-haired girl get up from the table on the other side of the room. For a second, Mama D thought the dad was going to go with her, but then thought better of it. An awkward age. A little too old to have her go into the men's room with him. A little young not to feel a pang of doubt for sending her by herself. But the girl's younger brother threw a fit at the table so the dad sat, gave her a nod, and settled back into the booth, unaware that he would never see his little girl alive again.

Mama D stood, brushed her shirt and pants flat, and followed the girl to the bathroom. It wasn't much, but the pesh had a little of the gift. Enough for her to make Jimmy pull off the freeway as she honed in on the power source. No, it wasn't much, like a tiny bag of chips when what she craved was a five-course gourmet meal. Still, chips were better than nothing and Mama D was hungry.

With a quick sweep of the Waffle House, she saw that Jimmy was behind her. He would position himself outside the bathroom door in case anyone came poking around. She only needed a minute or two. It was, after all, just a snack.

She opened the door and called out, "Hello, child. Don't worry. Mama D's here to take care of you."

The door fell shut behind her and Jimmy stood nearby, leaning against the wall with practiced nonchalance while the little dark-haired girl's soul was devoured in the bathroom behind him.

Chapter 39

S arah fell into her bed and thought it was the best feeling she'd ever experienced. Between Ichote and the episode in the car, she felt totally spent. It had taken everything she had not to fall asleep in the car while Lonetree and Sorenson completed a circuit around the property and then searched the house. Once they declared it clear, her dad drove the SUV down the driveway and parked it at the front door.

When she got out, her legs were rubber, the same way they'd felt after she ran a half-marathon last year. Only this feeling of tiredness somehow ran deeper than anything she'd experienced before. It felt like the air was heavy and pressed her down, making every movement burn her muscles. Her bones felt old and brittle, as if they might break from the smallest fall.

Buddy, their yellow lab, ran toward her once the door was open. He moved stiffly, his white muzzle showing his age. But his tail beat side-to-side like some out-of-control motorized toy, until he got closer to her. Sensing something, he lowered both his head and his tail and let out a long, slow whine. It wasn't fear, but concern. Buddy curled up at her feet and rolled on his back. Sarah reached down to scratch his belly and he carefully licked her arm.

"You know how I feel, don't you, Buddy?"

Buddy whined again and the sound pierced her ears, more painful than it should have been. A headache throbbed behind her right eye, a marble-sized point of pain that pulsed with her heartbeat. She knew it was just a headache, but it felt like an insect crawling around in her brain, scratching and scraping the backside of her eye, trying to dig its way out.

She nudged Buddy and the lab slowly climbed to his feet, looking excited to be let off the hook so he could go pee on the grass. Sarah just needed sleep. She'd begged for it, even if only an hour or two. Reluctantly, and only after a discussion among the adults about how safe they were in the house, her parents agreed to let her get some rest before they left but warned it would be minutes, not hours. Her feather-top mattress swallowed her up whole and she drifted away easily into a black, uncomplicated nothingness. For a while, she had peace.

But the nightmare waited in the dark recesses of her mind, coiled with ruthless energy, biding its time to inflict its horror.

213

Chapter 40

Jack fought back the sense they were making a huge mistake as he lugged two large suitcases up from the basement. Lauren came from the mudroom with a pile of jackets, gloves, and hats. Jack threw the suitcases on the dining room table, then propped one open so that Lauren could drop the pile of winter gear into it.

Lonetree stood to the side, leaning against one of the decorative pillars separating the kitchen from the great room. He shook his head. "I told you, running isn't going to work."

"Yeah? Well, maybe it's the least bad out of a lot of really bad options," Jack said. "Like you said, we can't go to the police or the FBI. They'll think we're nuts. If we stay, we're just targets and they have the initiative."

"Maybe, but at least we can fight them where we know the area," Lonetree said.

Sorenson walked in from the garage carrying a large, heavy duffel bag. He hefted it onto the breakfast bar and unzipped it, revealing an arsenal of weapons. "He's right, Jack. If you run, they'll track you. The attack will come, only it will be when you don't expect it. At a gas station. Or a hotel room. Maybe they storm your car while you're getting McDonald's drive-through."

At the mention of an attack at the drive-through, Lauren headed to the kitchen and started throwing food items into one of the suitcases. "Then we go off the grid. Far away from anyone or anything."

"This isn't some pop-fiction spy novel," Lonetree grumbled. "These people aren't tracking you with computers and access to surveillance cameras. Using cash instead of credit cards isn't going to do shit, okay?" He pointed to his head. "Mama D's up here. She can sense Sarah no matter where she goes."

Jack zipped one of the full suitcases. "No, Sarah said she can erect a wall around that stuff. Make sure nothing gets out. Ichote showed her how."

Lonetree shook his head. "It's just a matter of time before she uses her power again. It's the very nature of power that it demands to be used. The greater the power, the more certain it's going to not only be used, but eventually used in the wrong way."

Lauren stared at Lonetree. "She didn't mean to hurt Ichote."

"How about the girl at school? Her mother?" Lonetree asked.

Lauren shot Jack an accusatory look. Jack held his ground. "These guys are putting their lives on the line for

215

us. They deserve to know everything."

Lauren looked away, but the flash of anger that had been there seconds before slowly transformed into grudging acknowledgement. Jack knew she was having a hard time reconciling the idea that their daughter put two people in the hospital. He was having the same problem.

"There is one thing we haven't considered," Sorenson said.

Jack looked over. He was amazed to see that his breakfast bar had been turned into a display of semi-automatic weapons and stacks of ammo.

"What's that?"

"The date. The map we found had a specific date on it. Tomorrow. Why? What's so important about tomorrow?" Sorenson asked.

"Could be anything," Lonetree said. "Might be arbitrary."

"But what if it's not?" Sorenson asked. "I mean, what if this thing they want to do to Sarah has to get done tomorrow for some reason? If she's as highly prized as all that, seems weird to me that Mama D would wait to come get her unless there was a real good reason."

Jack and Lauren stopped packing, thinking through the implications of what Sorenson was suggesting. It may have been grasping at straws, but at least it was something to grasp for. Lonetree stood silently, arms crossed, thinking.

"If you're right, then we just need to evade them for one day, right? Just get in a car and don't stop until the day's over," Lauren said hopefully.

Lonetree shook his head. "No, that's not it. Mama D can always use Sarah. She'll always crave her and seek her out." He looked back to Sorenson. "This could be useful though."

Sorenson noticed Jack and Lauren's confused looks. "If the enemy has a hard deadline, they'll be willing to take more tactical risks," he explained. "The trick is to use their urgency to force them to take enough extra risks that it's fatal."

Jack was getting it. "If there wasn't a deadline, they would wait us out for weeks. Months even. Until we let our guard down. But if tomorrow is that important to them, they might risk a frontal assault in public."

He saw Lauren's eyes shift to the guns on the breakfast bar.

"So, what? We turn this place into a war zone? Fight it out like it's the Old West?" Lauren asked, incredulous.

Lonetree left his spot against the pillar and walked toward them. "Yes and no. Sorenson might be right. The date could be specific. Some kind of condition for a ritual."

"Full moon tonight," Sorenson said, looking up from his phone.

Lauren let out an involuntary snort. "Come on, a full moon?"

Lonetree looked at her curiously, but didn't argue with her. Jack guessed what the big man was thinking. How could any of them discount anything as being too odd or weird after everything they'd seen in even the last twelve hours?

"The full moon is central to a lot of rituals across the world," Sorenson added. "Whether it makes an actual impact isn't really important."

"It doesn't matter whether it makes a difference,

only that they think it does," Lauren finished, getting it quickly. "Okay, just for the sake of argument, how would we use this?"

Lonetree and Sorenson eyed each other. Jack tried to follow the body language between them as they seemed to have an entire conversation with only a few looks, a shrug of the shoulder and a slight nod of agreement.

"First, we start knowing this is a long shot. We don't even know if the date tomorrow matters enough to push them to do something stupid," Lonetree said. "But if we decide to roll the bones on this one, then here's how we play it. Sarah would have to make noise. A lot of noise. Like she did at her school today and again in the car."

"And at the cabin with Ichote," Jack added.

Lonetree shook his head. "The catchers stopped most of that from getting out."

"The catchers?" Jack asked.

"You saw those things strung up in the trees around the property? Made out of bent tree branches and rope?"

"Yeah."

"Those are catchers. They protect Ichote from being discovered by other people with the gift. People like Mama D," Lonetree said.

Lauren perked up at the idea. "We could do that. Surround the property to block her from seeing Sarah."

Sorenson looked up from the weapon he was cleaning. "You saw how she lived. Is that what you want for Sarah? Hiding from the world in the middle of the woods somewhere?"

"If it kept her alive, yes," Lauren said.

Lonetree shook his head. "You saw Ichote with Sarah. Just contact with her almost killed her. Sarah's already more powerful than Ichote will ever be. There aren't enough catchers in the world to contain her when she loses control."

Jack put an arm around Lauren. Both of them felt it. Hell, they cringed when a teacher made a mild comment about Sarah's need to focus more in class, or to try a little harder to socialize with other kids. Hearing someone talk about their little girl's inevitable telekinetic outburst felt like a punch to the stomach. Worst of all, they both knew it was true.

Sorenson shot Lonetree a warning look, but diplomacy wasn't Lonetree's strong suit, so he missed the signal and soldiered on. "Like I was saying, Sarah makes as much noise as she can. Hopefully without tearing the house apart by accident."

Sorenson put his gun back on the table a little harder than necessary and Lonetree looked at him oddly. Jack knew the big man had no idea he was making his and Lauren's stomach turn over every time he talked about Sarah like she was some kind of monster.

"It's all right," Jack said, mostly to Sorenson who seemed ready to check Lonetree's delivery. "Keep going."

"After that, the three of you hightail it out of here. Sarah locks down her thoughts. Builds a wall around herself. She knows how to do that. Eventually, the wall won't hold her in, but she can pull it off for a day or two. That's the theory anyway."

Jack was about to ask how he knew that was the case, but decided to leave it alone. This was the first plan of the night that didn't include his family staying around to meet the enemy head-on. He didn't want to derail the momentum.

"So, they key on the noise," he said. "They show up here, but then what?"

Sorenson pumped a sawed-off shotgun dramatically with one hand. "Then Mama D and her friends get to meet me and Lonetree. If we capture her, we might need you guys to stay away for a few days. We're gonna want to pay her back a little for some of her past transgressions, if you know what I mean."

Jack checked in with Lauren. She bit her lower lip, a habit she had when thinking a problem through. After a few seconds, she said, "If we leave right after she draws them in, then it's not like we're using her as bait, right?"

"But it's still a big risk," Lonetree said. "If they don't go for it, if somehow they figure out you're on the move, then you'll be on your own against them. Sorenson and I will be here, out of the fight," Lonetree said.

Jack nodded. "This is the best plan we have. I think it's a risk worth taking."

Lauren looked up from her own phone, the color draining from her face. "The date you saw was tomorrow, right?" Lonetree nodded. Lauren held up her phone. "The full moon reaches its zenith tonight, right after 3am. That's tomorrow's date."

They all stared at her, each of them adjusting to this new information. Sorenson checked his own phone then looked up, embarrassed. "She's right."

Jack spoke first. "Okay, nothing changes. We load up right away, have Sarah make some noise, and then get the hell out of here."

Lauren stiffened. "What if Sarah can't use her powers on call? I've only ever seen her use them when she was agitated."

The four of them considered the idea, but no one had an answer.

"And we need her to be loud so there's no doubt they've heard her," Lonetree said. "If she can't figure it out, we'll just have to agitate her somehow."

"Agitate her?" Lauren said, anger in her voice.

Jack took Lauren's hand, gave it a squeeze. "Come on, let's get the last few things packed. We'll worry about that if it's an issue, okay?"

Lauren nodded and got busy closing up the bags, pointing Sorenson toward the ones ready to take to the car. Jack walked quickly to the front of the house, feeling the new sense of urgency from their stepped-up timetable.

He was in the front entry, about to zip up the last suitcase with hiking boots and winter coats, when Lonetree approached and threw a Glock on top of it. Jack picked it up and turned it over in his hands.

"Remember how to use it?" Lonetree asked.

"Does this one have blanks in it?"

Lonetree grinned. The first time they'd met, Lonetree proved his trust by handing over his handgun to Jack, a gun the ghostly presence of Nate Huckley later forced Jack to turn on Lonetree. Fortunately for them both, Lonetree hadn't really trusted Jack all that much and had given him a gun filled with blanks.

"No, I gave you big-boy bullets this time," Lonetree said. "Before this is done, you might need to use that. You might need to make some tough choices."

"What do you mean? What choices?"

Lonetree looked toward the stairs, then back at Jack.

"You were in the cave," Lonetree whispered. "You saw what happened. What Sarah's capable of doing."

"Yeah, but—"

"Ichote told me a few things back at the cabin."

Jack rocked back, remembering the look on Lonetree's face when he first walked out of the cabin. "Okay, like what?"

"Like how in most kids the power decreases with age. They repress it and it goes dormant after time. Only Sarah's gotten stronger since the cave," Lonetree added. "A lot stronger."

"But that's not—"

"And there's something else," Lonetree said, cutting him off. He opened his mouth, but the words stalled. Lonetree looked away. "Damn it, I wasn't going to tell you this, but I feel like I have to if we're separating."

Jack braced himself. He'd felt there was something Lonetree was hiding from him. And for him to hide it probably meant it wasn't something Jack was going to want to hear. He thought back to the last thing Ichote said. *The devil's already inside her.* He stared Lonetree down, almost daring him to continue with his thought.

"C'mon," Jack said. "If it's about Sarah, you can't keep it from me. I deserve to know."

Lonetree took a deep breath. "There's a chance, not for sure, but a chance that…" Lonetree trailed off, cocking his head to one side. "Do you hear that?"

At the back of the house, Buddy started to bark. Vicious, snarling tones like his life depended on it. Before either of them could react, Sarah screamed from upstairs. Jack immediately imagined the worst, but his imagination fell far short of the real reason Sarah was screaming.

NIGHT TERROR

Chapter 41

Sarah's eyes bolted open and she gasped for air as if someone had been holding her head underwater and she had finally struggled loose. She panted heavily and fought back a sense of disorientation in the dark room. It took her a few seconds to realize that the room she was in was her own. The cheap boy-band posters tacked to the walls, her dirty clothes strewn across the floor, the Santa Claus night-light she still insisted on keeping out year-round because she liked the idea of Santa watching her sleep and keeping her safe.

Only now it felt like there was more than the flat, plastic Santa face sharing the room with her. Something else was in there with her.

She went to push off the bed, ready to run to find her parents. But she couldn't move.

She was flat on her back on top of her bedsheets, still wearing the clothes from their road-trip. Her legs were straight and her arms were crossed on her chest.

Like I'm in a coffin.

A shudder passed through her body, but that was the only movement she could manage. That and her choppy, rapid breathing.

She tried to cry out. If she couldn't run to her parents for help, then she would bring them to her. Certainly with everything that was going on, they couldn't be far away. She drew in a lungful of air and screamed as loud as she could.

Nothing.

Not even a whisper. Her throat constricted, cutting off the flow of air until her lungs burned and she felt the blood building up in her face. Soon, she felt dizzy from the exertion and stopped trying. She gasped for air again, then chugged in shallow breaths. Inexplicably, the temperature in the room dropped and short plumes of white burst from her mouth as she hyperventilated. Terror began to take hold.

She was trapped in her body. And something was in the room.

Her head was propped up on a pillow that angled her forward, chin digging into her chest. This gave her a view of her unmoving body and most of her room. Whatever strangeness had frozen her body into place, it did not seem to have the same effect on her face. Her mouth gaped open in horror. She frantically shifted her eyes from side to side, desperate to see what or who was in the room with her.

At first, she didn't see anything. Her bed was against the wall, so she felt confident that there was

225

nothing behind her. Straining her eyeballs to each side until it was nearly painful, she thought she had a good idea of the areas in her periphery. Under her bed was always a possibility, but that was only a six-inch clearance, making whatever might be using it for a hideout at least small. Her breathing slowed a bit and she felt like she moved her head ever so slightly to the side. She had just touched on a glimmer of hope that her imagination had run away with her, when she saw something.

A flash of movement. Really, more a flicker from the Santa night-light blinking off and then back on as something moved in front of it.

She craned her neck to get a better look but her ability to move her body at all was just wishful thinking. Even so, she rolled her eyes in their sockets, trying to take in the whole room at once.

Another flicker of light. Then another.

A sound came next. A high-pitched squeaking noise. Not loud. Kind of hushed, like a whispered language.

The squeak was answered by others. Urgent. Impatient.

Then she saw them. Rats. At least a dozen of them. Crawling across the floor of her room. Others coming in from her closet door. From out of the heating vents on the floor. One crawling out from a recessed light in the ceiling, hanging there for a second, then dropping with a thump to the carpeted floor. There was a scraping sound. They were in the walls. Hundreds of them.

Mom. Dad. Sarah screamed with her mind. *Lonetree. Help!*

The second she thought the message, every rat turned toward her. Where before they wandered the room in a random frenzy, every one of them suddenly oriented to her bed and ran toward her.

She struggled with everything she had against whatever was immobilizing her, but she couldn't break its hold. The covers pulled and stretched around her as the rats climbed up the sides of the bed.

Then one reached the top of her bed, down near her feet. It crawled up her leg and stopped on her stomach, rising up and down with each short breath she took.

It was hairless, nothing but pink skin pulled tight across its emaciated body. She could see every bone of its ribcage. Its face looked shrunken and mottled, like vacuum-sealed meat abandoned to freezer burn. Two black beads bulged from its head and stared her down. The rat hissed at her, almost like a feral cat, opening its mouth to show a row of tiny fangs.

Movement all around her bed now. Pressure on her legs. Her stomach. They were covering her.

She opened her mouth and let out a silent scream.

The rat on her stomach closed the distance in only a few jumps, then forced its way into her mouth. She pushed against it with her tongue. Bit down on it until her teeth drew blood. But the rat was too fast. It clawed its way down, deeper, past her mouth, into her throat. Scrambling and straining.

Sarah gagged, tears pouring from her eyes. Her brain screamed for someone to help her. But no one came.

She looked down and saw only the long scaly tail sticking out of her mouth. It whipped back and forth as the rat climbed deeper into her chest, disappearing inch-by-inch. Beyond the twitching tail, the other rats were gone. Replaced by men on their knees around the bed, each of them gorging themselves on part of her body. Even in the dim light, she saw blood glistening on their faces as they ripped and chewed her flesh.

One of the men looked up. It was Sorenson.

He stood up from his knees and moved up toward her head, still crouched over, his blood-covered face leering at her as he licked his lips.

Oh my God. He's one of them.

Sarah heard the voice in her head. In her panic, she thought it was her own voice. She could only manage a whimper as Sorensen came closer.

You can kill them. Kill them now.

The voice was all wrong. Deeper and throaty. It was a man's voice. One she didn't recognize. But it didn't matter to her where the voice came from. It was right. She had to stop Sorenson. She had to stop the men ripping the flesh from her legs and arms.

Do it now.

Sarah closed her eyes and summoned as much power as she could muster, feeling the freedom to move her body come back to her.

That's it, the voice hissed. *Kill them all.*

Chapter 42

Lonetree watched in horror as Sorenson tried to shake Sarah awake. They had been the first up the stairs once Buddy started barking. They found Sarah lying ramrod straight in her bed, hyperventilating. Her eyes were wide open, jerking side to side. Seeing something, just not what was actually in front of her.

Jack and Lauren were only seconds behind them. Sorenson stepped back to make way for Lauren, who reached out with the deft, systematic hands of an emergency room doctor.

It was freezing cold in the room, their breath showing in large white plumes in front of them.

"She's freezing," Lauren said. "Is there a window open?"

Lonetree glanced over at the only two windows in the room. Both shut.

"What's wrong with her?" Jack asked.

"I don't know," Lauren replied, looking into Sarah's eyes.

And now you kill them. Kill them all.

Lonetree heard the voice. He looked around the room for the source. Buddy still barked like a maniac down in the living room. He wondered if he had misjudged and if the voice came from one of Mama D's henchmen outside the house. Maybe it was an order to kill everyone inside.

"Her body temperature is too low. Hypothermic shock. Jack, run a hot shower. Go."

Jack ran to the girls' bathroom and Lonetree heard the water come on.

Do it now.

This time Lonetree was ready for the voice. He spun away from the door and back to Sarah. The voice wasn't hers, but there was no mistaking that it had come from her.

"We need to give her some space," Lonetree muttered.

Sarah closed her eyes. Lauren reacted to it.

"No, no, baby. Come on. Stay awake for me." She called over her shoulder, "Jack?"

"Ready," Jack said, running back into the room.

"Lonetree, grab her," Lauren said.

That's it, the voice hissed. *Kill them all.*

Lonetree froze. No one else reacted. They didn't hear the voice. He looked down at Sarah. Her eyes were closed, chest heaving, eyebrows narrowed in concentration. He knew that look.

"Everyone get down!" Lonetree yelled.

Sorenson hit the floor without hesitation, dragging Jack down with him. Lonetree grabbed Lauren and threw her to the floor, rolling on top of her.

She screamed in surprise, but the sound only lasted a second.

A roar ripped open the air around them, as loud as a freight train. The floor shuddered and then shook violently. Books toppled off shelves. A mirror fell and smashed into pieces. The bed slid across the floor, carrying a still-prone Sarah, who seemed oblivious to the chaos raging around her. Lonetree dragged Lauren out of the way just as the bed flung across the room at them. The roar grew louder. The two windows shattered and burst outward. The shaking grew worse, drywall falling in chunks from the ceiling. Sparks burst from the lights.

"The house is going to come down," Sorenson yelled.

"Sarah, stop," Jack shouted, crawling to the bed. "Sarah."

The bed spun back across the floor. Sorenson shoved Jack out of the way and the thick bedpost slammed into Sorenson's side, sending him to the floor.

Sarah jerked her head to one side and her eyes jolted open, staring at Sorenson. But they weren't her eyes, not really. They were full of pure hate.

Sarah looked over to a desk next to her bed. Lonetree followed her eyes and saw what she was looking at. A pair of scissors.

"Watch out," Lonetree yelled.

Too late. The scissors flew through the air like a bolt out of a crossbow. It hit the meat in Sorenson's upper chest and sank in up to the handle. Sorenson

231

grabbed at the scissors and scrambled out of the way as the bed charged toward him like a living thing. He reached to the small of his back with his other hand and brought out a gun. Jack reached for Sorenson's arm and forced the gun into the air.

"No!" Lauren screamed. "Sarah, wake up."

Lonetree closed his eyes and tried to clear his mind of the chaos raging around him. He took a deep breath and willed his body to settle.

Sarah. It's Lonetree. He pushed the thought outward with as much concentration as he could muster. *Can you hear me? This is just a dream. You're going to hurt your mom. Your dad. You don't want to hurt them, do you?*

Lonetree thought he felt the house shake a little less for a second, but then it came back even harder than before.

Lauren screamed, breaking his concentration, and he opened his eyes.

The bloody scissors that had impaled Sorenson were floating in the air six inches in front of Lauren's face. Sarah stared at the scissors, her expression slack.

Lauren moved to her right, but the scissors darted in the same direction.

"Wake up, Sarah," Lauren cried. "Oh God, please wake up."

Chapter 43

Sarah stared at the man in front of her, hate burning inside of her. He was tall but slouched over with a hunch. He was dressed in an old moldering suit, parts shredded and hanging like rags on his thin frame. His bald head was stained with inkblot birthmarks and cancerous sores. The face was what she hated most. Beady eyes, a hawk nose, thin lips pulled back in a sneer over bloodstained teeth, the man looked like a nightmarish version of a scarecrow. But that's not why she hated him. That was because she recognized the face from Lonetree's memory. This was one of the men who ate Charlie Winters. And now she'd caught him feasting on her flesh.

But she was stronger than Charlie. She wasn't going to let them take her like that. Somehow they had started on her while she was unconscious, but once she woke up to it, she'd showed them who they were dealing with.

Sorenson had been the first order of business. He deserved the scissors just for being one of them, but he deserved to die slowly for being a traitor too. She guessed that he must have killed Lonetree too, otherwise these men would never have been able to get into her room. He deserved all the suffering she had in store for him.

But this one, the bald man with the long scarecrow face, didn't need any special treatment. He was a garden-variety kid killer. Just your regular monster feeding off souls, stealing their energy while they writhed in unimaginable pain.

She focused her attention on the pair of scissors she levitated through the air. It was as easy as if she held them in her hand. She would stab the man through the eye, then force the scissors open and rotate them in a circle. The man moved side-to-side, as if he might dodge his fate, but she corralled him in. He deserved what was coming to him.

Just like he deserved it when Lonetree had cut his head off the first time.

Sarah hesitated. The memory stormed through her head. The long-faced man's head on the floor next to Charlie's body. The body with the torn suit lay a good distance away, so the head must have rolled across the floor and come to rest against Charlie's chewed torso.

Sarah looked back at Sorenson. He had a gun now, but one of the other men was trying to wrestle it away from him. That man looked just like the bald scarecrow man too. More than that, it *was* the bald scarecrow man.

Don't let them fool you, the man's voice said. *Kill them before they kill you.*

Sarah looked back at the man in front of the floating scissors. Instead of the tooth-baring scowl on his face from seconds before, the man's expression was a strange mix of fear and sadness. Especially in his eyes. They reminded her of someone else, but she couldn't put her finger on it.

Do it now!

The voice was right. Sarah refocused her energy on the scissors. She wanted them to go deep, right into the bald man's brain.

But just as she was about to let the scissors fly, the bald man did the strangest thing. He spoke in a woman's voice.

"Wake up, Sarah," the voice cried out. "Oh God, please wake up."

The man's face flickered, like on a TV screen. Between the flickers she saw another person, as if two people were occupying the same space, one layered on top of the other. Sarah focused harder and the flickers grew longer so that she could see the other face.

Realization hit her all at once.

It was her mom.

Lonetree's voice burst into her head. *...a dream, kid. Just a dream. Wake up, Goddammit.*

Panicked, she looked around the room. All the men flickered. Some of them blinked out of existence entirely.

With a tremendous push of mental energy, she shoved outward, yelling at the top of her lungs. It wasn't a word, but at some primordial level it said more than any word could. The air rushed around her, the freight train roar peaked, the house shook with a mighty jolt and then…

…nothing.

Like a switch being thrown, the chaos disappeared.

The house was still. Scissors dropped to the floor with a dull thud. Nothing moved. No one made a sound. Even Buddy stopped barking.

Her mom stared at her from the foot of the bed. Around her were her dad, Lonetree, and Sorenson. The last had a patch of blood blossoming out from a wound on his chest. With a horrible realization, she knew that she was the one who had done it to him. More than that, she realized she hadn't just wanted to hurt him, she had wanted to kill him. She had wanted to kill them all.

Still, no one moved. As if they were unsure if the danger had really passed. Whether she was back to being herself.

She was herself again. But she didn't think that meant the danger was over.

"Baby?" Lauren asked softly.

The gentle love in her voice caused tears to spring to Sarah's eyes. She sobbed and reached out for her. "I'm sorry. I'm so sorry."

Lauren and Jack rushed forward and gathered her up in their arms, all three of them crying together. For that second, wrapped inside their embrace, she felt safe.

"Well, on the bright side," said Lonetree, looking around the destroyed room. "We needed Sarah to make some noise. I'm pretty sure this did the trick. You okay?" he asked Sorenson.

"Yeah, it's not bad," Sorenson replied, wincing. "A few stitches and it'll be fine."

Her dad stood, keeping a protective hand on her shoulder as she clung to her mom.

"Then we need to get out of here," Jack said. "Get some distance before they get here."

"Agreed," Lonetree said.

Sarah felt the four adults' eyes on her. She lifted her head and wiped her eyes. "I'm okay."

Then Lonetree's voice was in her head. *You did good, kid. You were strong.*

I almost killed you all…

No, the thing inside you almost killed us all, but you controlled it. You were stronger than it was.

Lonetree?

Yeah, kid?

This thing. This "it" you keep talking about. Even though it was just a thought, her voice quavered. *It's something bad inside me, isn't it?*

No answer.

Sarah stood from her bed and crossed the room to Lonetree. She put her hand on his forearm. "And what if next time I'm not stronger than it?" she whispered. "What happens then?"

Chapter 44

Just when Mama D thought the walls she'd erected around her mind were high enough and thick enough to withstand any onslaught, she learned a new lesson at the feet of this little bitch Sarah. Fortunately Jimmy was driving the car when it happened. At first, it felt like being slammed by a wave in the ocean. Hard enough to make her stagger back a couple of steps and doubt her footing, but not enough to make her go down.

But then wave after wave crashed over her and her mental walls trembled, cracking from the strain. Mama D had rolled up into herself, pulling all the resources at her disposal to the defense. She plunged deep into her fire and pulled out white-hot embers, using them to forge metal reinforcements at the weakest parts of the wall.

The effort paid off. After only a few minutes, the mental blast disappeared. Mama D held up the defense for another ten minutes, worried that the little bitch might just be trying to get her to take her guard down. Except the attack hadn't felt specific. There was rage directed at her and her kind, but it felt more like a shockwave from an explosion than a projectile aimed at her. Slowly, she relaxed and decided that the attack was truly gone. Before coming back out to the world, she spent some time fortifying her defenses, learning from the experience so it would be impossible to surprise her the next time.

When she finally opened her eyes, Jimmy's face was right in front of hers.

"You okay, Mama D?"

Mama D looked to her right and saw the others gathered outside the car, nervously staring in at her. She counted five. So the entire group had pulled off the road in what looked like a rest area off the freeway. So all six cars, usually carefully separated, gassing up at different stations, keeping a few miles between them so there was no apparent connection, were all parked in the same small area together.

She looked back at Jimmy. Her expression must have conveyed how she felt because he turned pale with terror. Carefully, he held up a hand towel she hadn't noticed before. It was still white at the corner where he held it, but the rest was a glistening crimson, heavily soaked with blood.

"What the hell did you do to yourself, Jimmy?" Mama D asked.

Jimmy didn't say anything. He just nodded toward her.

She was slow in understanding, but finally looked

down at her own chest. It was slick with a blood trail that went the length of her shirt and onto her lap. She raised a hand to her mouth and nose. They were hot and sticky.

"You was gushin' blood," Jimmy said. "I didn't know what else to do."

Mama D angrily grabbed the towel from him, intending to use it to clean herself. But it was already saturated, blood dripping from it in long, viscous strands.

"Give me another towel. Jus' a Goddamn nosebleed is all."

Jimmy turned in his seat and grabbed another towel from the back. Mama D snapped it from him and held it to her nose. Then she looked at the towel, satisfied with the minimal amount of blood she saw there.

"See? It's all gone."

"But...you're a mess. If she did this to you, then maybe—"

Mama D shot him a look that froze the words in his mouth. He turned away from her and looked out through the windshield.

"Tell the others to get," Mama D whispered. "We got a ways to go yet and it's getting dark."

"You know where she's at now?" Jimmy asked, his fear melting at the promise of a feast.

"Sure do. But I know they're gonna run too."

Jimmy's disappointment just made Mama D want to rip into him even more. It showed an unhealthy lack of respect for her hunting skills that he thought a pesh on the run would be hard for her to track down. Still, the visitor had felt the same way. That's why he'd given her a little gift.

"But I know how to stop 'em. Bring 'em back to us so we don't have to chase them all over creation. We need to have the girl under this full moon," Mama D said, leaning back in the seat with her eyes closed, wincing at the headache that had grown from a dull pain to feeling like someone was driving nails into her skull with a ballpeen hammer.

"How's that?" Jimmy asked.

The headache was too intense to spare the anger for Jimmy's continued insolence. She just murmured, "Tell the others to get. Follow us outta here."

"Where should I tell them we're going?"

"Just have them follow us," Mama D said, weary now. "Go on now, tell them."

Jimmy slid out of the car. Mama D turned away from the window, away from prying eyes. She managed to turn around enough to look to the backseat at the sleeping teenage form lying lengthwise with a blanket pulled tight around. Mama D knew it was more than sleep. She felt bad for drugging her Pesh. But it was for his own good, whether he knew it or not. But with this girl, this Sarah, she hoped to fix all that. If things went as the visitor promised, she would finally have her son back.

And, for Mama D, that was everything.

Chapter 45

They rushed downstairs to gather their bags. Believing that a group of killers with psychic powers was on the way over to feast on their daughter's flesh was a great motivator.

Jack was amazed at the destruction throughout the house. He didn't know why he'd thought that the shaking was limited to Sarah's bedroom; of course the whole house had been shaken by her energy. Cracks crisscrossed the drywall. Artwork either hung cockeyed or lay scattered on the floor. The drawers and cabinets in the kitchen were all thrown open, plates and silverware dumped onto the floor. It reminded Jack of the horror movies he and Lauren liked to watch together before the kids came along. The ones with the poltergeist tearing the house up to scare the living owners out so the dead could have the place to themselves. Only those movies didn't seem so scary now that they were living their own nightmare.

Lauren and Sarah got into the car, both of them sitting in the backseat so Lauren could hold onto her little girl. Lonetree tossed the last bag into the back and Jack slammed the door shut.

"Sorenson all right?" Jack asked.

"He's had worse injuries than that from his girlfriends. And they liked him," Lonetree said. The attempt at humor fell flat. Neither of them were in the mood.

"You were going to tell me something," Jack said. "Before Sarah started, you know…"

Lonetree shook his head. "I think you already know now. Her power, it can have a mind of its own. When that happens, if that happens, it's not Sarah anymore." Lonetree seemed to want to say more, but then stalled. "Just be aware," he said.

Jack nodded. "Are you sure you can handle these guys? We don't know how many people are coming."

"We're SEALs," Lonetree said. "We hope they bring an army just to make it fun."

Jack grinned. There were a few wrinkles at the corners of Lonetree's eyes and even a few grey hairs in the ponytail pulled back into a knot, but the man's aura of pure confidence was unchanged from their first meeting.

"You've taken a lot of risks for my family," Jack said. "I appreciate it. I always have."

Lonetree looked back to the house, trying to brush away the emotion of the moment. "You have the gun I gave you?"

"Yeah. And enough ammo to fend off a small army."

243

"Okay then." He fixed his eyes back on Jack. "You're a good man. You're the father I would have wanted to be if I had kids."

Jack started to pull his hand back, ready to reply with some innocuous comment, when Lonetree pulled him in tight.

"That's why I know, if it comes down to it, you'll do the right thing for Sarah. If there's a choice that has to be made. You have to be strong enough for her. You understand what I'm saying here?"

Jack stared at him, sorting through the layers of meaning. Lonetree's body language and his face told him this wasn't just about doing whatever it took to protect his daughter. This was deeper. This was asking something fundamental of him.

Would he be able to take his daughter's life to prevent her suffering?

He didn't know if he could ever do that, but that wasn't the answer Lonetree wanted. Part of him wondered if the big man would try to stop him from leaving if he admitted that no, he probably couldn't kill his own daughter if it came down to it. Of all the terrifying things that had happened in the cave with Huckley and the Source, the decision he made to end Sarah's misery with a gun instead of giving her to the Source was the moment that replayed in his mind most often. He'd made the decision, felt the rightness of it, felt a kindred spirit with the hundreds of skeleton mothers in the cages around him who had chosen to kill their children as well rather than let them slowly starve to death, mewling in the pitch black of their underground tomb. But despite all of that, he hadn't been able to do it. And thank God. Even though he hadn't acted on it and they had survived, he carried the guilt of that decision with him every day.

So, with Lonetree asking that question of him, Jack answered the only way he could think to do under the circumstances. He lied.

"Of course. I'll take care of it."

Lonetree searched his eyes and seemed unsatisfied with the answer. "If they get her, they will feast on her for days. Maybe even weeks. And she won't lose consciousness the entire time. She'll feel everything," Lonetree said. "And there are scenarios at work here that are worse than that. So I need to know for certain that you can you do it."

Jack swallowed back the bile rising in his throat. It was impossible to hear what Lonetree had just said and not have an image come to mind. Men eating his daughter's flesh as she thrashed and screamed. He couldn't think of what could be worse than that. He didn't want to think of it.

"Yes," he said, meaning it this time. "I can do it."

Lonetree gripped Jack's hand tighter, shook it once, then let go. "Now let's make sure you don't have to make that choice. Go on. Get out of here. Don't stop except for gas."

"We're going to get Becky at school and then—"

Lonetree held up his hand. "Better if I don't know. Be safe, Jack."

"You too," Jack replied. "If you meet this Mama D character, give her a couple kicks for me, will you?"

"Oh, I plan to do more than that. But sure, I'll put in a few with your name on them."

Jack opened the car door and climbed in. He looked in the rearview and saw Lauren had wrapped a seatbelt around both herself and Sarah, as if the vinyl strap would somehow keep her little girl safely attached to her. He noticed Sarah turn to look outside at Lonetree. Her lips moved, barely, and he had the strangest feeling that somehow she and Lonetree were talking.

He put it out of his mind and started the car. He took one last look at the house. Despite the bizarre dramas that had played out here, it had been a good home. It marked the renewal of his marriage and of his focus on life instead of work. As he pulled out of the driveway, he couldn't help but wonder whether any of them would ever see it again.

Chapter 46

L auren felt relief with each mile they put behind them. She cuddled with Sarah, talking to her quietly about fun things they had done together as a family when she was younger. Anything to keep Sarah's attention away from the danger she was in and, hopefully, to keep her mind preoccupied so she didn't send out any signals that might be used to track them on the road. And she wanted to keep Sarah awake. None of them wanted to see a repeat of what had happened back at the house.

Sarah leaned against her and Lauren brushed her fingers through her hair, happy to feel Sarah's body relax as they made progress down the road. She hated herself for what she was about to say.

"Jack, we need to stop at the hospital on the way out," she said softly.

Sarah tensed. Jack turned to look at her. She couldn't see much of his face in the low glow of the instrument panel, but she guessed his expression was something she wouldn't want to see anyway.

"You can't be serious," Jack said.

Lauren continued to stroke Sarah's hair, willing her to relax again.

"We don't know how long we'll be gone, right?" Lauren said.

"And?"

"There are things in my lab. Things that I'm responsible for."

Sarah sat up and separated herself from Lauren.

"What's in your lab?" she asked.

Lauren flashed a look at Jack. He knew everything but she didn't want to go into details in front of Sarah. "I'm doing experiments. I'm in animal trials."

"Have someone else look after them," Jack said.

"You know no one else has access," Lauren said.

"Then you let the rats die," Jack said. "It's not worth—"

"Rats?" Sarah asked, her voice catching. "What kind of rats?"

Lauren looked at her, noticing the calm demeanor she'd had for the last ten minutes crumble in front of her. She reached out, but Sarah pulled back.

"They're just lab animals, honey. Nothing scary about them," Lauren said.

"Are…are they hairless?" Sarah asked, shuddering. "Just skin?"

"You've never been to the lab," Lauren said. "How did you—"

248

"It's fine," Jack said calmly from the front seat. Lauren guessed he was trying to defuse things but his tone came across like he was an orderly talking around a mental patient. "Let's none of us worry about the rats today."

"It's not about the rats," Lauren said. "There are things in the lab that could be dangerous if someone got in there. If we leave for a few weeks, people might get hurt. It'll take all of five minutes to dispose of the active cultures and..." she hesitated, feeling Sarah's glare, "...take care of the test animals."

"You mean you're going to kill the rats, don't you?" Sarah asked.

Lauren caught a look from Jack in the front seat. Before she could reply, Sarah grabbed her hand.

"Good," Sarah said. "You should do that. You should kill them all."

A pit formed in her stomach. Jack was silent. She realized neither of them knew how to react to their daughter right now. She also knew he just wanted to go pick up Becky at her school and then get as far away from Prescott City as possible. They had talked only briefly about where they might go. New York, too many people. Maine, getting to be too cold. They even considered going cross-country to California, but decided it was best to go where they had no ties. Where no one could guess at a destination. Maybe they'd just head to the nearest airport and buy tickets to the Cayman Islands and stay there until their sanity returned. If she closed her eyes, she could almost feel the warm blue waters lapping against her feet as her toes dug into the powdered-sugar sand.

Only when she opened her eyes, she was still in the car in the middle of the night, running from a band of lunatics who wanted to kill her daughter. The Caymans seemed a million miles away.

"I want to get out of here as much as you do," Lauren said. "I wouldn't ask unless I thought it was really necessary. You guys can stay in the car. Five minutes is all I need."

Jack didn't reply, but Lauren knew his body language. If he wasn't going to stop, they would still be talking. Silence was consent, even if it was grudgingly given.

Twenty minutes later they pulled into the Midland Hospital parking lot. It was almost four in the morning and the parking lot was empty except for a handful of cars. The only entrance open was the emergency room. Jack pulled under the covered area where ambulances could offload patients in bad weather.

"Five minutes," Jack said.

"If that," Lauren replied. She turned to Sarah. "I'll be right back, okay?"

Sarah nodded but didn't say anything. Lauren wasn't sure if she was more mad or scared. Not that it made much of a difference. Either way, she had to close down her lab so that no one got hurt. If Hofstra broke into her lab, Lauren wondered whether the woman would call the CDC or poke around on her own to find out what Lauren was doing. She decided Hofstra would take the opportunity to gather as much information as she could before involving any outsiders. Having someone without proper training in her lab was precisely the scenario that scared her. There were too many variables in the equation for such an intrusion to end well. With a last look to Jack meant as a reassurance that she would hurry, she opened the door and climbed out of the car.

She hurried across the driveway and passed through the automatic sliding doors into the bright fluorescent eternal daytime in the emergency room. In the inner-city hospitals where Lauren had spent time, the ER waiting rooms teemed with humanity regardless of the hour, showcasing everything from frantic parents holding a child with a rasping cough, to a few souls who had cut or impaled their bodies in unexpected but interesting ways, to a chest pain or two, to the requisite junkie readying their performance art in the hopes of scoring a hit off an overtired doc. But Midland General was empty except for Ned Brickman swabbing the floor with a heavy antiseptic. He looked up with sad, unfocused eyes, and Lauren imagined he had been a million miles away before she walked in, his body working on autopilot while his mind was somewhere else entirely. Recognition came slowly to his eyes, like someone getting their bearings after being awoken from a sleep.

"Hey, Ned," Lauren said, trying to act as normal as possible under the circumstances. Her unplanned absence was going to cause enough rumors; she didn't need the sighting of her at the hospital to be her running to her lab in full panic mode. She smiled but didn't slow her pace. "Working the late shift, huh?"

Ned grinned as his typical sunny disposition dropped into place like a mask that had been pushed up on his forehead while he worked. He gave her a wink. "Sho 'nuff, Doc. Gotta do whats you gotta do."

"I hear that," Lauren said, looking over her shoulder as she passed him. "We're heading out of town so I need to check on the lab."

Ned clucked his tongue in a disapproving way and shook his head slowly. "That place causin' all kind of problems, Doc. Not that you heard it from me."

Lauren nearly lost her balance on the newly mopped floor as she came to a stop. She walked back to Ned and looked him up and down. "Okay, spill it."

Ned shrugged his shoulders. "I was workin' up by Hofstra's office, sweeping, you know. Not meanin' to overhear nothin'. But she's talkin' this and that about your lab. Usin' words like illegal. Unethical. Moral."

"Immoral?" Lauren offered.

"Yeah, probably," Ned said. "Anyway, she said she was goin' into the lab with or without permission. I don't know who was on the phone wit' her, but she was shoutin' at them. A couple a screws loose, if you ask me."

Lauren felt a surge of panic. "When was this? Did she go in?"

Ned shrugged. "I dunno. This was jus' this afternoon. You know, yesterday. But she left the hospital, I guess, 'cause no one's seen her since."

Lauren figured the sick feeling in her stomach registered on her face because he looked at her with concern.

"You okay, Doc? You don't look so good," Ned said. "Maybe I shouldn't a told you, but I thought you'd want—"

"No, thanks," Lauren stammered. "I'm sure it's fine. I'm just going to run up and check on some things and then head out. Thanks for letting me know."

She glanced at her watch. It'd already been five minutes. Jack was going to kill her. She walked through the emergency room, giving a brisk wave to the on-call staff as she marched through the door that led to the back stairwell and up to the third floor.

The lights in the hallway flicked on as the motion sensors picked up her movement. She came to the lab door and checked the security pad. It had been tampered with.

"Shit," Lauren mumbled.

She punched in her code and the door unlocked with a click. She opened it, reached inside, and flicked on the lights.

"Hello?" she called into the room. There was no response. The florescent lighting bathed the room in stark relief. Hard shadows lined the floor and crawled up the walls. Lauren stepped inside and closed the door behind her.

It wasn't until she cleared the row of tables in the middle of the room that she knew something was very, very wrong.

Chapter 47

Mama D sat in the car and took a drag off her cigarette. She didn't like the set-up and she certainly didn't like being told what to do. But once the voice had come to her and told her that the Tremonts were planning to run and that Lonetree and his sidekick Sorenson were still in the picture, she knew she had better listen.

But she also knew better than to force things. When things were forced, they tended to go to shit. And when things went to shit, people got killed. Or at least went to prison. Neither was an option for Mama D. But losing Sarah Tremont was also unacceptable.

Still, if it was only up to her, she would back off, wait for things to calm down. The Tremonts would be vigilant for a month or two, maybe longer, but they would let their guard down eventually. Then it would be a low risk abduction. No fuss. But the voice was adamant that it had to happen that night. The full moon had something to do with it, but Mama D wondered if the urgency was that the voice was just hungry, desperate for a jolt of power.

So there she was, watching the car in the parking lot, waiting for her next move to present itself. She exhaled toward the crack in the window and took a deep breath. The moving parts to this venture were piling up, making her vision of how it would all turn out increasingly complicated. She cursed the voice even as she wondered at its power and its seeming omniscience. It not only knew what the Tremonts were doing, but what they planned to do. Or at least it was her judgment that the voice had spoken true when it visited her. And Mama D knew true when she heard it.

So, a simple matter of finding the girl now that she was more active with her powers had become something much larger, with more interested players in the game. She saw the benefit of joining forces rather than competing, especially given the power behind the voice, but she had no intention of sharing. For someone who knew true when she heard it, she was equally adept at the lie when it suited her purpose. A nagging part of her wondered if the voice had seen through her already. She assumed that it had and was biding its own time until it double-crossed the partnership. Mama D intended to beat it to the punch.

But this was taking forever. The occupants of the car just sat there, the car running, the interior too dark to make out anything. Approaching the car wasn't the best play, especially at this time of night. If it was the more respectable side of midnight, then it would be reasonable for Jimmy or even herself to approach the car with a story of a broken-down vehicle or a flat tire. With a little effort, they could talk the driver out of the car and then, with the escape cut off, it would be open season on the girl.

But at four in the morning, a stranger roused more suspicion. More likely to prompt the driver to offer to call the police for help than to get out. Using force was an option. A gun barrel rapping against the window might get the driver out of the car. But it could just as easily send the driver speeding away into the night, with them giving chase. Not something she wanted to do. She considered shooting the driver through the glass. They didn't need him anyway. It would be loud and messy, but better than the interminable waiting.

Just when she was about to suggest they shoot the driver, the car door opened and the girl got out.

"Jimmy," Mama D said.

"I see it," Jimmy said. He held up a walkie-talkie and pressed the button. "She's on the move."

"We're ready," said a man's voice, crackling over the talkie.

Mama D opened the car door. The dome light was disengaged so there was no light. She almost brought her sword but thought better of it and climbed out and crossed the manicured lawn that stretched between her and the girl, putting herself on an intercept course with her. Halfway across, a wave of pressure filled her head as if she were suddenly a hundred feet underwater. The voice blared into her mind.

Do you have her?

Mama D forced a wall up in the direction of the voice, but it came again. Louder this time.

Don't try to block me, girl. Do you have her?

Mama D stifled an angry grunt. She hated the feeling of violation. She hated her own weakness. She hated being called "girl."

I'm walking up to her right now, Mama D said in her mind.

Good, said the voice. *Don't fail me.*

Then the pressure was gone, and the voice with it. Mama D spat onto the ground and then stepped on the gob of spittle with the heel of her boot. It was an old custom, deep in her bayou roots. She whispered the words. "To hell with you, to hell with me. The death of you, will set me free."

It was just a schoolgirl curse and she knew the words didn't matter. There were no magic words to make the voice go away. She would have to do that the old-fashioned way. Still, the words made her feel better as she restarted her walk toward the girl. She glanced over and saw the car slowly pull away and turn a corner. Good thing for the boy in the car, chivalry was dead. Because if he had walked his date to the door like a real gentleman, then he would have been too.

"Becky?" Mama D called out quietly. "Becky Tremont?"

The girl jerked her head in the direction of the sound. On seeing that the voice belonged to a young, well-dressed woman, she let her guard down. She looked more embarrassed than scared. Mama D noticed she wore a boy's jacket a few sizes too large for her. At least the little punk making out with her in the car had given her that for the quick walk back to her dorm room.

"I thought that was you," Mama D purred.

Becky stopped walking. "I'm sorry, do I know

you?"

Mama D stopped in front of her and breathed the girl in. Not even a whiff of power in her. She hoped the voice knew what it was doing. A white van with its lights off turned the corner behind Becky and rolled toward them.

"I said, do I know you?" Becky asked again.

Mama D flashed her most genuine smile. "No, honey. But you're going to."

Chapter 48

The cages were open. All of them. The heavy-gauge wire doors hung loose on their hinges, frozen in place in the still air of the safe room where they had come to rest. Lauren was about to activate the outer door of the airlock, but her intuition stopped her. Instead, she sidestepped away from the door and peered into the room.

It was a disaster. Trays of serum samples were scattered across the floor, the centrifuge knocked over on its side. The refrigerated drawers gaped open, the individual plastic boxes opened and thrown around. Computer displays were smashed, glass catching the bright lights at odd angles. It looked like a team of addicts had been let loose and told the drug of their choice was hidden somewhere in the room.

Only Lauren knew it wasn't a drug addict that had broken into the safe room. It had to be Hofstra. But why would she cause this kind of damage? Especially since she had no idea what the experiment was about. If the CDC had shown up, the place would be on lockdown with armed guards while a team of scientists slowly pieced together what they were dealing with. No, this was something else entirely. And where in the hell were the lab rats?

A sound came from the far side of the outer room, in the area behind the safe room where the electrical cabling and ventilation lay in the gap between the plexiglass wall and the regular wall of the room. It was darker there and Lauren couldn't see anything in the shadows.

"Hello?" Lauren called out. "Who's there?"

The sound came again. A wet, sticky sound, like a toothless old man slowly moving his mouth open and shut. Lauren fought the urge to turn and run. Back to the car. Back to Jack and Sarah just to get away. But she knew she couldn't do that. Especially now that the safe room was compromised.

The serum was an unknown pathogen, one that killed every test animal injected with it. So far she had detected no transmission mechanism for the virus during her trials. But that didn't mean one didn't exist. Years of justifying the unsanctioned tests came crashing down around her. She'd taken such precautions, convinced herself she was doing the right thing to protect Jesse Dahl but now, looking at the ruined lab, it suddenly seemed like madness. Perhaps she was no better than Dr. Mansfield, who had performed his experiments with the Source in the name of science.

"Jesus, what have I done?" she whispered to the empty room.

The sound came again, this time joined with a heavy *thump*. Whatever was back behind the room was bigger than a rat.

Lauren searched the area immediately around her, suddenly feeling the need to arm herself. The scalpels and other instruments she used for dissections were inside the safe room. The only things out here were a computer terminal for taking notes and a couple of potted plants. She thought about going into the safe room to get a weapon but shoved the idea aside almost immediately. If there was someone in the room, she needed to keep her line of escape open. Going into the safe room was like putting herself in a corner. She had to be smarter than that.

If I was smart, I'd get the hell out of here.

The noise came again. She grabbed one of the potted plants and held it up as if to throw it. She felt ridiculous. "Who's there?" she called out. "Come out where I can see you."

Nothing.

"I have a gun," she added.

She winced at the words, hearing the obviousness of her lie. But whoever was in the room with her didn't seem to care about her idle boast. The wet sucking sound filled the air once again.

Lauren eased her way down the length of the safe room, one hand on the plexiglass wall and the other holding the pot high. Her breath grew more shallow with each step. Adrenaline pumped into her blood and every sense felt heightened. The *whirr* of the furnace. The *tick-tock* of the large clock on the wall. The dank, salty taste in

261

the air.

She tried to look through the safe room, hoping to see to the other side of the transparent walls instead of having to turn the corner to see what was there. But that side of the room was stacked with cabinets, blocking her view of what was beyond.

Lauren slid her hand, palm down, along the wall until it reached the edge. She was panting now, almost hyperventilating with short, shuddering breaths. Sweat trickled down between her shoulder blades and ended in the small of her back. She forced a deep breath and turned the corner.

At first, she wasn't sure what she was looking at. The cabinets inside the safe room blocked most of the light, casting the space in shadow. But within the shadow, piled up on the floor, was a darker shape. Lauren squinted, trying to make out what it was. Perhaps a pile of clothes? Or blankets?

But then the shape moved and the wet, sucking sound came with it.

The mass lurched forward and something on one side of it stretched out from the center and attached to the Plexiglas wall. Where it connected to the wall, there was a shaft of light that came through a gap in the cabinets. Not much, but enough to highlight the shape of the thing. Lauren felt her throat constrict in terror as she realized it was a hand. It slid on the smooth surface, leaving a streak of blood behind.

Oh my God. If that's a hand, then...then...

The dark mass rose slowly, jerking in fits and starts. It was a person, facing away from Lauren so she only saw its back. It sat back on its heels as if gathering strength.

"Are you hurt?" Lauren called out. "I'm a doctor. I can help you."

The body twisted, arms, chest, and head moving in weird, spastic movements, like a marionette being made to dance with tangled strings.

As it turned, it pushed itself forward with a sickening wet sound and entered the light. The sight of Lauren seemed to give the thing strength. It grunted and raised itself up, still on its knees, but otherwise fully erect. A hospital gown hung loose over the body and it held its head low, chin to chest, hiding its face. Still, Lauren shrank back in terror as she realized who it was. The hair, burnt orange with blond highlights, stuck out stiff and rigid. The overly tan skin had a grey, peaked pallor. And if that wasn't enough, Lauren could see the rose tattoo tangled in barbed wire on the woman's chest.

Debbie Berlin.

Mitzy's mom. The one Sarah's power had put in the hospital. That had seemed impossible only a day before but now struck her as a cold, hard fact. But what was she still doing here? And what was she doing in Lauren's lab?

"Debbie, it's me. Doctor Tremont." She took a hesitant step forward. "Lauren. We met yesterday. Can you tell me what's wrong? Are you hurt?"

One knee jerked up so that one of Debbie's bare feet planted on the tile floor. There was a wet sound, like she'd stepped in a puddle. The other knee spasmed upward and she ended up in a low crouch. Slowly, with great strain, fighting for balance the entire time, Debbie stood. As she did, the hospital gown came loose and fell to the floor, exposing her naked body.

Debbie didn't react to her sudden nakedness. She

was far beyond any sense of shame. But Lauren reacted for both of them. First, with embarrassment for the woman and then in horror as she pulled back, a hand going to her mouth on reflex.

The body was riddled with holes. Uneven tears with shredded flaps of skin hanging at odd angles. In her torso. In her legs and arms. All over. It looked like the damage Lauren had seen in war-torn countries where bodies were decimated by large-caliber munitions. Only she knew immediately these were not gunshot wounds.

There was no blood.

Not a drop spilled from any of the dozen or more gaping holes in Debbie's body. Even though the holes were deep enough that she saw flashes of white bone in some and a string of intestine hung out of another, it was as if the blood had been drained completely from her body. But that wasn't the worst of it.

Something moved inside of her. A lump bulged under the skin near the woman's hip and migrated slowly across her abdomen. It stopped halfway across and then turned up toward her chest, and then disappeared. Other bulges appeared under the skin of her bare legs, moving erratically, rising and falling. Debbie, or whatever was left of her, lifted her head off her chest to look in Lauren's direction. It swiveled loosely as if unhinged from her neck, until it found a balance and stared at her. Although staring wasn't really possible. Both eyes were missing from their sockets, leaving only black stains where they'd once been.

In her work with the CDC, Lauren had seen the horrific results of nature's viruses before and her training locked into place. This was something terrible, but it was something to be studied, to be contained and, hopefully, to be treated.

But then the woman's mouth opened and all that changed. A thin snake slid out, curling onto her cheek. But on a second look, it wasn't a snake. It was a tail. A rat's tail.

At that moment, something poked through Debbie's left eye socket. A quivering pink nose. Whiskers. Beady black eyes.

There was movement in the hole in the woman's side. Lauren's eyes darted there in time to see the smooth, pink wet flesh of a hairless rat slide by the opening.

"Oh God," Lauren whispered, her voice sounding hollow and distant in her own ears. She backed away from the woman. "It can't be."

Chapter 49

D ebbie Berlin's right leg jerked forward with a wet
sucking sound. Lauren looked down and finally
saw that the floor was covered with a thick pool
of blood, tacky and viscous as if it had been there a while.

The other leg flung forward and Debbie took a
full step toward her. The bulges under the woman's skin
roiled as she did, almost breaking through. The rats were
inside of her. Somehow they were inside of Debbie Berlin
and causing her to move. This had nothing to do with
science. This was something else entirely. And it was time
to get the hell out of there.

As she went for the door, the rat-infested body
lunged at her, moving fast but erratically. Lauren ducked
and rolled to one side but ended up next to the entrance

to the safe room with Debbie between her and the way out.

Debbie spun, snarling, each step more coordinated than the last. Whatever the rats were doing inside her body, they were mastering it.

Lauren turned and punched in the code to enter the safe room. The door hissed open, the pressurized antechamber still intact. She rushed in and closed the door just as Debbie staggered forward. The rats miscalculated. Debbie's face slammed into the glass window and her head cocked back from the force. She sagged to the floor.

Lauren hit another button to open the inner door to the safe room, hopeful that Debbie had knocked herself out for good. As she entered the inner chamber, she looked over her shoulder and saw that it was wishful thinking. Debbie rose awkwardly to her feet, her nose broken and bent to the right. Her arm rose toward the control panel and Lauren fought down a rising sense of panic.

Of course, it can get in. Half the things in here are smashed. It's already been here.

The outer door opened and the rat-filled body lurched into the antechamber. Lauren scrambled through the lab, looking for weapons. She grabbed for a tray of scalpels and cleavers used for dissections, and accidentally knocked it onto the ground. Lauren dropped to her knees and grabbed a scalpel for each hand.

She wheeled around to the door just as Debbie entered the chamber. Slits in her skin were opening now, giving in to the stress of the rats pushing against it. Little claws and sections of tail hung out from her torso.

In a flash of insight, Lauren saw that there was

too much of the body destroyed to think of Debbie as human any longer. This gave her options.

"Come on," Lauren yelled. "Come and get me."

The rats must have understood because the body rushed forward, hands out to strangle her. Lauren crab-crawled down the length of the middle table that held the abandoned lab cages.

She waited a beat and then snuck down an aisle. She prayed for the monster to chase after her. As she did, she heard a small squeaking sound right next to her head. She looked over and saw a rat sitting in an open cage. It slunk to the back, shivering, but exhibited no sign of disease. *What made this one different?* she thought. *Why hadn't this one joined the rest? Was it the serum?* No sooner had the thought formed than a guttural cry from behind her shocked her back into the moment. The creature was almost on top of her. Lauren grabbed at the rat in the cage, but it squirmed out of her hand. She glanced at the label on the rat's cage, 34E2, and then threw herself forward out of the creature's grasp.

She spun around the end of the table, then clawed her way to her feet. There was a clear shot to the door now. And the containment protocol button was just outside. All she had to do was run out, hit the button, and the creature would be consumed in a phosphorus fire. But the rat in the cage stopped her. Number 34E2. What if the serum worked? A single serum that could stop disease. All disease. Who was she to destroy it?

She ran forward, toward the refrigeration unit where the serum trials were stored. The creature thrashed behind her, but she tried to concentrate on the rows of tiny vials. 29, 30…34. Then five rows back. The second layer. 34E2. She grabbed the vial of bright red liquid and jammed it into her pocket. She turned and…

…took a direct punch across the face. The creature's power was incredible. She left her feet and crashed into the Plexiglas wall. Then the Debbie creature grabbed her with one hand wrapped around the shirt at her waist and the other around her ankle. It lifted her up into the air and threw her across the room. She smacked into the metal cages, pain radiating out from her side and streaking down her legs. For a second, she worried she'd broken her back. But then she remembered if she had she wouldn't feel anything. As it was, her body was on fire.

The creature reached out and picked up a scalpel in each hand, copying Lauren earlier. Then it charged, scalpels slicing through the air.

Lauren rolled, barely escaping a blade. She hit the edge of the counter and spun off of it. Using her momentum, she staggered to the door. She reached out and hit the button to the antechamber. It whooshed open and she fell into the room. The door slowly closed behind her as the creature rushed at her.

The other door wouldn't open until the interior door closed. If the creature got to the door, Lauren was trapped.

"Come on," she cried.

The door wasn't going to close in time. The creature would easily make it first. Lauren braced herself to fight back, but after experiencing the creature's strength, she didn't think it would do much good. She screamed as the creature advanced, her fists up.

Then the creature took a false step on its own bloody trail, lost its balance, and slipped to the ground. It righted itself quickly, clawing at the ground. But it was all

269

the time Lauren needed. The door closed shut with a beautiful hydraulic hiss. The creature pulled and pounded at the door, but it held firm.

Lauren punched the control on the wall and activated the decontamination unit. The walls and ceiling came alive with high-pressure sprays. Lauren removed the single vial of serum from her pocket, amazed that it had survived through the ordeal. She shed her clothes until she stood naked and scrubbed her hair and skin with scouring pads. Through the spray, she saw Debbie Berlin's eyeless face staring in through the window, cocking her head side-to-side, as if still able to watch her.

Lauren knew that whatever controlled Debbie wasn't likely something that could be knocked back by a decontamination unit, but she wasn't about to take the chance of taking whatever this was into the world with her. She also didn't want to go another second with the creature's blood on her bare skin.

Lauren finished the decontamination shower and hit the button to open the outer door. She ran out, grabbed a chair, and stuck it in the door to keep it from closing because, if it did, the inner door could open. Lauren had no intention of letting that thing out into the world. In fact, she had no intention of allowing it to even exist any longer.

She walked over to the control panel for the fail-safe protocol and typed in a code with a shaking hand. Sprinklers inside the safe room came to life and soon the room was filled with a fine mist. The creature looked up and sniffed the air. Somehow, it realized what was coming. Suddenly, hairless rats, coated with bits of internal organs, muscle, and blood, poured out of Debbie Berlin's body, leaving through the holes in the skin, through her mouth, ripping new holes in her abdomen. Her body sagged and fell to the floor like a deflated plastic doll. The rats crawled over one another, forcing their noses into corners, desperate to get out.

"Too late," Lauren said. "Die you little rat fuckers."

She shielded her eyes and threw the final switch. The safe room flashed like a thousand cameras going off at once. The phosphorus caught fire and incinerated everything in the contained space in a matter of seconds. The rats were destroyed, along with Debbie's body. She felt a pang of guilt about that. As terrible as the woman had been, she was still a human being, still someone's mother. But how in the hell had she gotten not only into the lab but into the safe room? And what force had controlled the rats?

She realized that she was breathing too hard. Her side vision was blackening and she was dizzy. She took a long, deep breath and forced herself back under control. There would be time to sort all of that out later. She had to get out of there. Back to Jack and Sarah.

She snuck out into the hallway, thankful the floor was empty. She ran to a nurse's station and found a clean set of scrubs, which she pulled on. She double-checked that the door to the lab was locked and then headed down a corridor to the back stairway. She managed to avoid any of the night staff except for Ned, who she saw as she walked quickly through the sliding doors to the parking lot. He still mopped the same spot where he'd been when she'd talked to him on the way in, scrubbing the same section over and over again. He looked up and saw her. If he registered the change in her clothes and wet hair, he didn't show it. He only smiled softly, gave her a nod, and went back to his work.

Lauren raced across the parking lot to where Jack had moved the car. Her cell phone and watch were back in the decontamination unit so she had no idea how long she'd been gone. She guessed fifteen or twenty minutes. She just hoped that Jack had stayed in the car.

She opened the door and climbed in. Jack was on the phone, the color drained from his face. Sarah sobbed quietly in the backseat. Neither of them asked what had taken her so long or why she was wet and smelled of chemicals. Jack hardly acknowledged that she was in the car.

He nodded his head. "Yes, I know where that it." A pause. This time he shot her a look. She'd never seen him so terrified and it scared her.

"What?" she asked.

He ignored the question. "I understand. We'll be there."

Jack lowered the cell phone and stared at it. She reached out and grabbed his forearm. He flinched and looked straight through her.

"They have her, Lauren. They have her," Jack mumbled.

Lauren spun in her seat. "No, Sarah's right…" Her voice trailed off as she realized what he meant.

Jack nodded. "They have Becky. And they're going to kill her."

Chapter 50

Mama D hung up the cell phone. Jimmy was driving but he said nothing in the silence that hung in the air. Mama D turned in her seat. They had switched out of the sedan and taken one of the group's other cars, a black GMC Yukon with three rows of seats. Each spot was taken. The far back row had three men she had known for over fifty years.

They were foot soldiers, all of them Korean War veterans, although their appearance would have made that connection impossible to make. They were smooth-faced and muscular, with sharp eyes and posture that demonstrated how tightly wound they were. Their military bearing was unmistakable to those familiar with such men, but they looked like veterans of the Iraq war, the second one even. For this they owed Mama D and they never failed to pay their debt when she came calling.

In the next row, a man and a woman sat on either side of Pesh. Her Pesh. Her beloved. They each had two hands firmly on his arms, ready for the next round of thrashing. Mama D knew the journey would be hard on him, but she'd underestimated his stamina at fighting against the institutional-grade straight jacket she'd put on him. The jacket was meant to protect him from himself, but he refused to be calm. For hundreds of miles of highway, he'd jerked and strained, trying to get out. It reminded her of a trapped animal, flopping around senselessly until it was utterly exhausted.

At least she didn't need to worry about Pesh chewing his leg off. He wore a helmet with a full-metal face guard. Without it, his two minders likely would have been missing a few fingers and maybe an ear by now. Even with the cage, Pesh snarled and chomped the air with his teeth.

Mama D hated seeing him like this. Trussed up like something less than human. More than once on the trip her eyes had welled with tears as he kicked and struggled. No matter what she said or how hard she tried to penetrate his mind to connect and soothe him, he thrashed and mewled like a dying thing. She knew it was for his own good but it was still hard for a mother to endure.

She thought about the Tremont girl tied up and hidden under layers of blankets in the SUV's cargo space. If she fed her to Pesh, he would be happy for the rest of the trip. Maybe even take a nap for the last hour to Prescott City.

But she knew it was a bad idea. The voice had warned her Sarah would know if her sister was dead, the blood bond powerful enough to override any protections they raised to hide from the little girl's awareness. Besides, the plan was working perfectly. Jack would bring his little girl to the old farmhouse like the voice wanted. Certainly he would have some plan to try to rescue both of his girls, but he would fail. Especially since she would know his exact plan before he arrived.

The warning she'd given Tremont not to call Lonetree or allow Sarah to try to communicate with him in any way wasn't a bluff. She knew everything that was happening in their car now and she planned to make good on her threat to kill the sister if they defied her.

The fool probably hoped Lonetree and Sorenson would come to their rescue, but she already knew those two were back at the Tremont house to set a trap for her. Only they were the ones in a trap. A group of her men were closing on them already and, as an insurance policy, the local police had been tipped off to the location of the federal fugitive. Lonetree and Sorenson would never get out alive.

A cry came from the backseat and Mama D's seat pushed forward as something strong hit it from behind. Snarls and grunts filled the car as Pesh jerked and flailed, arching his back. Throwing his head at his minders like a battering ram. Mama D didn't need to look back, she knew what it looked like and it broke her heart.

Even though she knew his mind was too confused to hear her, she silently sent him a thought. *Shhh, Pesh. It'll be over soon. You'll be my boy and have a real life. This will all be over soon. I promise you that.*

As the car sped through the night, she hoped she could deliver on that promise. If not, if this turned out to be another dead-end, then there would be hell to pay.

And she relished the idea of making Sarah Tremont be the one who paid it.

Chapter 51

Sorenson called out from the kitchen. "They're here."
Lonetree jogged across the living room and
looked at the bank of monitors set up as their
command center on the breakfast island. The screens
were all the eerie green of night vision, the wireless feeds
coming in from the cameras Sorenson had positioned
around the property. They showed armed men crouched
low to the ground, moving with military efficiency,
exchanging quick hand signals as they moved forward.

"Ex-military," Lonetree murmured.

"Ex-paintball champs if we're lucky," Sorenson
replied.

Lonetree scowled. "When's the last time you
remember us being lucky?"

"Good point," Sorenson said. "Look, they

277

stopped. They're just holding positions."

Lonetree leaned in and studied the screens. Obviously there weren't enough cameras out there to give them complete optics, so they had to make do with limited information. On a couple of views, they actually were lucky and the men were nearly in the middle of the screen, as if they were posing for them. But in the others, they had to squint and parse the image to pick out a leg here and a shoulder there, hidden in the forest. But it looked like Sorenson was right. No one was moving.

"Maybe their job is just to contain us," Sorenson said.

"That means they know Sarah's not here," Lonetree pointed out. "That's not good." He picked up the phone and dialed Jack's cell. It immediately went to voicemail. He tried Lauren's and got the same result.

"Can you reach Sarah?" Sorenson asked. "By, you know…" Sorenson dangled his fingers in front of his forehead like he was sending out signals.

Lonetree gave him an incredulous look and Sorenson lowered his fingers. "No, I've tried. I'm pretty sure she could reach me if she wanted."

Sorenson glanced back at the screens and then to Lonetree. "So, what's the play? We can't just sit here."

"These guys are the real deal. We're not going to be able to just crawl out the back door and sneak away without a fight." Lonetree tapped the screen. On one of the camera angles where they were given an unobstructed view, a two-man team set up a .50 cal gun on a tripod. "They came dressed for the party."

Sorenson gave a low whistle. "Why do they get all the good toys?"

"A quick breakaway by car is out. That thing would shred us to pieces. Any ideas?"

Sorenson shrugged. "We can put up a pretty good defense if they come at us. Depending on the breaks we get, it's possible we slip through during a firefight."

Sorenson's words said everything Lonetree needed to know. When the best plan was to let the bad guys attack first and just hope something worked out, it meant they were pretty much screwed. Lonetree picked up the landline and dialed three numbers. Sorenson looked at him oddly but didn't say anything.

"911, what's your emergency?" came the voice on the other end of the line.

"I'd like to report the location of known federal fugitive Joseph Lonetree." Lonetree went on to give the address and a few pertinent details to make the call stick, then hung up the phone.

"Classy," Sorenson said. "Talking about yourself with strangers like that. Will she do anything with it?"

"She perked right up halfway through the call. Must have accessed the APB and figured out the gift she was getting."

"And the trace on the landline will confirm the call came from this address but it won't prove you weren't just some kid blowing smoke. You know they'll still only send a unit or two to size things up. Doesn't seem fair to drag some local beat cops into the middle of this."

Lonetree nodded. "These guys don't want to get into a firefight with law enforcement unless they have to. Hell, half this house is made of glass. If they wanted they could have let us have it already. No, they're on defense. I can feel it."

Sorenson tapped the screen with the .50 cal as if

doing so might make it go away. "Let's hope you're right about that."

Lonetree checked his watch. "We should know soon enough. Even out here in the sticks, the response time should be under ten minutes. Let's get ready. If these assholes open fire on the cops, then we're guns blazing."

"And if they don't?"

"If they don't, I have an idea."

He explained the idea to Sorenson who smirked and then shook his head.

"You're crazy," was the only analysis Sorenson offered.

"So you keep telling me. Come on, let's get ready."

Ten minutes later, a single cruiser wormed its way up the Tremonts' long driveway. Judging by the lack of manpower, it didn't look like they were taking things too seriously.

"One cruiser," Sorenson sniffed. "Guess they're not too worried about facing down the big, bad fugitive from justice, Joseph Lonetree."

Lonetree gave him a grunt but didn't take the bait. He nodded to the bank of monitors. "How are they reacting?"

"They look a little fidgety, but they're holding position."

"Okay, let's see how this goes."

Chapter 52

Craig Peters took a deep, slow breath to steady himself. He forced the tension that had worked its way into his shoulders to fade and allowed himself a shift in position to redistribute his weight more evenly on the damp forest ground. His eye never left the scope attached to his M40 sniper rifle and the crosshairs inside that scope never left the young police officer's blond head. These cops had unexpectedly crashed their party and he didn't like it one bit. He hated police and he wanted nothing better than to see the man's head burst open like a watermelon. But he knew Mama D wouldn't like that. And keeping her happy was all that really mattered.

Well, all that mattered was getting juiced. And the juice only came if Mama D was happy and alive. Craig wasn't so sure anything could actually kill the woman, but he didn't intend to let anyone find out. All he knew was that she was the one thing that had kept him alive for all these years. Hell, more than alive. He was a fuckin' twenty-two-year-old god, even though he'd celebrated over eighty birthdays. Seeing men his actual age, ones who didn't know anything about the juice, made him sick to his stomach. They were so frail, all hunched over with their paper-thin skin and their yellowed eyes and their rotten teeth. More than once he'd become so disgusted at the sight of one that he had no choice but to lash out. The old men's bones cracked and snapped with hardly any effort. Their stupid eyes always looked so shocked when he attacked, the rightness of the state of nature among real men worn down by a lifetime of wear and tear and nagging wives and asshole bosses.

He'd killed a few of them. Not many. Not as many as he wanted to. But he wasn't an animal and he knew how to control himself. Just like he controlled his finger even as he pressed lightly on the trigger, probably only a pound or two of pressure away from causing Deputy Dawg's brain to disappear in a puff of red mist.

The blond cop walked to the door with his slightly overweight partner, a Mexican by the looks of him. God, Craig hated them too. Taking over the country with their refried beans and their Tejano music and their skanky girls that just got fat once they started popping out kids. He shifted the crosshairs to the Mexican's head and quietly mouthed the sound of firing the gun, "Pah, pah, pah..."

The police moved a little warily, looking through the windows as they approached the house, but they weren't tense. The blond pulled out his gun but held it at his side, just following protocol. Craig knew what it looked like when a man drew a gun because he intended to use it. These guys didn't have that look. He wondered what the hell they were doing here at this time of the morning.

Craig opened his left eye and watched for any sign of light or movement inside the house. Nothing. The cops knocked on the door and stood back. After a few minutes, the door opened. Even with his night-vision scope Craig only caught a glimpse of the person inside. It wasn't Lonetree but the other one. Sorenson. Craig knew all about him. Once Mama D finished whatever business she didn't want these two interfering with, she'd promised Craig could do whatever he wanted with these two. He was looking forward to it.

Sorenson had a beer in his hand, shirt untucked over boxer shorts. He leaned against the doorjamb as the cops peppered him with questions. The cops looked agitated now, more angry than combative. He heard snippets of the conversation float through the air.

...report of a fugitive
...how long are you housesitting
...Mr. Tremont's cell phone number
...filing false report
...search the premises

Sorenson made a dramatic sweeping gesture and invited the cops in. The cops entered the house and the door closed behind them. Lights came on.

Craig looked up from his scope and whispered into his throat mic. "Steady, boys. No one makes a move, right?" He knew most of the men in this group well enough, but there were a few late additions that made him nervous. Young pups just back from the war who missed the freedom of action a little too much. They were hooked on a juice of a different kind, the burst of adrenaline that came from combat. Craig just hoped that didn't cause one of them to do something stupid.

Mama D had been specific about holding Lonetree down until she gave him the signal. The rule of engagement offended him. The only way to interpret it was that Mama D didn't think he could handle Lonetree and Sorenson in a fight, not even with the element of surprise and a squad of seven other men at his disposal. He burned at her lack of trust, the professional insult, especially after decades of proving himself. He'd already decided that if he had clear shots on both of the targets, he'd take them. He'd make up some story about how Lonetree had forced his hand. As long as the deed was done, he didn't see how Mama D would care. Besides, he didn't want to miss out on the feast with all the juice that was supposed to be there.

But he didn't have a shot yet so, for the meantime, he did as he was told and sat still as the cops searched the house.

With so many windows, he had a pretty good view as the cops walked through the house. Sorenson followed behind, opening another beer. He picked up a pair of jeans slung over the couch and dug into a pocket. The cops didn't like that at all and reached out to stop him. Sorenson slowly pulled his hand out of the jean pocket to show them his wallet. He pulled out what looked like an ID and handed it to the Mexican. The fat cop pointed to a chair and Sorenson obediently sat.

Craig had a clear view into the great room and saw the blond cop climb the open staircase to the second floor while the Mexican called in the ID on his radio and then made a couple of calls on his cell. By the guy's body language, it seemed like whoever he was calling didn't pick up. Something must have squawked on the radio because the cop acknowledged it and then handed the ID back to Sorenson. He called upstairs and the blond came back down, gun in his holster now.

Craig grinned. He had to hand it to the kid. He was playing the cops perfectly. Must have had a solid fake ID for them to check. Perfect. He almost felt bad about having to kill him later. Almost.

Sorenson stood and shook hands with the cops. They walked back toward the front door, out of his line of sight. When the door didn't open when he expected it to, he activated his throat mic.

"Anyone have eyes on the target?"

"There's a door in the back of the kitchen. They went in there," one of his men replied.

Six other replies came back negative. Sorenson and the cops were in a blind spot. It wasn't surprising. They were lucky the rich puke Jack Tremont didn't care about his heating bill and made a house mainly out of glass to give them as much access as they had.

"I see them," came the call in his earbud a couple minutes later. "Coming to the door."

"Okay, all eyes on the house. Once the cops leave, Lonetree might come out. It might be our one chance with lights on. If we have coordinated shots on both targets, we execute."

He felt his stomach twist. Even though he'd thought this scenario through, he had a rush of nerves now that he was about to go against Mama D's direct order. But she couldn't have predicted this opportunity. He convinced himself that if she were here, she would change the order. If they had a shot on them both, this could be over in a few seconds. Sure, he'd miss out on

285

making Lonetree suffer the way he wanted, of holding his superiority over the man, but he also wouldn't risk losing any men. It was grudging respect that led him to want to shoot him on the spot.

He ignored the cops as they walked out of the house, climbed into the car, and rolled out. Craig conducted a sweeping search of the house through his scope, seeking out movement. He imagined Lonetree coming in from a side room and he and Sorenson having a laugh at the cops' expense before turning the lights back off.

The minutes ticked by and nothing happened.

"Can you see Sorenson?" Craig asked into his mic.

Seven negative responses. And suddenly something didn't feel right.

"Did he come out of the back room with the cops?" Craig asked.

Silence this time.

Shit.

The twist in his stomach was an ice ball now, churning in place. He wasn't an indecisive man, but he felt locked up, unsure of his next move. After another five minutes, he made the call. "Move in, take it slow. If you get a visual, call it and go back to positions if possible."

Immediately, seven men dressed in black tactical gear emerged from the forest, closing in on the house in a tightening circle. Craig had the longest open run to make. If his feeling was wrong, then it would likely be the last run he ever made. He crouched low and ran the distance across the Tremonts' front yard and driveway, ducking under the front door patio. The fact that he'd made it that far terrified him.

"Go in on my count," Craig commanded. "One…two…three."

Craig kicked in the front door. He heard the other men breaking in through different parts of the house. But no gunfire.

He paired up with the man to his right and they worked in tandem, clearing the rooms. Craig knew exactly where he needed to go. Through the great room, into the attached kitchen, and to the door that led to the back room. It was locked. He fired at it, the need for stealth gone. He kicked in the splintered door and knew what he'd see before he saw it.

The two cops tied up with gags in their mouths, lying on the ground in their underwear.

"Goddamn it!" Craig screamed.

A few of his other men leaned into the room. No one dared to say anything. Craig punched the wall. "Bring them," he said, pointing to the cops.

His men dragged the struggling cops out to the great room and forced them to the ground. Craig pointed his gun at the blond's head. He yanked out the gag.

"Where did they go?" Craig demanded.

"I…don't…how would…" the blond cop blubbered.

"Waste these guys and let's go," one of Craig's men said. "Lonetree and Sorenson are miles from here by now."

The cops dropped flat to the floor without being asked to. Craig squinted, thinking it through. With a flash, he figured it out. He looked up at the wall of glass facing the woods.

"Lonetree, you son-of-a—"

The windows exploded with rounds from the .50

cal machine gun. The barrage of metal tore through the room, shredding furniture, walls, flesh. Craig saw his team decimated in the first few seconds. The cops were on the ground in front of him, their hands shielding their heads.

In his last act of defiance, Craig raised his gun to kill them. If it was so important to Lonetree to save these cops that he risked telling them his plan, then he would at least take that away from him.

But when he raised his arm to point his gun he was surprised to see that his hand was no longer there. Instead, there was only a stump where a .50 cal round had ripped through him. In the second before the next burst hit him square in the chest, he felt a profound sense of loss and regret. He'd imagined this moment before and worried he might realize he'd wasted his life. Blown the opportunity to do good things with the extra time he'd been given. But he didn't. He just thought about the juice and how much he would miss it. With that last craving, a shell slammed into him and threw him across the room, sending him on his well-earned trip to hell where he knew he belonged.

Chapter 53

A few minutes later, Lonetree and Sorenson, still dressed in the cop uniforms, picked their way through the destruction that was once the Tremonts' home.

They checked on the cops first. They were scratched up a little from flying debris, but otherwise in good shape. Physically anyway. Emotionally, they were having a tough time with it, both of them shaking uncontrollably, the blond cop weeping in ragged gasps. These were cops in a mostly rural area. Busting kids for drugs and an occasional highway fatality was about as extreme as things got out here. Being in the middle of a massacre with a heavy-caliber weapon was outside their experience.

But they were alive, Lonetree thought. And the bad

guys were dead. It was a pretty good turn of events in his mind.

He crouched down next to the cops. "Easy, guys," he said. "You're okay now. If we wanted to kill you or hurt you, we would have done it already, right?"

The Hispanic cop nodded. He seemed to be handling things better than the other one. "Now what?" he asked.

"We're going to leave you here. You'll be safe. We're taking the squad car so your dispatch will think you left here, but they'll piece it together before too long."

"You...you killed them all..." the blond cop said.

"When you run their info, you're going to be glad I did. These men are killers."

"Don't kid yourself," the Hispanic cop said, mustering some courage. "You are too."

Lonetree put a hand on his shoulder and met his eye. "Yes, I am. But, as it turns out, I'm one of the good guys."

Chapter 54

Jack squinted through the windshield, trying to pick the best path over the rutted dirt road. He'd turned the headlights off when they first made the turn off pavement onto the dirt path in the small hope of maintaining some element of surprise. There was a full moon and no clouds, so the landscape glinted silver and blue. Still, the SUV bounced hard when he hit potholes or larger rocks.

He knew the way even in the dark. After the incident in the cave, the police had brought him out here on numerous occasions to walk the property and recount his story. He didn't begrudge them for doing their jobs, but by the sixth or seventh time he had to answer the same questions asked by some skeptical FBI hotshot obviously looking for the smallest discrepancy in his story, he was done. The road had been in bad shape back then, but with the area blocked off, it was in worse shape now.

They got to the chain-link fence blocking the road. Someone had cut a hole in it large enough to walk through. Jack stopped the car but didn't turn it off. He dug into the center console and brought out the Glock Lonetree had given him. He removed the clip, saw it wasn't full, and put it down to look for the box of ammo. A heavy silence filled the car.

"They're going to kill us all," Lauren finally whispered. "If we go in there, that's all that's going to happen."

Jack stared into the night, gripping the box of ammo he'd found.

"What do you think's going to happen?" Lauren asked. "We have a good chat with Mama D, appeal to her better nature? Threaten her with the one gun we have and she lets us all go? She's done all this to get Sarah. Do you really think she's going to just give that up?"

"No, and that's why I'm going in alone," Jack whispered. "Mama D said she'd sense if we ran. Well, she can sense Sarah's nearby, but that doesn't mean she has to go all the way. This is our one chance. That's why once I leave, you're going to drive back to the road and get Sarah out of here."

"No, Dad," Sarah said from the backseat.

But Jack's attention was on Lauren. "You know it's the right thing. If we call the cops, they kill her. Like you said, if we all go in there, they'll just kill us all."

"But what do you think you're going to accomplish by yourself?" Lauren asked, but there was no fight in her words. She wasn't trying to persuade him on anything. Her voice was soft and laced with sadness. A lover saying goodbye.

"I don't know. But I have to try." He reached out and put his hand over hers. "And if I wasn't willing to, I know you would go yourself. No matter the risk. But we have two daughters. So one of us has to stay."

Tears welled in Lauren's eyes and Jack saw that she knew the truth of it. Their futures seemed to roll out in front of them as inescapable roads bordered with high, unassailable walls. Jack down the path to rescue Becky, most likely to be captured and killed. Lauren, on the run with Sarah, driving down isolated back roads, to small towns and cheap motels. Running and running until the inevitable day that Mama D and her group found them.

Lauren turned her hand so that hers was palm to palm with Jack's. She squeezed it tightly and Jack found comfort in the strength there.

"Save our baby, Jack," she said. Then, swallowing hard, she added, "Or at least kill the bitch who stole her from us if you have the chance."

Jack leaned over and kissed Lauren, sensing that he was feeling her lips against his for the very last time. For a moment, the nightmare they were in was gone, the terrors that filled the night were silenced in his head, and all he felt was his connection to her. Even inside the reprieve from the world around him, he registered a sound that wasn't quite right coming from the backseat. He stiffened, and he felt Lauren do the same. Before he could pull back from her, the inevitable follow-up sound filled his ears and made his stomach drop.

The first sound was the back door quietly opening, followed by it slamming shut. Sarah was outside.

"Sarah!" Jack shouted. He reached for the handle

293

to his door and pulled it.

The door locks all around the car clicked into the locked position. Jack tried the electric lock and then pulled at it with his fingers. It wouldn't budge. He tried the windows. Nothing.

You can't get out, Dad. I'm stronger than that. And I've twisted the locks inside the doors.

Jack jerked his head up. It was Sarah's voice in his head. She stood just outside his window, staring in at them.

I'm sorry it has to be like this, but I have to face her. I'm the only one who has a chance to save Becky.

"No, Sarah!" Lauren yelled.

"Let me at least come with you," Jack shouted through the window.

You'd try to stop me. I know it.

Jack reached for his gun, ready to shoot out the window. He didn't care if it gave away their position. But he couldn't find it. Slowly, he looked back outside.

Sarah held the gun in her hand. She placed it on the hood of the car. Along with the keys to the car.

Jack looked down at the ignition, half-expecting to still see his keys there. But they weren't. If Sarah was able to twist the metal locks in the door, it made sense that she'd been able to float the keys to the backseat when he hadn't been looking.

Jack sent her the strongest thoughts he could, begging her not to go. To wait and make a plan for them to work together. But it felt false, because really the only thing he could think of were ways to stop her. Ways to get her back in the car, by force if necessary, and have Lauren drive her away from this mad idea.

Lauren sobbed in the seat next to him. "Baby, don't do this. W…w…we can get away. Let's just get out of here, all right? All of us."

Sarah shook her head. *I love you both. I'll do everything I can to save Becky. I promise.*

Then she turned and jogged down the path, quickly making a turn so that she disappeared into the tree line, swallowed up by the night.

"Sarah!" Lauren shouted to no avail.

Jack stared through the windshield in disbelief. Their little girl was gone.

Chapter 55

Mama D sat on the porch swing next to Pesh on the wide verandah of the dilapidated farmhouse, her sword balanced on her lap. The place was not much of a house anymore, more of a ruin. The earthquakes during the cave-ins had seen to that. The rear rooms had collapsed completely, and were now just a jumble of splintered two-by-fours and plywood, accented by the odd interior detail that had ended up exposed to the world. A swatch of wallpaper with tiny red roses. A half-shattered mirror. A bedpost that still glistened with thick lacquer, notched with lines by someone likely long since dead, the reason for the dutifully carved lines dead with them.

The front façade of the house was mostly intact, like an old Hollywood movie set. But it only appeared so when viewed from the front. With the slightest angle, it was apparent that the second story leaned backward fifteen or twenty degrees from center, showing that it was just a matter of time and weather before the entire thing collapsed onto itself.

Mama D idly wondered how the whole thing was left standing at all by the powers that be. The empty beer cans, shattered glass, and graffiti attested to its attraction to teenagers in the area. She would have thought some agency or another would have at least bulldozed the property down. Probably some kind of jurisdiction issue. Mama D appreciated those.

The lack of information-sharing between law enforcement entities had always been a help to her group. Back in the good old days, it was rare to have word of an abduction reach more than a few towns away. Then, later, when everyone suddenly had a car and a telephone, word would spread to the next county over. Maybe the next two counties if the sheriffs had a relationship. Even when the FBI got into the business and the Internet promised to make all information open and free, law enforcement remained full of alpha males who didn't want anyone taking a piss in their yard.

Mama D was glad they hadn't torn the place down. Even if they had, she thought maybe this covered porch with its swing would have remained standing. It was solid and well-built, maybe added after the main house. The floorboards were wide, irregular planking, probably cut and milled on the property. In a world where everything was disposable, she liked how the porch gave off a sense of both timelessness and solidity. Like it had always been there and always would be.

It was exactly how Mama D considered herself.

Once this was over, she decided she would build a porch just like this on her place in Texas. Pesh would be himself then. A regular teenaged boy. They could sit on the swing together and talk about the world. Tell stories and jokes to entertain one another. She knew he would be a smart boy once he was fixed by the girl. Such a clever boy. Funny too, she was sure of it. They would laugh together and drink sun tea as the hot Texas sun drifted through the sky until the world caught fire with its glow. Then they would eat their dinner together in the cool breezes of the night, taking turns reading their favorite books out loud. It was going to be magnificent.

Pesh jerked next to her, lunging at her with his head as if forgetting he still wore a helmet and that his wrists and ankles were shackled together. A chain ran through the wrist and leg irons, attached to the floor with a shiny metal hoop screwed into the wood there. He jammed the facemask of his helmet against her body, snapping his teeth, long strands of saliva pouring from his mouth and hanging from his chin. He howled as he pulled at the shackles, twisting and arching his body.

Mama D wondered if he felt the presence in this place the same way she did. She couldn't quite place it, more like an echo of something old and powerful that lingered in the air, seeping up from the soil all around her.

"Shhh...Pesh," Mama D said. "It won't be long now. You won't have to be like this anymore. I promise. Mama promises."

A wave of pressure hit her, her ears popping like she'd suddenly changed altitude. It wasn't painful like the times before, but she felt the voice before she heard it. *She's here,* the voice in her head bellowed. *Get ready. Don't underestimate her.*

Mama D petted Pesh's arm even as he continued to flail at her, his eyes rolling wildly in their sockets. "People should take care not to underestimate *us*, isn't that right, Pesh?"

She picked up her sword and unhooked the shackles from the ring in the floorboard. She rose from the porch swing and gave a tug until Pesh stood and followed her to the top of the stairs. The full moon glowed bright enough to give the false sense of day. Even so, Mama D had ordered bonfires to be set around the property. She liked the ambiance and the additional light and heat. She looked out over the rough landscape of broken ground. Deep ruts and valleys created a pattern of light blue-grey open areas checked with dark shadows. It was from one of these shadows, less than a hundred feet from the house, that Sarah emerged.

How did she get so close without me knowing? Mama D wondered, a little unnerved. She realized that she gripped her sword too tightly.

Sarah walked slowly toward the house. As she did, Mama D saw four of her men step from the shadows as a loose escort, Jimmy among them. She noticed that they kept their distance. She didn't know whether they felt the danger radiating off of her or if they were just feeding off her own nervousness. To her men, she was a goddess. The thing that the goddess feared was a thing to fear indeed.

Mama D felt a pang of burning hatred for Sarah Tremont. After she got what she wanted from her, Mama D planned to have some fun with the girl. She'd use her sister, maybe send Jimmy to track down the girl's parents, and prolong the agony as long as she could. Maybe even bring them all back to Texas so she could take her time with them. Just thinking about it made her feel better. She walked down the steps, if nothing else than to prove she was not afraid of her. They closed the distance between them quickly and then stopped with only ten feet between them.

Everything was silent. Even Pesh seemed to feel the tension as he sniffed the air in the girl's direction and then gave a barely audible growl. The girl spoke first.

"I'm Sarah Tremont. You have my sister."

Mama D stared back at her and said nothing.

"Give her to me and I won't kill you," Sarah said.

Mama D noticed her men shift uncomfortably on their feet, looking to one another and then to her. All of them had guns trained on Sarah. She didn't like their uncertainty. She decided to play it big.

"You have nerve, girl, I'll give you that," Mama D laughed. "Your sister's inside the van. The white one over there," she said with a nod of her head. She watched as the girl looked in that direction, focused for a few seconds, then turned back to her.

"No she's not," Sarah said. "She's in the farmhouse."

"Good, very good," Mama D said, wondering if the girl knew she was giving away information about her powers. "You're strong. I need that. You're going to help my son, my Pesh. Because of you, he's going to find himself again."

"A trade, then," Sarah said. "You let Becky go and promise she'll be safe, and I'll cooperate with you."

"But why would I give something to you when I can just take what I need?" Mama D asked.

"Because I know I'm going to die tonight. Part of me wants to die, to be done with these dark thoughts in my head. To stop hurting other people. But I want my sister and my parents to live."

Mama D grinned. "You still haven't answered my question. Why should I care about what you want?"

"Because if you don't do this deal, then neither of us gets what we want," Sarah said.

"Hey, what's going on?" Jimmy called out.

Mama D looked over and saw him straining to lower the gun he held in his outstretched hand. He slowly raised it so that it was pointed at Sarah's head.

"Jimmy, what are you doing?" Mama D shouted at him, raising the tip of her sword in his direction.

"I can't control it," Jimmy yelled. "She has control. I can't stop her."

Mama D looked back at Sarah, realizing what the girl meant to do. "You wouldn't dare."

"You want to find out?"

Chapter 56

J ack braced himself against the center console and kicked again at the driver's window. His ankles throbbed as the window held, looking no worse for wear.

"How can it be this hard?" Lauren said.

"I'm doing the best I can," Jack snapped, harder than he intended. They'd been trapped in the car for five minutes. They were both scared and frustrated, but he knew fighting each other wouldn't help anything. "I'm sorry," he said.

Lauren ignored the comment. Her attention was outside the car. "Jack, what's that? There in the woods?"

Jack followed the direction she was looking and picked out a light weaving through the trees ahead of them. He turned out the dome light and motioned for Lauren to get down.

"Mama D's people," Jack whispered. "Who else would be out here this time of night?"

"Do you think they heard us?"

Jack didn't reply. He grabbed her hand and squeezed it. If they were found locked up in the car and without a weapon, they were as good as dead and they both knew it.

Seconds passed and they strained to hear anything outside the SUV. Briefly, Jack thought he heard the low murmur of voices but it fell away and he was unsure if it was just his imagination. They remained crouched down for a full minute. Nothing.

"Are they gone?" Lauren whispered.

Jack motioned that he was going to raise himself up to take a look. He took a deep breath and slowly lifted his head up over the edge of the window. Nothing but dark forest stared back at him.

"I think—"

A hand slapped against the window, followed by a brightly lit face. A flashlight came on, held underneath it, like something done at a campfire when telling a scary story. And the face fit the part. It was a man, pale and drawn with thin lips and an impossibly long chin. The eyes glowed in the light like a cat's and were too large for his skull. His hair hung to his shoulders in heavy, greasy strands. The man grinned and revealed a row of tiny teeth filed into points. Worse than the man's bizarre appearance was the gun he held next to his cheek, which he slowly turned to aim directly into the car.

Lauren let out an involuntary scream. Jack pushed back away from the window and tried to cover Lauren's body with his own. As he did, a second man banged on the passenger-side window. A quick check told Jack all he needed to know. There was a second gun pointing straight at them. There was nowhere to hide.

He put his hands up. "Wait," he shouted. "Just wait."

The first man, the greasy man with the long hair, licked his lips. He looked through the car and out the opposite side. "What you think, Nettle? These got to be the girl's parents, right?"

There was no answer from the second man named Nettle, but his flashlight moved slowly back to the rear of the car, the finger of light systematically searching the vehicle. Finally, he grunted. "Nothing here, Carl."

"Where's the kid?" the greasy man named Carl shouted.

So they don't have Sarah. Thank God, Jack thought.

"Somewhere safe," Jack shouted. "Not here."

Carl leaned forward, his flashlight shining right into Jack's eyes. After a few seconds, he said, "And I think you're lyin' about that." He stood up and called out over the top of the car. "Shoot the woman. In the leg. We'll need her to make this one talk."

"No!" Jack shouted, twisting and lunging toward the passenger side, trying to get his body between Lauren and the window.

An explosion erupted and glass shattered everywhere. Jack felt a searing pain in his arm as he fell on top of Lauren. He heard her grunt from his weight, but she wasn't screaming. The bullet had missed her. He reached to the spot where the pain radiated from his arm and felt the hot blood pouring down his arm.

"Lauren," he said.

"I'm okay," she replied.

"That was a warning," the greasy-haired man said. He had walked around the car and now stood outside the shattered window. "Nettle here enjoys women like your wife here. I'm inclined to give her to him. Whether I force you to watch or not is up to you. Now where's your girl?"

"I'll make you a deal," Jack said. "Let my wife live, and I'll tell you where Sarah is."

"Jack," Lauren hissed.

Jack mouthed the words *I love you* and pushed himself up, awkwardly trying to show the two men his hands in the universal sign of surrender. "Just let me get out of here and I'll tell you."

Carl hesitated, then nodded to Nettle and the big man reached in through the window, grabbed Jack by his wounded arm and dragged him out of the car. Jack cried out, the pain so intense that the edges of his vision darkened. He gasped for air, the pain temporarily the only thing that existed in the world for him.

Now, he screamed at himself. *Your best and only chance is now.*

Jack fell hard to the ground, slumping into a heap in a way he hoped caused the men to let their guard down, even if only for a second. His one hope was to catch them off guard and somehow wrest away one of their guns.

"Aww, look at his arm, Nettle," the greasy-haired one said. "You shot him and he—"

Jack kicked behind him and smashed the heel of his boot into the side of the man's knee. There was a satisfying *crumph* as ligaments gave way and the knee broke. The man cried out and dropped to the ground. Jack spun and half-crawled, half bull-charged Nettle, ramming his shoulder into the large man's abdomen.

Thick arms wrapped around Jack's midsection and lifted. His feet came off the ground and suddenly he was airborne. He smashed into the side of the car and slid off it to the ground.

Instantly, Nettle was on him, pulling him up by his hair. Jack swung and connected a right cross to the man's face. Nettle didn't flinch and Jack's hand throbbed with pain.

"Break his fuckin' legs," Carl roared. "Break his arms too."

A scream came from behind and Jack felt Nettle let him go. He rolled and got up as quickly as he could to see Lauren holding on to the man from behind, one arm locked around his neck in a choking maneuver.

"Lauren, no," Jack cried.

But it was too late. The big man lunged backward, slamming her into the side of the SUV. The impact loosened her grip. The second she did, Nettle bent forward, flipped her over his head, and tossed her through the air. Jack tried to break her fall, a move which only succeeded in both of them falling to the ground. When he looked up, the greasy-haired man stood over them, his gun pointed at Jack's head.

"Enough of this bullshit," he said, cocking the gun. "Sayonara, mutha—"

The gun went off twice, and Jack jerked back on reflex. It took his brain a full second to catch up and for him to realize he hadn't been shot at all. But he'd heard the shots. How could the man have missed at such close range?

A fissure in the greasy-haired man's forehead dripped a single line of blood that rolled over his left eyebrow and passed over the man's open eye. Jack realized whatever light had been on inside the man was gone. Impossibly, he stayed upright, swaying. His friend Nettle collapsed to the ground behind him, a geyser of blood pouring from a crater in his chest.

Two police officers walked up. The younger of the two swatted away the gun still in the greasy-haired man's hand and looked him over curiously.

Despite facing death seconds before, Jack couldn't help but break out into a wide grin.

"Like you were saying," the young cop said. "Sayonara mutha fucka."

He pulled a knife and dragged it across the man's throat. Frothy blood bubbled out from his windpipe and the air filled with a wet gargling sound. Finally the man sagged to his knees, and then fell face-first into the ground.

Jack blinked hard, certain his eyes were playing a trick on him.

The young cop was Sorenson and Lonetree was right behind him.

Lonetree was helping Lauren to her feet as Jack got up, favoring his arm.

"What took you guys so long?" Jack said.

Sorenson grinned. "Oh you know, fighting military-trained mercenaries, evading arrest, the usual."

"Looks like you did more than evade arrest," Lauren said. "You didn't—"

Lonetree shook his head. "Don't worry, we just borrowed their clothes. They're fine."

"Which is more than he can say for your house. Lonetree lit it up with a .50 cal machine gun. Pah-pah-pah," Sorenson said, acting out the part. Lonetree shot him a look. Sorenson shrugged. "Well, you did."

Lonetree ignored him. "What the hell are you two doing here? Where's Sarah?"

"Mama D has Becky. Said she'd kill her if we didn't come, and that she could tell if Sarah was getting closer to her or farther away. We had no choice." Jack paused as Lauren wrapped a makeshift tourniquet above the gunshot wound on his arm. "I planned on only bringing Sarah this far and then going down myself. But then Sarah left on her own." Lonetree raised an eyebrow. "She took the gun and locked us in the car. She twisted the locks inside the door somehow."

Lauren cinched the tourniquet tight and he swallowed the pain down, black dots dancing across his vision. Even though Jack felt unsteady on his feet, he managed to walk in the direction Sarah had gone. "We have to find her. She went to face Mama D on her own."

"How long has she been gone?" Lonetree asked, following close behind.

"Too long," Lauren replied. "Ten, twelve minutes."

"What does she think she's doing?" Sorenson asked.

"Taking it to the enemy," said Lonetree, his expression grim. "I just hope she knows what the hell she's doing."

Chapter 57

Sarah concentrated her hold on the man's arm. Jimmy. That was his name. Jimmy. A simple name for a simple mind. Easy to read and control. Challenging only because of his blind devotion to Mama D. It completely stifled his basic instincts for self-preservation. Sarah quickly gauged that he would fight back harder if she tried to make him turn the gun on Mama D. Still, she took a chance and tried to make him swing his arm toward the woman. As expected, he fought back hard, his hand shaking violently.

Make him kill himself then, came the voice in her head. *It's easy. You could do it. Open his head and splatter his brain.*

She shuddered at this uncontrolled thought coming up from inside of her. It was the foreign voice, the unclean part of the fire inside of her that felt like pure hate. The voice scared her.

She focused on Jimmy, still straining from the

309

effort because of how delicate she had to be. A little too much pressure on the wrong tendon and he would pull the trigger.

"Put the gun down, Jimmy," Mama D growled.

"I can't…can't move…" Jimmy whispered.

Sarah was aware the other men had their guns trained on her. She felt their confusion and fear pulse out from them like waves of heat.

"You shoot the girl and I'll rip you limb from limb, you understand me?" Mama D said to them.

Jimmy whimpered and Sarah felt him struggle against her will. She pushed back too hard and the gun jerked to the side and went off, kicking up dirt where the bullet slammed harmlessly into the ground. She quickly brought him back under control.

"Dammit, Jimmy," Mama D growled.

"She's too strong," he yelled back, fear in his voice.

Deep down, he wants me dead, Sarah realized. *He's afraid of how Mama D will change if she takes my fire for herself. That's why I can control him.*

"I want my sister," Sarah said calmly.

Mama D turned to the boy who stood next to her, stamping his feet impatiently, sniffing the air toward the new arrival. "What do you think, Pesh? Is she bluffing? Will she really sacrifice herself for her sister?"

Pesh grunted and wheezed, agitated now, clawing at the air with shackled hands.

Sarah allowed part of her focus to shift to the creature chained next to Mama D. When she'd first walked up, she'd thought the thing to be some kind of primate. A monkey or an ape dressed in human clothes because of the way it hunched over and loped next to her in a sidelong gait. The helmet and faceguard obscured its face from a distance, but now she could see it more clearly. It was a boy, probably her age or a little older. And, despite the animal-like contortions of his face and the vacant, mad eyes that burned with hate and hunger, the face was really quite beautiful.

She pried into the boy's mind and it was like stepping from inside a building out into a raging storm. Only this storm wasn't wind and hail and lightning. It was hate, terror, and an all-encompassing lust for blood.

Mama D stepped between Sarah and Pesh. "No, no, no. Don't go pokin' around where you're not wanted. You leave my Pesh alone."

My Pesh? The way she said it gave her an insight. And insight was power.

"That's your son," Sarah said, making the guess a statement. Mama D said nothing but a single line appeared between her eyes as she concentrated harder on Sarah. It was all she needed. "So it is your son. And you chain him up like an animal?" She paused and looked Mama D over, a look of mock sympathy on her face. "Oh, I see. You're afraid of him, aren't you?"

"Shut up, girl," Mama D spat. "You don't know anything about it."

"I know something about it. I know what you did to Charlie Winters. I know about the others. So I know you're a monster and that's why you gave birth to one."

Sarah winced as Mama D's mind slammed like a steel battering ram into the defenses she'd erected around herself. She heard the woman screaming and shouting, calling her names she'd never heard before, but it was muffled and distant, like someone shouting through the closed doors of a bank vault.

311

"How can this be?" Mama D asked, the first signs of fear flashing on her face.

Sarah wondered herself at how powerful she felt. Since walking out onto the field, the fire inside her raged like an inferno. In her mind's eye she saw power radiating out from her hands, off her skin. Her brain was on fire, sensing the world in infinite detail all at once. Each minute, the power grew stronger, the heat building inside her chest. A faint warning rang in her mind that it was too much, that she was being consumed by something she couldn't control, but she forced it into silence.

No. Something else forced it into silence. Something foreign rising from inside the fire.

"I will bargain with you, girl," Mama D said. "Your life for your sister's."

"No," Sarah snapped. Her voice came out in a rasping bark, deeper than she'd ever heard herself speak. "The game has changed. I'm not here to bargain anymore. I'm here to punish you."

For the first time, Mama D looked scared. "Shoot her," she cried. "Shoot her in the legs."

The other three men lowered their guns to her legs without hesitation. But they weren't quick enough. With a simple thought, Sarah wrenched each man's forearm and their bones cracked and broke through their skin in ragged tears. They dropped their guns and screamed in pain, cradling their arms to their stomachs.

Their hearts. Squeeze their hearts like pieces of spoiled fruit.

Sarah did as the voice commanded. She pictured each man's heart beating in their chests. Suddenly her hand was not only wrapped around one of them, but somehow around all three at the same time. She felt the beating muscles twitch and flex, slippery in her fingers.

Crush them. Snuff out their pathetic lives. You know they deserve it.

Even though she knew it was just an extension of her mind, she shuddered as the hearts throbbed in the palm of her hand. The power. It felt absolute. She was judge and jury for these men and her form of justice was death.

She squeezed the hearts slowly, afraid to end it too quickly. She didn't want this feeling to go away. Not ever.

The men clutched their chests, the agony of their broken forearms lost to the panic of feeling the pressure inside their bodies.

Kill them, Sarah, said the voice. *Burst their hearts and rip open their bodies. Pour their blood into the earth so I can drink.*

Chapter 58

The word *I* caught her off guard. From the beginning, the voice had felt foreign and strange, but another sensation washed over her, filling her with an assurance that everything was fine, that everything was just as it was always meant to be. But this feeling was a lie. Something was wrong. Very wrong.

So I can drink.

I.

Oh my God, she thought. *Someone is inside of me.*

BAM.

The gunshot roared from right next to her.

She let go of the hearts and pulled back into herself. For a confused second, she wondered where the gunshot had come from, but she quickly spotted the smoke rising from Jimmy's gun. She knew immediately what had happened. The break in her concentration had given Mama D the opening she'd been waiting for. Jimmy had pulled the trigger, but only because Mama D had climbed into his head and pushed Sarah aside.

She felt a rush of relief that she hadn't been hit by the shot. But her very next breath caught in her throat because of the white-hot pain tearing up her leg.

NO! screamed the voice in her head.

Sarah matched the scream and fell to the ground. She reached for her leg and felt the blood gush from the wound. Mama D came at her mentally, the power of her mind like a tidal wave. She fought through the pain and focused back on her defensive wall. Just in time, she blocked her from coming in, but the barrier was so thin, Sarah could hear her clearly.

I'll destroy you, Mama D yelled in her head. *I'll drink your blood and suck the marrow from your bones. Let me in. LET ME IN.*

Sarah looked up from the ground and saw Mama D standing with her eyes closed, her face twisted with concentration. Next to her, the creature Pesh clawed at the ground, tugging at his chain, snarling in a frenzy at the smell of blood.

She looked back at her wound. In the firelight, the blood shined like black oil. It drenched her leg and soaked the ground beneath her, but there was something unusual happening. The ground opened wherever her blood hit, pursing open like thirsty lips sucking the moisture out of the air. The earth was drinking her blood.

Ahhh… said the voice in her head. *Better than I could have imagined.*

Sarah kept the wall up to keep Mama D out, but still risked a look inward. Even though part of her didn't want to see what was there, she had to know.

She saw the tower of flame, the embodiment of the fire burning inside of her. Where it had once been a controlled blaze, fierce but contained, it raged like a wildfire, spitting out sparks and flame. Then, in the center of the fire, she saw a dark shadow. Indistinct at first, just tall and slender, taking shape slowly in front of her. Her breath quickened and then suddenly stopped, her throat constricted in terror.

The shadow took form.

Legs, arms, torso.

It was her nightmare made real again, the face that haunted her.

The shaman. The one Huckley and his band of murderers called the Source. Part of the monster was inside her. Had always been inside her since that night in the cave when he was destroyed beneath millions of tons of rock.

But he wasn't dead. He was alive, inside her soul, and getting stronger.

She looked at the blood seeping into the ground and knew that somehow the blood was giving him strength. She didn't understand it, but somehow there was a connection. She pressed her hand against the wound, desperate to keep any more blood from reaching the dirt, but it was no use. It was everywhere.

Too late, child, the shaman said. *What is done cannot be undone. There is nothing you can do to stop me now.*

The shaman spread his arms and he grew in size, blocking out more and more of the column of fire. Sarah fought back a surge of panic. She felt the rising force he gathered to himself. It was a massive bow being pulled back, vibrating with tension. Like so many things that had happened to her, she found that she knew something impossible for her to know.

He's about to consume me. Take over my body and soul and I will be gone forever.

Fear gave way to anger. She heard Lonetree's voice in her head. *So, that's how it's going to be? You giving up? What happened to taking it to the enemy?*

Sarah knew she only had a few seconds before her destruction. She searched the fire that was still accessible to her for a way out. An idea came to her that was so impossible that she knew it had to come from deep truth found inside her power. Not in a million years could she have come up with the idea with her imagination. The same truth told her the act, even if it worked, might kill her. But she had no other choice. Besides, death was coming for her either way. At least this way she could deny the creature what it wanted from her.

The shaman grew massive before her mind's eye, nearly blocking the fire from view and casting her into darkness. She had to try it.

"I'm sorry," Sarah whispered, giving in to the premonition that she was about to die. She pushed out the message with her mind. *Mom, Dad, Becky. I'm so sorry I let you down.*

A new sound rose behind her, a roar like a freight train materializing out of nowhere and hurtling full speed down the track toward her.

She was out of time.

Sarah forced her mind to split from her body, pulling out the roots that traveled to every part of her body through miles of veins, arteries, and nerves. She gathered it all together and held it to her chest. She closed her eyes and imagined a blank wall with an open door.

The power of the roar was a physical thing behind her as she sprinted to the door and jumped into the void on the other side.

As she jumped, she said a single word and closed her eyes, picturing the attractive boy with the bloodthirsty eyes of a maniac.

Pesh.

Chapter 59

Jack ran through the brush, pushing aside the low branches blocking his way. His heart pounded as he ran, both from the exertion and the adrenaline pouring into his system. Even with it, the pain in his arm burned with each step. He didn't care. Not one but both of his daughters were at risk. As far as he knew, they could both already be dead. He pushed the negative thought away and focused on keeping his feet under him on the loose rock path.

Then he heard the gunshot.

All of them stopped. It came from the valley to their right. He crouched against a rock outcropping and Lauren slid in next to him. Lonetree was there, the only pair of binoculars in the group already up. Jack tried to get a read off of the big man, but it was like reading stone.

"Four men, armed. Handguns. Mama D with some kind of creature on a chain next to her."

"Sarah," Jack said. "Do you see her?"

Lonetree lowered the binoculars and Jack saw a flicker of emotion on his face. It was small, just an involuntary curl of his upper lip, but Jack didn't like the look of it. He reached out and grabbed the binoculars from Lonetree.

"Wait," Lonetree said.

Jack raised the binoculars to his eyes. They were powerful and at first he couldn't orient them properly enough to find his target. Eventually, using a few landmarks, he zeroed in on the figures in front of the old farmhouse, well lit by the tall flames of the bonfires.

He didn't see Sarah until the flames shifted with the wind, revealing her standing behind one of the fires. Lauren must have caught a glimpse of her with her bare eyes too because she drew a sharp breath next to him. Sarah stood in front of Mama D, defenseless and alone, ringed by four men with guns, one pointed at her head.

"Can you get a shot off from here?" Jack hissed, not moving the binoculars.

"If I had my M40, this would all already be over," Lonetree said. "These handguns and the shotgun from the cop car won't do anything from this distance."

Jack was about to throw the binoculars back to Lonetree so he could race down the hill toward Sarah, when movement caught his eye and held him in place.

Three of the men around Sarah dropped their guns and grabbed at their forearms. Their painful screams reached all the way across the field and up to their position. Sarah held out a hand toward them and the men writhed on the ground, holding their chests. Jack knew what was happening. Sarah was killing them.

"Do it," he whispered. "Finish them."

He felt bitterness that he would wish such a thing on his daughter, but more than anything else he wanted her to live. If that meant she had to use her powers to rip these men to pieces, then so be it.

Then the fourth man, the one with the gun still pointed at Sarah's head, lowered his gun and fired. Lauren screamed next to him and stood, hitting his arm in the process. The image in the binoculars danced around and he desperately scanned the area, looking for Sarah.

"No, no," he mumbled.

Then he found her. On the ground, holding her leg. Jack breathed a sigh of relief and then immediately felt the ridiculousness of his response. His daughter had been shot. Perhaps not fatally, not yet anyway, but she had still been shot. Whatever power Sarah possessed, it was not going to be enough to best Mama D and her cohorts.

"We need to get down there," Jack said.

Lonetree nodded. "Sorenson, circle wide on the north side and come in from behind the farmhouse. We'll spread out and come in from the front, Jack to my left, Lauren to my right. If we're lucky—"

"If you're lucky, Mama D will only kill you," said a voice behind them. They all spun around and saw a man dressed in black tactical gear fifteen feet behind them, a M16 up against his cheek. He flipped a selector switch and a laser sight flared on, lighting up a red dot on Lauren's chest. The second he did so, three other laser sights appeared, one on each of them.

Chapter 60

S arah had no idea where she was. Dizzy and disoriented, she held her hands to her ears and pressed them as hard as she could to block out the howling screams that swirled around her, every bit as real as physical torrents of wind. Her stomach folded over on itself and waves of nausea drove her down to one knee. She crouched low to the ground, sobbing from confusion and terror.

Where am I? she thought.

The screams around her turned to cackling laughter, mean and penetrating. Beneath the laughter, coming in undulated waves, a mocking voice mimicked her thought.

"Where am I? Where am I?"

She recognized the voice. It was the same voice that echoed in her head whenever she had a nightmare about her ordeal in the caves. The same voice that had lured her to his hospital room where she was abducted. Ten years later, it was the voice she could never forget.

Nate Huckley.

Stop it! she screamed in her mind. *Get out of my head.*

Huckley found this hilarious and shrieked with pleasure, sending great gusts of wind crashing against her, threatening to rip her from the ground and send her spiraling up into the air. Huckley sang his taunts like a kid on a school yard.

"Get out of my head. Stop it! Stop it!" he sang.

Sarah ran. She didn't think of a direction or of where she might escape to. Her destination was simple. Away. Anywhere that was away from the wind and the voice and the screaming laughter. As she ran, the wind acquired new texture. Gritty dirt. Wet, moldering leaves that smelled of decay. Twigs and small branches that stung when they *thwacked* against her body.

I'm in the forest, she thought, thinking of her body in the real world outside her mind. *I made it that far. But they're probably right behind me, he's probably right behind me, so I can't stop. I have to keep moving. I have to…*

She froze in place and looked carefully around her, squinting into the wind. There was a tickling sensation in her mind, similar to the kind that came before she was able to make things move with her mind. But this felt different. This felt like…*knowing.*

She squeezed her eyes shut and willed herself to clear her mind. She tried to remember how she got here, where "here" was. There was Mama D and the man

Jimmy with the weak mind and the gun. Huckley wasn't there. He was dead, buried under a mountain of stone. The last thing she remembered was the feeling of the force hiding inside her fire, that thing that rose up to consume her before she…

…jumped.

I jumped.

Pesh.

I'm in Pesh's mind.

The thing that felt like knowing that had slouched in the dark corner of her mind finally stepped forward. As she crouched against the buffeting wind, everything became clear to her. There was no wind. Or voices. Or even ground for her to stand on.

None of what she saw was real, not in the usual sense of the word anyway. This was Pesh's diseased mind, filled with the confusion and terror that had gripped her when she'd first arrived. Why Huckley was here, she had no idea. Maybe something she brought with her? Her greatest fear tagging along for the ride?

She risked opening her eyes and had to shield them with her hand as debris flew through the air. It was as if she were in the center of a tornado. The screaming pierced her head and made her dizzy. Her body, no matter if it was real or not, sagged under the strain of bracing against the wind. She'd only been there for minutes but the place was already wearing her down.

She looked down at her feet and was shocked to see that dirt had piled up to her knees without her even noticing.

She looked at the hand covering her eyes and saw a trail of sand stretching off of it into the air. Only it wasn't sand. It was her hand. The cells of her body drifting off into the wind.

If I don't do something, I'm going to become part of this madness. I'll go insane and never get out.

She yelled and refocused her mind. The trail of particles streaming off her hand snapped back into place. She yanked her feet out of the dirt and ran.

Within seconds, she heard a chorus of snarls and barking. She spun around and three dark shadows materialized out of the storm. They were dogs, but not like anything Sarah had seen before. They had no skin, just raw flesh covering their bodies. They snapped their massive box jaws at her and sprinted her direction.

Sarah ran. Blind, staggering over the uneven ground. She heard the dogs behind her. Felt them there. And she knew if they reached her, she would be ripped to shreds, her blood and bones scattered into the maelstrom of Pesh's mind. She couldn't let that happen. She had to run.

Harder and harder, she sprinted. The debris was so thick in the air that she had no sense of movement. For a horrified second, she wondered if she was moving at all, or just running to stay in place like in countless nightmares she'd had. Only in those dreams it had been Huckley and the Source chasing her. Now it was the dogs, their snarling so close that she expected the pain of the first bite to come at any second.

This is it. I'm not going to make it.

No sooner did she have the thought than the ground fell away from beneath her feet and she found herself tumbling down a steep decline. The dogs were close enough that she heard them yelp, caught off guard the same way she was. Sarah wrapped her arms around her head to protect herself as she rolled uncontrollably down the hill.

After what seemed an endless fall, she smacked into something solid. She opened her eyes and saw a smooth white wall. Not a single blemish on it, even though the storm seemed even more intense here. She looked up and the wall disappeared into the storm above her. In a fleeting break in the debris cloud, she thought she caught a glimpse of it extending up hundreds of feet into the air.

But of more interest to her was the door in the wall just to her left. Made of the same white material, it had a seam that outlined the edges of the door and, strangely enough, a matching shiny brass knocker and doorknob.

The three dark shapes of the dogs smashed into the wall farther down the wall to her right. They appeared disoriented, but only for a moment. They clambered back onto their feet, sought her out, and then keyed on her position. They spread out next to one another and walked deliberately toward her, as if taking care not to let her get away again.

Sarah took the few steps to the door and tried the knob. Locked. But somehow she'd known it would be. She lifted the doorknocker, slammed it down, and it boomed like thunder. She did it again and again. Harder each time, glancing over her shoulder at the approaching dogs.

"Please," she screamed. "Let me in. I won't hurt you. Please let me in."

She hammered the knocker again, this time so hard that it broke off in her hand. It didn't stop her. She clutched it and used it to beat on the door.

"Please, they're going to kill me," she begged. "Let me in."

The dogs were so close she could smell the odor of rot and decay on them. Another second or two and it would all be over.

She turned to face her death. The nearest dog jumped, its front paws stretched out and its mouth wide open. Sarah braced herself, willing with everything she had inside of her to make it stop. But her power didn't work in this place. All that was left for her to do was die.

"NO!" came a voice behind her. Then a hand grabbed the collar of her shirt and dragged her backward.

She passed through the door, still facing the pouncing dog, feeling the breeze from its massive claw as it swiped past her face, missing by only an inch. Then the door slammed shut and everything went quiet. The screaming stopped. The wind was gone. Sarah expected a heavy thump on the door behind her as the dogs tried to pursue her, but nothing came.

She realized her eyes were squeezed shut. Slowly, she opened them, already guessing what she would see there.

Chapter 61

Jack struggled against the handcuffs as he walked. One of Mama D's thugs jammed the business end of his gun into his ribs to hurry him along. He cast a sidelong look at Lonetree. The SEAL was stone-faced and unreadable as always. Jack just hoped there was a plan cooking in the man's head because based on his own evaluation, things seemed hopeless. Lauren let out a small cry next to him.

"Sarah!" she screamed and ran forward.

One of their escorts grabbed her by the hair and jerked her backward. Jack lowered his shoulder and rammed the man in the chest, then rocked his head back and caught the man under the chin. He heard the satisfying crunch of shattered teeth. But the victory was a small one. The other guard rewarded him by slamming the butt of his gun between his shoulder blades. Jack fell to the ground, sputtering for air.

When he looked up, he saw what had caused Lauren to cry out. Sarah stood next to Mama D, her leg soaked with blood. But it was what she was doing that made his stomach turn over on itself. Bile rose in his throat and he thought he might scream, only no sound would come from his throat. All he could do was stare, mesmerized by the sheer horror at what he saw.

Mama D stood with her right arm outstretched, the soft, white skin of her forearm nearly translucent in the glow of the fires. Sarah stood next to her, most of her weight on her uninjured leg. She held Mama D's arm in front of her, fingers curled into claws that gripped the flesh. Sarah's mouth was pressed to Mama D's wrist, suckling like a hungry baby at its mother's breast.

Mama D grimaced, appearing to be simultaneously in ecstasy and in pain. Sarah raised her head and blood dripped out of the corners of her mouth. She looked right at Jack and a wicked grin spread across her face, showcasing bloodstained teeth. Her eyes reflected the dancing light of the bonfires and regarded him with such hatred that Jack felt the hair on his neck stand on end, a primordial response to a primitive evil.

It was as Lonetree suspected all along. There was something else inside of his little girl.

No, not something else.

Some*one* else.

He knew those eyes after so many hundreds of nightmares.

It was the shaman.

Chapter 62

The room was circular, perhaps forty feet in diameter. It was well lit, although Sarah couldn't see any source of light. There were no lamps or wall sconces. And there could be nothing from above them because there was no ceiling. The slick, white walls soared into the sky over them as far as she could see, lit by the strange light all the way up so that the immense height gave her a sense of vertigo.

She looked back down and noticed the floor was the same material as the walls. In fact, it was hard to determine where the floor ended and the walls began. Other than the boy, there was nothing else in the room.

The boy. Sarah stared at him, trying to reconcile him being locked in this room with the storm raging outside.

But as she studied the steel-grey eyes that searched her face as if she were an alien being, as she took in his chin line, the full lips, the scattering of freckles across his nose and cheeks, she realized that his presence made sense. With Huckley's voice dominating the world on the other side of the door, this place was a refuge for the body's true owner. The boy standing in front of her was a prisoner in his own mind.

"Hello, Pesh," she said.

The boy withdrew from her and shuddered. "Don't call me that."

She felt a pang of sadness for the boy. His reaction had been so visceral, like she'd slapped him with the name. "I'm sorry," she said. "What should I call you?"

"Why are you here, Sarah? How *can* you be here?" he demanded.

Sarah rocked back. "How do you know…" her voice trailed off as the boy stared at her. She stood slowly, taking note of the boy's physical appearance. She understood now that everything she saw in this place was a manifestation from either her mind or his. So every inch of his appearance told a story.

She saw him as he saw himself in his mind's eye. He wore weathered boot-cut jeans, a faded vintage Rolling Stones t-shirt, and Converse sneakers. His hair was long enough that he had to toss it to the side with a flip of his head. He could have walked the halls in her high school and fit right in. All of these cues told her that although Pesh, this real Pesh, was hidden away in this shelter, he was somehow still connected to the outside world.

"I came to find you," she said, aware that it wasn't the entire truth.

The boy shook his head. "Lying doesn't work here," he said. "Even half-lies."

Sarah thought about her connection to Lonetree and how lying had been impossible between them. It made sense that in his own mind, even this small, cordoned-off section, Pesh could sense a lie when it was thrown at him.

"I came here to escape," Sarah amended.

"Ha," he barked. "Who escapes *into* a prison?"

"Is that what this place is?" she asked. "A prison?"

He ignored the question. "What were you escaping from?" he asked.

"Since you already know my name, I think you already know the answer to that, don't you?"

He didn't reply. Instead, his brow furrowed and his eyes turned dark.

"You do," Sarah said. "Or at least some of it." She had to tread carefully here. Pesh's feelings toward his mother were a wild card. Even though the Pesh in the real world was a blood-craving creature, Sarah had counted on the boy's mind to be that of a simpleton, something she could easily dominate and take over. She had miscalculated on two scores.

First, she'd underestimated just how terrible the torment in his mind really was. She had no doubt that if she had been subjected to it for even a few more seconds that she would have been lost in it forever. The dog-creatures that had chased her were simply manifestations of the power the boy's insanity had to tear her apart. Secondly, she had never guessed that the real person might be buried somewhere safe inside the maelstrom. And now she had only guesses and intuition as to how he would react to her.

"My mother," the boy said. "You're running from my mother."

"I'm running from her and you're hiding from her," Sarah replied, careful that no tone of judgment entered her voice.

Pesh turned red-faced and Sarah thought it was anger, but it wasn't. She realized it was embarrassment. Right in front of her, the boy's body shrank, his face thinned and his hair shortened into spiky tufts. Ten years of age melted away and for a few seconds, the boy in front of her was a five-year-old kid, nervously wringing his hands. Then the teenager was back.

Sarah recalled that what she was seeing was how Pesh saw himself. She felt a spur of hope that the mention of his mother's name caused that nervous inner child to appear. Perhaps there was a chance here yet.

"What is this place?" Sarah asked, wanting to move away from talking about his mother until she got a better sense of him. "How long have you been here?"

Pesh looked around the barren room as if just now seeing it for the first time. "Sorry. Here," he said. "Is this better?"

Instantly, the room was transformed into an outdoor garden bursting with flowers, the air buzzing with all manner of insects and a creek tumbling over smooth rocks. The floor was now lush, thick grass. In the middle of it all was a picnic table made of rough-cut wood set against a row of apple trees bursting with perfect fruit. A tall, glass pitcher of lemonade and ice sat in the center of the table, beads of condensation covering the glass surface. At the table was a single chair, and one empty glass.

"Do you like it?" he asked.

Sarah recognized the place. It was the table where she had sat with Ichote. Only instead of the dying days of fall, it was in the full bloom of spring.

"It's rude to go into someone's mind without their permission," she snapped.

The garden grew dark, as if a thundercloud had crossed in front of the sun. A cold wind kicked up. The leaves turned brown and lifeless as the fruit browned with decay.

"I didn't…I just wanted…" the boy mumbled.

"It's okay," Sarah said, glancing around at the worsening weather. "I like this place. It was a good choice."

Pesh smiled and the sun reappeared, the cold wind replaced with a gentle breeze that smelled of jasmine and sage. The trees returned to their splendor.

"You can make this place anything you want?" Sarah asked.

Pesh walked toward the table, obviously pleased that she was impressed with his power. She followed him. "We're in my mind, after all. It's not much different than learning to control a dream."

They got to the table and there was only one chair and one glass. "Sorry," he said, embarrassed. "I'm not used to having company." A second later there was a second one of each. "Are you thirsty?"

She was actually, parched as if she'd walked through the desert for days before reaching this place. But it didn't make any sense. Her body wasn't with her mind. It was still out there, in the open field next to the crumbling farmhouse. Shot and bruised and likely completely taken over by the shaman by now.

335

She felt the importance of remembering that her body was not in this place, that if she wasn't careful, she would get comfortable here and reality would just drift away. How easy would it be? She replaced the now empty glass of lemonade on the table, her thirst satisfied even though she didn't remember picking the glass up.

"How long have you been in here?" Sarah asked, hating the small tremble in her voice.

Pesh shrugged. "How long has anyone been in their own head?"

"You know what I mean. In this room."

Pesh fell into the chair and slumped there. He looked back and forth across the garden, and then finally at Sarah. "I know all about you," he said. "You're the one my mother thinks will finally cure me. Calm the storm out on the other side of the door. Is she right? Can you do that?"

Sarah felt her heart skip a beat as missing pieces of understanding clicked into place. Mama D had sought her out to save her son. Her mania to consume the fire of others was of course narcissistic self-preservation, but also a mother willing to do anything to save her child. All the power she consumed was meant for Pesh, a vain attempt to transform him into a human being instead of the grunting animal Sarah had seen chained and muzzled by Mama D's side.

But the force she had sensed inside of her before she jumped into Pesh's head had no intention of sharing Sarah with Mama D. It meant to possess her only for itself.

Even though a small part of the shaman had been festering inside of her, buried deep in her fire, the creature had waited until now to grow strong enough to consume the rest of her, to possess and feed off of her. Suddenly she realized the shaman hadn't been waiting to get stronger for this day, he'd been waiting for her to get stronger so her powers could transform him. Still, she didn't feel capable of fighting the ancient powers swirling around her.

"Well?" Pesh asked. "Can you?"

"I don't know," Sarah said. "But I think if I could have, I would have been able to save myself in the storm out there."

Disappointment registered on his face, but there was something else there too. Relief?

"How is it that Nate Huckley's voice is in your head?" Sarah asked.

This new direction surprised the boy, but he simply nodded. "I forgot you knew him." He looked up at her quickly. "It's not that I saw him in your memory. I won't look again without permission. I promise."

Sarah smiled softly, finding something sweet and simple about the boy. "Thank you."

"Mama told me how you were in the caves with him. With Huckley."

Sarah barked out a laugh that was too loud. "That makes it sound like we were having a nice picnic together. He abducted me and was going to feed me to a monster down there. He was pure evil and I was happy to see him die."

"I agree with you," the boy said softly. "Even though he was my father."

Sarah's mind whirled again, finding it hard to keep up with the changes she was being forced to digest. Nate Huckley and Mama D. What were the chances? But that was the wrong way of thinking about it and she knew it.

There was no coincidence here. Mama D was in her life because of Huckley. It wasn't chance, it was cause and effect. Even from the grave, Huckley had found her.

"He's the storm out there, not my mother," Pesh whispered. "He's why I'm in here."

"But why can't you control it, the way you do in here?" Sarah asked.

Pesh shook his head. "He's too strong. Too terrible. When my mother...feeds me," Sarah noticed he seemed to choke on the word, "Huckley takes the fire and just gets stronger. He makes me into the creature you saw out there in the real world."

Acting on an impulse she didn't quite understand, Sarah reached out and grasped the boy's hand. He froze at her touch and then tried to pull away, but she wouldn't let him.

"No," she said, leveling her eyes at him. "This is who you are. Right here. And it's time you remember that. It's time you use that."

"Use it to do what?" Pesh asked.

"I think you already know," Sarah replied, squeezing his hand tighter. "In fact, I know you do."

Chapter 63

"What if it doesn't work?" Pesh worried. "If I leave, I might never get back in here. No, I know I won't. If I leave, I'll die."

Sarah pointed to the garden around them. "But this place isn't real," she said. "It's no better than a dream."

"And what's so great out in the real world that I'm missing?" Pesh asked. "I see through my eyes still. I know what's there." He made a casual gesture and the world around them blinked out of existence, replaced immediately with a busy Manhattan street, perfectly replicated with cars and crowds, but no sound. Another flick of the hand and they were on a beach in California, watching breakers roll onto the sand, the sun nearing the horizon in the distance. "In here, I can have it all at my command."

Sarah thought back to the look she spotted when she told him she didn't think she could stop the storm raging in his mind. It was relief. "You don't want to leave," Sarah said.

Pesh raised his chin and stared her down. "No. I don't think I do."

She processed this information, thinking it through, trying to work out how to reach him. As she looked out over the false Pacific Ocean stretching in front of her, smelling the salt in the air, feeling the breeze caress her skin, she wondered why she cared to convince him of anything. Why couldn't she just stay here with him and forget the outside world altogether? Maybe his question bore all the truth they needed: what was so great out in the real world that they were missing here?

She looked up and the sun was halfway below the horizon. It was as if time had passed without her notice, just like when she had taken a drink of the lemonade. A warning bell rang in her brain and she knew that she could get lost in here if she wasn't careful.

"We could stay here," Pesh said. "It's not that bad, you know."

She looked up and he was holding her hand. They stood on the edge of the Grand Canyon, the sun rising in the east, turning the rocks around them afire. She breathed in the fake air and, as she did, willed away her awareness of its falseness. It was pure and real. It was perfect.

Sarah, you can't stay here, said a voice. It was a boy. Quiet and sad. *It's not finished. You promised you would see it through to the end. It's not finished. It's gotten worse.*

Sarah drew in a sharp breath and it felt like ice filling her lungs. She knew the voice. Charlie Winters.

"Who is that?" Pesh called out. The Grand Canyon blinked out of existence and they were back in the circular room with smooth white walls.

"Charlie," she called out. "Where are you?"

"Here," the voice said to their left. "Here." This time to their right. "Here, here, here," the voice bounced around like an echo. Only it wasn't an echo at all, but the voice coming at them from every direction. "I'm everywhere. *We* are everywhere."

A cacophony of voices rose up like a wave and crashed over them. Dozens and then hundreds. Perhaps thousands, but it was impossible to know. That much noise should have deafened them but it didn't. It simply passed through Sarah and Pesh like rushing water through a sieve.

Sarah felt every voice pass through her and she knew who they were. Each of them an individual, not a complete being, just a sliver of the original. Like a spark rocketed out from a fire to drift up into the sky. And just as a spark retained its power to scorch and burn, so too did these fragments of souls still possess their power to sear themselves to her mind.

She felt each death. Their terror. Pain. Suffering. Humiliation. All at the hands of Mama D and her minions.

When the final voice passed through her, Sarah fell to the floor, hands wrapped around her stomach, sobbing.

Slowly, she was able to regain her mental balance and calm herself. When she did, she turned to see Pesh kneeling on the ground next to her. At first glance, she thought he might be praying. But then she noticed his white-knuckled fists on the ground in front of him. This was no prayer. This was the birth of resolve.

He turned and looked at her. "There were so many."

She nodded. "You said before that your mother was trying to cure you. These fragments of souls are what she was feeding you."

"I didn't drink from her," he said. "It was Huckley. And now these souls are trapped here."

"Just like you," Sarah said.

"But my body still exists. It's different for them. Their souls have been shredded, the remnants spread all over the place. They can never have peace."

Tears rolled down his cheeks, each sparkling like a diamond. Sarah marveled at them, knowing they were manifestations of his mind and all the more beautiful because of that fact.

"If we don't stop them," Sarah said, "they'll keep killing. More than we can imagine."

Pesh wiped his tears away. He looked up at the cylinder that extended up into the sky above them, the smooth walls stretching out to eternity.

"Will you help us?" he called.

"Yes, we will," came back the chorus of souls, amalgamating into a unified voice.

And then a single voice rang out over them all. Sarah recognized Charlie Winters. "This Huckley is powerful. He's not part of a soul. He's burned into your genetics. Burrowed deep into every cell. He will fight to survive. And part of Mama D is here too, in the background. I don't know how we can defeat them both."

Sarah noticed Pesh tense. She saw the years melt off his face the way they had when she first arrived in the room and mentioned his mother. It was fear turning him back into how he now pictured himself, defenseless and weak.

"You never told me your name," Sarah said. "When I first got here, you told me not to call you Pesh. Is your name Nate Huckley?" He shook his head. "Do you have the same name as your mother?"

"No," he said, his body image returning to normal. He smiled, understanding her point. "My name is Daniel and I'm not my parents. I'm me."

"You're damn right," Sarah said. "Now, if you don't mind, Daniel, I'd like to get the hell out of this room and back into my own body before it's too late."

Chapter 64

Mama D fought down her panic, certain the shaman would feel it through her blood if she didn't control it. She eyed her sword on the ground next to her, careful not to allow a fantasy of using it to enter her mind. How was it possible that he was inside the girl already? How had she not sensed it?

Even with these questions, other parts of the puzzle made sense now. The shaman had known the Tremonts' every move. Known what the girl's parents were doing every step of the way. Anything the girl knew, the shaman had known. The spy among the Tremonts had been Sarah Tremont herself.

But what of the presence she felt out here above the collapsed caves? What of the blood that was sucked into the ground? She sensed an ancient force there too.

"I am here and I am there, witch," the shaman said through Sarah, the voice coming out impossibly deep, resonant with layers of low tones and hissing. "In time, I will be everywhere."

"We had an agreement," Mama D said, trying to hold her voice steady. "I will hold you to your part of the bargain."

The shaman inside Sarah's body laughed, the deep, bass tones unnerving coming from the little girl. Mama D saw a flash of movement as Jack and Lauren both made a vain attempt to run to their daughter but Mama D's men slammed them back to the ground.

"Things have changed," the shaman said. "The girl has left and taken what I need with her." Sarah's body turned toward Pesh, still hunched over in his odd, simian posture, his face obscured by the helmet and facemask. The shaman nodded toward the boy. "But she didn't go far."

Mama D froze. She looked back and forth between Pesh and Sarah's body animated by the shaman. "What do you mean, she left? That's not possible," Mama D said.

"It's no matter," the shaman said. "I can sense her in the boy. I'll rip him apart and pull her out of his carcass."

Mama D grabbed her sword and stepped in front of Pesh, blocking the shaman. "Wait, we can get her back out. You don't have to hurt him." She tried to push into the presence in the girl's mind, probing to see if she could exert control over it.

The shaman bared Sarah's teeth and hissed, more animal than human. Mama D cried out as what felt like a thousand nails were driven into her mind. Her muscles betrayed her and she threw her sword to the ground as she grabbed the sides of her head, whimpering.

"I can destroy you with a single thought, woman," said the shaman. "Try me again and you'll see the truth of that."

Just then, Pesh fell to the ground, his body spasming. Bizarre, guttural sounds came from his throat, like he was choking and trying to speak at the same time. His eyes rolled up and the lids fluttered to reveal only the whites of his eyes.

Mama D's first thought was that the shaman was doing exactly as he'd threatened and was tearing Pesh apart to pry the girl out. But with a look, she saw that it wasn't the shaman. She could see it reflected on Sarah's face; the shaman was as confused as she was.

Better than that, she realized the shaman looked afraid.

As Mama D turned back to her Pesh writhing and bucking on the ground, she wondered at the revelation and tried to figure out how to use it to her advantage.

Chapter 65

"Come on, father," shouted Daniel. "Come here and try your best with me."

Sarah watched in horror as Daniel stood on an outcropping of black rock jutting out over a chasm so deep that the bottom couldn't be seen. His hands were raised over his head, clenched into fists. Feet spread apart to brace against the hurricane-strength wind raging around him.

"Daniel, no," Sarah cried. "Not like this."

But it was no use. He was lost in his anger and his grief. In his self-pity and his hate. There was no reaching him now. It would have to play out.

How quickly their plan had fallen apart. The second they opened the door and stepped outside the room, the storm was upon them. Only this time, there was more than wind and debris. There was both cold rain and drops of fire that burned and singed with each touch.

Within seconds, the storm had separated them. Sarah had called out for him, tried to reach his mind, but he was lost to her. She ran frantically through the storm until the earthquake came. Massive, jolting movements of the ground that threw her down, scraping her elbows and knees.

As she winced at the pain, she forced herself to remember this place wasn't real. But the truth of that didn't lessen the pain. The real truth was that her mind, her soul, whatever label was placed on the thing she had transported from her body into this one, was being battered and injured. The blood trickling from her aching knee may not have been real, but the damage being done to her psychic core was.

She noticed the ground beneath her was black rock. As it shook from the earthquake, fissures opened up, venting bursts of steam. She tried to stand, but as she did, the ground all around her fell away into a dark chasm. She tumbled forward and fell headlong into the dark canyon.

Can this be it? she asked herself in a more reasonable tone than she expected at the moment of her death. *Can this be all there is for me to do?*

Down, down, she fell, the rock walls closing in around her.

Then, with a screaming sound, the voices of the murdered souls flew up out of the cavern beneath her like a swarm of birds. She felt them as a physical thing, a force that first slowed her, held her, and then carried her up and out of the chasm.

"Are you all right?" Charlie Winters asked urgently in her ear.

"I lost Pesh…I mean, Daniel," she said, correcting herself.

"Over there," Charlie said.

The swarm jerked to the right and then lowered her to the rock ground. That's when she saw Daniel standing on the finger of rock over the edge of a different chasm as the world around him fell apart. All except the rock on which he stood.

And that's when she understood. Daniel was the one destroying the world around them.

"Where are you, Huckley?" Daniel shouted. "Come and face me."

From deep in the chasm there came a mewling howl. A red glow appeared, growing in brightness as Sarah watched. A wall of fire raced up the rock walls and she felt the heat on her face. She crawled backward just as an explosion jettisoned out of the pit, up into the air, forming a wall of flames along the rock edge.

"Daniel!" Sarah screamed.

He stood only inches from the wall of flame. Not touching it, but not being moved by it either. She looked up and saw the wall of fire cresting over like a wave hundreds of feet in the air above them. There, in that crest, she saw Huckley's face take form, grinning at them. This was the splinter of Huckley's soul he'd embedded into his son's body, enough to control him and turn him insane. Powerful enough to exile him to a fortress in his own mind.

That was it. In a flash of inspiration, Sarah knew what they had to do.

"Charlie, we need your help." She quickly told

him what she needed the murdered souls to do.

Instantly, half the swarm flew to Daniel and the other half lifted her from the ground and carried her back to the door of Daniel's fortress. She twisted around and saw Daniel fighting off the voices trying to help him, but there were too many of them and he was carried toward her. Impossibly, it looked like her plan was going to work.

But the wave descended toward them, faster than the voices could carry them. They weren't going to make it.

"Remember your promise," Charlie whispered in her ear. "Stop them all."

Before she could reply, he was gone, leading part of the swarm of voices up to the crashing wave. Thousands of them flew into the flames, each emitting a flash as it hit, winking out of existence. And it worked. The wall of fire slowed momentarily as the souls collided against it, giving her and Daniel enough time to reach the door to the room.

"What are you doing?" Daniel shouted. "Let me fight him."

"No, the only way to destroy him is if you destroy yourself," Sarah said. "And that would destroy any chance we have of stopping the others." She pushed him into the room. "I have a plan. Just trust me."

He hesitated, but far above them, a massive rendering of Huckley's head formed in the flames, opened its mouth, and roared at them in frustration. Daniel ran through the door back into the room. Sarah followed and pulled the door closed behind her.

Only it didn't slam shut. A piece of debris from the storm prevented it from closing.

"The door!" Daniel yelled.

Sarah ran toward it but the second she did, it banged all the way open with extraordinary force. She stumbled backward into Daniel as the sound of the raging storm pushed its way into the room.

Then, seconds later, a figure appeared. A man, appearing to be flesh and blood, with pale skin and thin, red lips and blond hair combed back flat against his scalp. Sarah knew him at once.

Nate Huckley.

"Hello, Sarah," Huckley said, licking his lips. "Look at you. All grown up. How's your dad?"

Sarah stood her ground even though every instinct she possessed screamed in terror. Daniel reached down and took her hand in his. Huckley noticed. He nodded appreciatively.

"That's my boy," he said, shouting the last word and grinding the air with his hips. His body image flickered as he paced back and forth in front of the door, unstable. Sarah noticed his face sag unnaturally, like it was made of wax that was too hot to hold its form. It was obviously hard for him to maintain the body. He reminded Sarah of a drug addict, pacing, eyes darting, sweating.

No wonder there's a storm outside these walls, Sarah thought. *He's barely holding himself together.*

"This is it? This is where you've been hiding out all this time?" He shook his head.

"Yeah, this is the prison you put me in," Daniel said.

Huckley smiled, his head jerking with a nervous tic. "But the good news is that she's here now. To set us free. Isn't that right?"

"You're half right," Sarah said.

351

Huckley froze, not understanding her meaning but sensing her confidence. Sarah sent him a strong mental image of her grabbing the piece of debris on the way through the door and jamming it into place.

The open door was a trap.

Huckley spun around. The door was gone, replaced with smooth white walls. By the time he looked back, Sarah and Daniel were already standing in front of the new door leading out of the room.

"You're part of me," Daniel said, "but not a part I'll ever let out again. You can rot in here."

Huckley's body shimmered and lost form. Small jets of flame shot out from under his skin. His mouth gaped open, the jaw unhinged, and a scream filled the air. It hit Sarah and Daniel, nearly blowing them off their feet. Quickly, they jumped through the open door and slammed it shut behind them, disappearing back into the smooth wall.

A massive thumping sound came from inside the room. Then the faintest sound of wailing and thrashing, as if from far away. And finally, silence.

"Look," Sarah said.

They turned. The landscape stretched out in front of them. It was a forest, alive, green, vibrant. Blue sky visible between the trees. The air smelled of fresh rain. Birdsong filtered down to them from the branches above.

"You're free," she said.

Daniel looked back at the walls behind him. It was an odd mix of triumph and loss. She realized he'd not known anything except the room. He was free but he'd lost the only home he knew.

"But it's not over, is it?" he said.

"I need your help," Sarah said.

Daniel nodded. "I won't let her hurt you."

Sarah met his eyes. "She's not the only one we have to worry about."

Chapter 66

Jack knew he had to kill Sarah. It was the second time in his life that he'd faced the terrible choice to let his daughter suffer or to end her pain.

Everyone else was focused on the bizarre boy they called Pesh. Both Mama D and the shaman in Sarah's body leaned over the boy. Jack couldn't hear what they were saying but it was clearly an argument. The men guarding them shifted their eyes nervously, obviously uncomfortable with the deteriorating situation.

Lauren had grown still next to him once the boy began having seizures on the ground in front of them, sensing there might be opportunity in all the confusion. He wondered if she was thinking of ways to kill their daughter too.

He chanced a look over to Lonetree who was already staring at him. The man nodded toward Sarah, the offer clear. If Jack wanted, Lonetree would take the burden from him. Do the horrific deed that needed to be done. Jack shook his answer. He had to be the one to do it. Lonetree answered with a barely perceptible nod.

A cry went up over where the boy was. Jack looked over on instinct. The boy was on his knees, then standing up, all of the strange posture gone.

A flash of movement to Jack's right drew his attention back away from the boy. Lonetree and Sorenson were on their feet, two of the guards already incapacitated. The third guard, the leader, swung his gun toward them, but Lauren launched herself upward and threw a double handful of dirt at the man's eyes. He blocked most of it, but the split second was enough for Lonetree to kick out the man's legs and get behind him to use his handcuffs as a garrote. With a violent twist, he snapped the man's neck.

The gun lay on the ground. Jack grabbed it. The thing felt cold and heavy in his hands. He swung it around and acquired Sarah, Mama D, and the boy in the sight.

Mama D saw him at the last second and threw herself in front of the boy. It strangely registered in Jack's mind as a valiant gesture, but it didn't stop him from pulling the trigger. The ground in front of her spit up dirt and rock, and he quickly adjusted up until her body jerked back with a satisfying rhythm as the bullets tore through her flesh.

The boy was on the ground, covered by his mother's body, but Jack didn't think of him as the real threat.

That was the shaman. Inside his little girl's body.

Everything seemed to slow down as he completed the arc around so the gun lined up on Sarah.

There has to be another way.

The thought was there and then gone. He knew better. He could see the devil inside her. He'd watched it suck the blood from Mama D's arm. No, Sarah was gone. And if he didn't do this thing, then it would use her body

355

to do terrible, unspeakable things. He knew this. But still he hesitated.

Then Sarah turned to him. The same eyes he'd looked into every day since her birth, the ones he'd seen fill with awe of him when she was small, with tears from playground scratches, with puzzlement as she grew and thought about the strangeness of life, those eyes which had always reflected back love now looked at him with unbridled hate.

"Jack, now!" Lonetree called beside him.

The shaman raised a hand toward Jack and he felt pressure around his forearms. The pressure turned to pain and the gun twisted in his hands, away from Sarah's body. He struggled against the force, knowing that if he didn't see this through, his daughter would be lost inside this monster forever.

With a yell, he heaved against the invisible force, staring the shaman down as he did.

Sarah's bloodstained face twisted into a maniacal grin, her hand now extended in front of her as a claw.

Then the expression changed. The grin disappeared, replaced with a look of shock, as if someone had shot the body from behind.

The hand dropped back to her side and the force on Jack's arms disappeared.

The gun swung back in line with Sarah's body and his finger was already pulling the trigger.

In the split second before the first bullet hit her body, Jack saw something that would haunt him the rest of his life.

The hate was gone from the eyes.

There was only acceptance and love.

Somehow, his little girl was back.

His brain screamed for the bullets to stop, but of course it was too late.

Bursts of red blossomed on her chest. The bullets picked her small frame off the ground and sent her flying backward to the ground.

Jack held the gun limply, smoke swirling from the barrel. He stared, not believing what he'd done.

For a second, the others stood in silence around him. He couldn't tell if it was shock from it being over, or if they'd seen the same thing he had. Maybe he imagined it. His mind playing the cruelest of tricks on him.

"Sarah!" Lauren screamed next to him. She ran to their daughter. He wanted to go with her, but he was frozen. He felt Lonetree reach out and take the gun slowly from his hands. Jack looked at him, questioning.

"Did you…I think I saw…" Jack said.

Lonetree shook his head. "I don't know."

The non-answer was all the answer he needed. He looked over at Sorenson, who looked down at the ground.

"If you hadn't done it, I would have," Lonetree said. "It would have been the same result."

But you might have stopped in time, he thought.

Then the reality crashed over him.

"Oh my God," he whispered. "It was her. She was back."

He staggered forward, found his footing, and ran to where Lauren sat next to Sarah on the ground, cradling their girl in her arms.

There was blood everywhere. Seeping through ragged bullet holes. Bubbling from punctured lungs. Every inch of her skin and clothing was dark and wet.

But, somehow, she was alive.

"Shh…baby," Lauren whispered. "Just look at me.

357

It's okay."

Sarah blinked away tears, opened and closed her mouth as if to speak. Jack, sobbing, leaned forward and kissed her forehead. "I'm sorry. I'm sorry," he mumbled, feeling the ridiculous inadequacy of the words.

Sarah turned his direction and smiled. Actually smiled at him.

"Hi…Daddy…" she whispered.

Jack broke down, pulling her into his arms, tears streaming down his face. Then he felt her body stiffen against him. Her words came out cold.

"It…it's…" Blood bubbled out of her mouth. "…over…"

A coughing fit interrupted her and Sarah writhed with pain.

"Yes, it's over now," Jack whispered.

He noticed Lauren digging through her pockets, a desperate look on her face. He assumed she was looking for a phone, some way to call for help. But they both knew it was useless. There was too much blood. The ground was covered with it.

And that's when he noticed it. The soil was alive, drinking in the blood as fast as it poured from Sarah's body.

Sarah spoke again.

"No…I said…it…it's…*not*…over…" she rasped.

Chapter 67

A stiff wind blew across the open field, whipping the bonfires higher. The hiss and pop of the wood filled the air. But beneath it was a low rumble, like a rush of floodwater gathering speed.

Lonetree stood next to Jack. "What is it?" he asked.

Jack shook his head. "I don't know." Lauren took his position holding Sarah and he stood, spinning around. The sound seemed to come from every direction. He registered that Lauren was pouring something into Sarah's mouth and hoped she had found some kind of pain medication for her. He was about to kneel back down to help her when Sorenson cried out.

"There," Sorenson said, pointing toward the pile of timbers that was once the barn that guarded the

359

passage down to the caves.

Jack saw it too. The pile of debris moved. Up in the air and then settling back. Up more violently, spilling wood beams from the pile, and then back down.

Something was underneath it, trying to get out.

Then, in an explosion of dirt, rock, and barn wood, a shape jettisoned up into the night. A dark shadow, thick and tall, jumped through the air toward them and landed in the clearing, now fully illuminated by the fires. All of them recoiled at the sight of a creature so grotesque that it awakened the most primordial instincts in them.

It possessed a humanoid shape, but its size made it clear this was no man. Over eight feet tall, it was packed with bulging muscles and thick tendons, all clearly visible because there was no skin. In fact, on closer look, there was no flesh.

The creature instead was made of every crawling and slithering thing imaginable from the rock and dirt grave from which it had sprung. Thousands of black, shiny beetles, slick worms, spiders, centipedes, slugs. There were rats and opossum. Bats that crawled blindly across the creature's chest. Snakes wrapped themselves throughout. The body was a living, slithering, crawling thing that simultaneously seemed to be part of nature and yet an abomination, in violation of every one of nature's rules.

The head held the greatest horror of all. It was massive, even for the size of the creature. And it had to be because, formed and shaped by densely packed insects, were not one but two faces, side-by-side.

The shaman and Nate Huckley.

Lonetree acted first. He raised the gun he'd taken from Jack and opened fire. Sorenson, who had grabbed a gun from one of the other guards, did the same. They moved with calm efficiency, as if their SEAL training had regularly included facing down supernatural creatures.

Their aim rang true. Chunks of the beast exploded with each hit, splattering bug juice and blood. But the other insects simply filled gaps, repairing the damage as fast as Lonetree and Sorenson could mete it out.

As if they were one mind, they shifted their fire to the creature's faces. The same result. A blistering salvo ripped open a massive gash in the head that closed seconds later with other slithering creatures.

Lonetree ran out of ammo first, and then Sorenson. Within seconds, the creature looked totally unblemished by the one-sided firefight. Only this time, when the head reformed, there was only one face. An old man with a weathered face, his mouth twisted in pain.

Lonetree dropped his gun and took a step back. "Old Swede," he mumbled.

Jack watched Lonetree continue to step back from the creature as Old Swede's face writhed in agony. He didn't know what the man meant to Lonetree, but he knew it meant the creature could get into their heads.

As if in answer to the thought, Old Swede disappeared and was replaced with the face of a young girl, only there was something wrong with it. The face was cut and dented, smashed inward. And Jack knew who it was. Melissa Rodriguez, the little girl he'd run over with his car in California. The one who had first haunted his nightmares and then come back to forgive him and save him from Huckley and the shaman the last time.

Still, the creature's message was clear. They were

all killers. There was no innocence among them.

Except for Sarah, he thought. *She's an innocent.*

The creature's face swirled and became Mitzy Berlin's. And then a woman he didn't recognize, mouth open in a silent, terrifying scream. He thought that it must be Mitzy Berlin's mother. The one Lauren told him about.

"But that was you," Jack yelled at the creature. "The evil you planted in her that night in the cave. It wasn't her."

The two faces returned, Huckley and the shaman. Huckley's face looked chastised and withdrawn. It was the shaman who spoke.

"Enough of this game," the shaman roared. "These people mean nothing. I must have the girl's fire before it goes out."

The creature strode to where Sarah still lay in her mother's arms. Lonetree and Sorenson charged at the figure and landed a few quick blows before being tossed to the side by the creature's massive arms.

Jack planted his feet and took a position in front of Sarah and Lauren. He looked around, desperate for a weapon of any kind, and found one in the unlikeliest of places.

Chapter 68

J ack saw the boy push the weight of Mama D's body off of him, shaking his head like he was trying to get his bearings. A streak of blood streamed from a gash above his eye. He let out a cry when he saw Sarah cradled in Lauren's arms. He stumbled toward her but the creature roared and stopped him in his tracks. Slowly, the kid bent down, picked up Mama D's sword, then walked over to take up a position next to Jack.

With the helmet gone and the odd, slouching posture replaced by an upright, confident stance, Jack saw that the kid was older than he'd thought. Probably fifteen or sixteen. Jack sized up whether he was a threat or not.

"I'm Daniel," the kid stated simply.

Jack nodded as if that explained everything and turned back to face the creature. If the kid wanted to make a stand, it was fine with him. Not that he thought it would do much good.

The creature came to a stop in front of Jack and Daniel. Huckley's face turned toward Daniel, screwing into a disgusted look.

"What are you doing?" Huckley asked. "You should be with us. If not me, then for your mother."

Jack eyed the boy's sword, seeing that he gripped it with white knuckles. The boy's face strained with effort as if he were lifting an enormous weight. Jack wondered what kind of mental pressure the creature was applying on the boy's mind.

"Yes," Huckley whispered. "That's right. Kill him for me. Do it and you can join us."

"And do what?" Daniel asked. "Kill more children? Drink their blood so I can live longer?"

"We won't only live," roared the shaman. "We will rule. Do as he says. Kill this man and show your worth. Or die along with him."

Jack watched as Daniel fought the pressure, sweat beading on his forehead from concentration. Jack wondered why it mattered to him what this kid decided. No matter what, he didn't see a way out. He'd already accepted that Becky must already be dead. The rest of them would all surely die at the creature's hands. So what did it matter?

Maybe it was that he'd thought the boy had taken a stand for Sarah. That there was good left in the world. Part of him wanted in his last breath to know that good had won a small victory over evil. That not all humans were willing to go to the devil's bargaining table with their soul to trade.

Daniel raised the sword and pointed it at Jack's throat. Jack felt the small hope crumble away. He braced for the pain, consoling himself in his faith that he would soon see Lauren, Becky, and Sarah on the other side.

But the pain didn't come. Seconds stretched out. He felt the boy twist in place to look behind them. He was checking on Sarah.

No, he was buying time.

The shaman reached the same realization. "Fool. He's just stalling for the girl. She's awake. End this."

Jack heard the boy whisper, "To hell with you, to hell with me. The death of you, will set me free."

Then there was a voice behind him that Jack never thought he'd hear again. It was strong and, more importantly, it was angry.

"Now, Daniel. Do it now."

The boy spun, sliced through the air with the sword, and took Mama D's head cleanly off her shoulders. The head rolled, eyes fixed in a distant stare, mouth wide open. A rush of sparks flew out of the mouth and swirled around the head, filling the air.

Jack spun as he heard Lauren cry out.

Sarah was on her knees, holding her stomach, her own mouth open and pouring out thousands of tiny sparks.

"No!" the shaman roared. "It can't be."

The tiny sparks didn't fade in the air, but rather kept their intensity. The sparks from Mama D and from Sarah joined together in midair. Jack wondered at the sight of it. In shifting patterns, he saw faces, then a body, more faces. All of them children. Children with a fire inside them that could have made them special had they not become targets for murderers.

These were the victims from so many eons of hunting, come to exact their revenge from the greatest hunter there had ever been.

With a great rush, the sparks flew forward and disappeared into the mass of insects and creatures composing the monster. For a moment, there was absolute silence. A single heartbeat passed and the shaman and Huckley looked directly at Sarah, as if wondering in that pause if they had won after all.

And then the creature exploded in a fireball that roared up into the night sky.

Jack threw himself over Lauren and Sarah and the heat blasted over him. When he turned, there was nothing left of the creature. Only the sparks remained.

They circled the area, as if searching for any remnants that needed to be destroyed. Finding nothing, they drifted over Jack's head toward Sarah. He resisted a childlike temptation to reach out and touch them. He saw Lonetree and Sorenson, hobbling from injuries but alive, follow behind them, as mesmerized as Jack.

Sarah was back on the ground, pale, breathing hard, the pain evident on her face. The sparks lowered themselves and spread over her. They congregated near her worst wounds. Hundreds passed into and out of her body, unrestricted by the laws of nature.

Soon, Sarah drew in a deep, cleansing breath. Her color returned and with Lauren's help, she sat up.

"Thank you," she said.

Jack half-expected a response from the glittering cloud, but none came. At least not one that he could hear. He looked over at Sarah and saw a smile spread across her face. If there was an answer, it came to her alone.

The cloud lifted, spiraling higher and higher into the night sky, until the wind took them and scattered them into the night.

They all stared at one another. Jack, Lauren, and Sarah. Lonetree and Sorenson. And, the newest member of their circle, Daniel. They had survived. They'd defeated an impossibly powerful evil for a second time.

Jack prayed it would be the last.

Epilogue

Sarah watched Daniel and wondered at the thoughts he must be having. In the last week, they had spoken for hours about their experience together, what had happened in the room in his mind, and their battle against Huckley. How they had split ways and returned to take control of their own bodies. It was as if each of them needed the comfort of knowing it really happened, searching for validation that they weren't just invested in the same shared delusion. But there was one thing they'd never talked about and now, as they neared the end of their time together, she knew she had to ask the question. Only she didn't know how.

The adults had been busy in the last week, quietly cleaning up the aftermath of the battle. Lonetree and Sorenson's particular skills of body disposal and creating reasonable alternative stories to explain away the evidence proved very helpful. Becky, thank God, had been found unharmed in the farmhouse. No physical injuries in any case, but like all of them, she would need time to heal her mind.

While the gunmen near the caves and Mama D were disposed of quietly, the destruction of the their house and the police eyewitnesses made that more complicated. Becky's kidnapping became the cover story for the dead men at their house. Her father admitted to authorities that he'd panicked when Becky was taken for ransom and he'd contacted Joseph Lonetree for help. The SEAL had gotten a little out of control. There was some question of whether her dad would have legal troubles because of it, but he didn't seem too worried. Sarah figured after everything they'd faced down, the local District Attorney didn't invoke any great fear.

During all this, Daniel's existence was kept a closely guarded secret. There was never even a consideration of turning him over to the authorities. He stayed with Lonetree and Sorenson at night and came over to the hotel where Sarah was staying during the days.

While the adults did their work, Sarah and Daniel fell into a routine of long walks in the woods near the hotel, sometimes talking about that night, sometimes talking about life, sometimes just walking in silence and enjoying the sounds of the forest. On the third day, he took her hand in his. The act caused an unexpected shiver through her body. She wished it was from the delight of his touch, but while certainly that was part of it, there was something darker. Part of the shiver was fear. Fear of the one thing neither of them wanted to discuss.

Huckley's soul still lived inside Daniel.

Sure, it was locked in a prison Daniel had forged for himself. But it was still there. Still part of him. Sarah couldn't help but wonder if it was simply a matter of time before it escaped.

It was the topic they never discussed. She had danced toward the subject, hinting at it, but each time Daniel had shut down, falling into a deep, brooding silence. And so she left it alone and it remained the dark shadow looming between them.

She considered probing his mind, but her abilities were so much lessened since that night that she wasn't sure she could even do it if she tried. She and Daniel had spent hours trying to make sense of what had happened to her power. The best guess they had was that Mama D's power came from taking parts of the fire from all the children she had consumed over the years. Part of them were in Sarah from when the shaman used her body to feed off of Mama D.

But the tipping point was the serum her mother had given her. That was from Jesse Dahl and those were the pieces of souls consumed by the shaman and Huckley. Once together, she used her own fire to spark them to awareness. When they left her to combine with the souls freed from Mama D, they took part of her fire with them, leaving her powers greatly reduced.

Or, at least that was their best guess after days of talking it through. Ultimately, they realized they would have to accept never really knowing exactly how they had survived that night, but to simply be thankful that they had.

It was on the sixth day of their walks in the forest that Daniel had wrapped his arms around her and kissed her on the lips.

Again, she had shuddered, thinking of Huckley inside of him. He felt it and pulled away. By the look on his face, she knew he recognized her fear. They walked in silence for the rest of the afternoon.

When she heard the plan of where Daniel would go to live, she panicked. She argued against the idea with whoever would listen. Her mom and dad. Lonetree. Daniel. But the decision was made and no one seemed more firm about it than Daniel himself.

Her dad made the final turn on the bumpy dirt road and the crooked old shack perched on a rock outcropping came into view. Lonetree and Sorenson were already there, standing on the covered porch with Ichote, waiting for them.

Her dad parked the SUV and they all got out and crossed the lawn toward the approaching Ichote. She heard Daniel take a deep, steadying breath next to her. Without hesitation, she reached out and held his hand. He smiled at her and then looked around them.

"Looks like the forest when we first left Huckley behind, doesn't it?"

She squeezed his hand sharply and looked up at him.

"I know it worries you," he said. "It worries me too." He nodded toward Ichote. "Lonetree thinks she can

371

help me control it. Maybe even get rid of him completely. What do you think?"

Sarah said nothing as the space between them and Ichote closed. Finally she stood in front of them. She gave Sarah a slight bow of the head, an acknowledgement of equals. Sarah returned the gesture.

Ichote held out her hands. "May I?" she asked.

Daniel nodded. Ichote raised her hands and moved to place them on either side of Daniel's head. Sarah's stomach felt raw as she remembered what had happened when Ichote had laid her hands on her own head.

Hurt him and you'll answer to me.

Ichote paused and glanced at Sarah. The old woman smiled her understanding. Sarah looked at her innocently, happy to know some of her power was still there for use when she needed it.

She pushed the thought away as Ichote placed her hands on Daniel's head and closed her eyes, concentrating. After only a few seconds, she opened her eyes and removed her hands.

"Then we are agreed, Daniel," she said. Turning to Sarah, she added, "No one will hurt you here."

Something in the old woman's voice held an accusation. Sarah remembered the kiss in the forest and how she'd reacted. She's the one who'd hurt him. She flushed with embarrassment.

"Thank you," Daniel said.

Ichote nodded, turned on her heel, and walked back toward the house.

"Just like that?" her dad asked.

The old woman didn't bother to turn around. "Daniel and I just had a long conversation. We reached an understanding. Say your goodbyes so he and I can get to work."

Her dad shook his head. "She's the strangest woman."

He reached out a hand to Daniel who shook it gratefully. Her dad pulled the boy into a hug. "You know you can stay with us if you want," he said. "That's a real offer."

"I know. I appreciate the offer. But this is best."

Her dad nodded and moved aside for her mom who hugged him. "Call us if you need anything."

Her parents stepped back toward the car to let her say goodbye. Daniel stared awkwardly at the ground. "I…uh…" he stammered.

She leaned in to him and kissed him. Not the soft, tentative brush of lips from the forest, but a passionate kiss that conveyed all of her worry and her care for him. She stepped back and didn't wait for him to say anything. She simply turned and walked back to the car.

She didn't want him to see the tears on her face because she knew he would see right through her.

The tears weren't because of their goodbye, they were because the kiss gave her the answer she sought about Huckley. And she didn't like it. Not one bit.

Author's Note

Dear Reader,

Thank you three times.

First, thank you for supporting a fellow human being's passion. I think it makes you a good person and makes up for that one thing you did in high school (you know what I'm talking about).

Second, thank you for being part of the community of readers. Each time you write a review, recommend a book to a friend or share a new novel through social media, you help keep the fire for books alive. Those of us who scribble stories late into the night are completely in your debt.

Lastly, thank you for your time. As a father of five and an avid reader (labels that can seem mutually exclusive at times), I recognize every book you open represents a hard choice among thousands of options. I'm awed and humbled that you chose to spend your valuable time within these pages. I hope that I proved to be worthy of your trust.

With appreciation,

Jeff Gunhus

About The Author

Jeff Gunhus is the author of the Amazon bestselling supernatural thriller, *Night Chill*, and the Middle Grade/YA series, *The Templar Chronicles*. The first book of the series, *Jack Templar Monster Hunter*, was written in an effort to get his reluctant reader eleven-year-old son excited about reading. It worked and a new series was born. His book *Reaching Your Reluctant Reader* has helped hundreds of parents create avid readers. His second novel for adults, *Killer Within*, was acquired by Thomas & Mercer. As a father of five, he and his wife Nicole spend most of their time chasing kids and taking advantage of living in the great state of Maryland. In rare moments of quiet, he can be found in the back of the City Dock Cafe in Annapolis working on his next novel. If you see him there, sit down and have a cup of coffee with him. You just might end up in his next novel.

www.JeffGunhus.com

www.facebook.com/jeffgunhusauthor
www.twitter.com/jeffgunhus

Lightning Source UK Ltd.
Milton Keynes UK
UKHW022002301018
331480UK00022B/739/P